MR. VANILLA

LISA DAVIS

MR. VANILLA

LISA DAVIS

Halo
PUBLISHING
INTERNATIONAL

Halo Publishing International
7550 W IH-10 #800, PMB 2069,
San Antonio, TX 78229

First Edition, September 2024
ISBN: 978-1-63765-648-8
Library of Congress Control Number: 2024914210

Halo Publishing International is a self-publishing company that publishes adult fiction and non-fiction, children's literature, self-help, spiritual, and faith-based books. We continually strive to help authors reach their publishing goals and provide many different services that help them do so. We do not publish books that are deemed to be politically, religiously, or socially disrespectful, or books that are sexually provocative, including erotica. Halo reserves the right to refuse publication of any manuscript if it is deemed not to be in line with our principles. Do you have a book idea you would like us to consider publishing? Please visit www.halopublishing.com for more information.

For my family, your support and love are all I ever need.

CONTENTS

CHAPTER 1

JULIE

It was a perfect New York night: the sky was clear, and the sun was just starting to set. We arrived at one of the top restaurants in New York for a romantic dinner, just the two of us. I was so excited for a night out, since work had been so hectic and demanding. I was an attorney at a law firm in New York, and our new clients had kept me busy with depositions and evidentiary discovery. I had been waiting for this night all week—a chance to catch up with my boyfriend and discuss anything but work. John was my normal; he kept me grounded and kept everything in perspective. John was your average good-looking man with dark hair and brown eyes, and I adored him. He made me feel special, and best of all, he wasn't a lawyer; he was a finance major in college when we met. Now, he was an investment broker. We'd been together almost two years. I should have seen things coming, but I had been so distracted by my career that he caught me off guard.

Dinner was fabulous. We had steak with baked potatoes, and here came my favorite dessert: chocolate cake. Anything covered in chocolate works for me, but cake is my favorite. The waiter dropped off the cake, and I began scarfing it down. Then I looked up, and John was on one knee. With my mouth full of chocolate, he asked, "Julie Ann Marks, will you marry me?" I was freaking out. If I could have gathered enough sense to run for the door, I would have.

At that moment, time felt like it stopped, and flashes of my past loves came flooding back like a bad dream. All of my bad decisions and indiscretions flashed through my mind like a bad movie. Was I dying? Was this my life passing before my eyes? My heart was pounding so hard, and I couldn't catch my breath. I'm not sure if I blacked out or just froze completely, but what was only seconds seemed like hours.

My past was filled with trainwrecks for relationships. I saw the terrible hair and fashion decisions in fast forward, followed by each boyfriend. In high school, my first true love was David. He was perfect in every way, and I adored everything about him. He was cute, with dark hair with dark eyes, and he was built. Clearly, I have a type. He played football, and I loved to watch him play. I was a cheerleader standing on the sidelines, drooling over him. Why did we break up? His family was in the military, and he moved several times after freshman year. I never saw him again nor heard from him. I assume he joined the military or went to college. I regret not keeping in touch. My heart still misses him. I searched everywhere to find him after high school. He just dropped off the face of the earth. My junior year, I met this cute guy at a football game from the opposing team. We dated for over a year. He was my first. We went to prom together and everything. He went to Arizona State on a football scholarship, and the long distance killed our relationship.

Then there was freshman year of college. His name was Jake. He was a player; I thought I was the only one until I walked in on him and my roommate. After that, I found out he nailed half the freshman class while we dated. How could I have been so blind and stupid? He hurt me so badly. Then, sophomore year, I met Jamie. He was so cute, and we got along so great. He had the sweetest smile. We dated for a month, then finally, we had sex. It was amazing! And Jamie never called again— he totally ghosted me. I never saw him on campus again, either. He just disappeared. I dated a couple guys in college after that, but I never really trusted any college guys. I was afraid they were always cheating or using me for sex, so I just gave up.

Now there was Joel, my best friend. Blonde hair, green eyes, built like a movie star. We met in our first year at law school and have been there for each other since. Joel is what I call my work husband. We have lunch all the time and talk about our cases, compare notes, and give each other advice. We both work for the same law firm, but Joel is on the fast track for Partner. Joel is also from a prominent New York family, which is probably why he is being fast-tracked. He is also married to a beautiful woman who most men dream of. Sarah is blonde and has gorgeous blue eyes. She could be a model. I swear she doesn't have an ounce of fat or a pimple. She is what all women envy and hate at the same time. Joel is lucky he has a great job and great wife. They seem to be perfect in every way. It really is annoying how perfect they are together.

Then there was John. I adore John, but I'm not sure I am in love with him. We have been together so long, and he is just comfortable and easy. John is like vanilla ice cream on my chocolate cake. We go great together, but John is so simple that I'm not sure he is the one. But I know I lost my one chance in high school, so my heart just built this wall around itself, and I never let myself feel. I knew I needed to say no to his proposal. I just didn't think I was ready. I didn't think I loved him enough to marry him. I did care a lot for him, but I just was not in love with him. Could I honestly be with the same guy for the rest of my life? He was Mr. Safe and Secure. We had no spontaneity, and my entire life was planned ahead, including sex. I kept thinking this, but then my mouth opened, and like the rest of my screwed-up relationships, it took over and said, "YES."

And then it happened: I was engaged to Mr. Vanilla. Wow, did I really just agree to marry John? Don't get me wrong: he was a great guy, but he deserved someone in love with him, not me. I wasn't ready, and I was a total mess in my private life. I had made so many mistakes, and I think saying yes to John was another mistake. How could I tell him no after I just said yes? The whole drive home, John was telling me how happy he is and how much he loves me, and I was thinking, *what have I done?*

My heart was pounding, and my mind was trying to make sense of everything. Then it hit. I said yes, so maybe it will be fine. Maybe I really could love him once I let the walls down. Maybe he was right for me. The 20-minute drive to John's apartment gave me time to think it through and talk myself into being Mrs. Vanilla. *I can do this*, I thought. *I'll just let the walls down, let him in, and find out I truly love him.*

We arrived at his apartment, a small studio with small closets and an even smaller bathroom. It was simple, but it was John. He has never needed anything extravagant. Since he was an investment broker, he tended to save all his money rather than spend it on material things. I looked down at my hand and saw this simple one-carat round-cut diamond that represented my new life. I wanted to cry tears of joy, but I just started crying, wondering, *what have I done?* John asked me what is wrong, and I lied and told him that I'm just so happy. John kissed me and told me how much he loves me and how happy we will be together. He grabbed my hand and led me to the bed. John made love to me missionary style. He never deviates from that position. It hit me when he finished: I would never have sex in any other position again. I laid in bed next to John, thinking about what my new life would be like: vanilla.

I flashed back to my college boyfriend Jake, who may have been a player but was the best sex I ever had. Jake was wild and spontaneous. We had sex in so many places and different positions. I have never been as sexual with anyone as I was with Jake. I think that is why I liked him so much: he wasn't much of a boyfriend, but he was great in bed.

I woke up early the next morning and went to work. It was Saturday, but I needed to get a jump on this new case I was working on. Honestly, I just needed to get away and think. I called Joel to tell him the news. He wasn't surprised; it turns out that John told him he was proposing. I asked him why he didn't warn me or tell him not to. Joel said he thought this would be good for me, and once I opened up and accepted it, I would be great. Joel thought that once we got married, John would unleash his vanilla side and get more adventurous. Joel said that was what happened to him and Sarah. I pointed out that not everyone has a hot wife and a great sex life all in one. I really didn't think John would change after we got married. Joel pointed out that I had to get married to find out. Besides, there wasn't anyone chasing after me besides John. I wasn't exactly supermodel material. Joel said that I remind him of an overdressed librarian. Joel thinks I'm too conservative, which is also why I don't attract men. The fact that I work 12-hour days doesn't help much, either. Maybe if I dress a little sexier, John will see it's okay to enjoy sex in more than one position. What have I got to lose at this point?

Joel came in to work just to help me get through the first round of discovery. I buried my head in this new case. It was a class action lawsuit, and we represented the MSC Group. I started going through all the complaints, looking for a way to bury my head in this mess. I finally decided to call John and tell him I was working all day and apologize for leaving without saying goodbye. I just told him that I was buried in this case and needed to get through it so I could plan our wedding and our lives together. John understood; he was a kind, caring man who never suspected that I had doubts.

I talked to Joel all day. He suggested we go interview witnesses, especially since they were out of town. It would require us being gone for a few days, giving me a break from thinking about my personal life. Joel said he could use a break, too, since his wife was driving him crazy. One day she wants to start a family, and the next day she wants him to give up his career and run away to a tropical island. Her mood swings were driving him crazy.

Joel was a family man, but his wife was so focused on her looks that she was afraid to have a child; it would ruin her figure. Then, she says she wants to start a family just so he will have sex with her. Lately she seems to be more worried about her figure. Joel swears she is losing her mind. All the Botox must be getting into her brain.

I made it through the day without thinking too much about my vanilla life. I went home to my one-bedroom apartment rather than going to John's. My apartment was a little further away, but I needed time to myself. I told John that I had to go check on my apartment. I didn't like leaving it too long just in case I left the stove on or water running. John believed me since I always forget and leave something on. I tend to be a little ditsy when it comes to turning things off. I can't count the number of times I've left the stove on after warming something up.

I really just needed to be alone and think. I went to bed early on Saturday and spent all night dreaming of my plain and simple wedding. I still hadn't called my parents to tell them I was engaged. They had met John months ago and seemed to like him. But what's not to like? He is simple and steady. He could really take care of me, and we could be a good fit. So why can't I convince myself that this is a good idea?

I called John on Sunday and told him I was making calls to tell everyone that I was engaged. Truth was I sat there all day in darkness, thinking. I just didn't know what to do. I liked John. I just wasn't sure he was the one. I should've said no or maybe. Now I had to marry John or break his heart. I sat down and talked myself into being happy that I was getting married. I found someone who loves me and whom I can make a life with. I told myself that you don't get true love all the time; sometimes you have to take love and make it true. I finally decided that this was my second chance. I was taking love and making it true.

I arrived at work on Monday. Joel was waiting for me. He had cleared our trip to Washington to interview potential witnesses as well as take a few depositions for our case. He told that me we leave Wednesday and return Friday, so I needed to pull myself together.

I told him I was great. I just had cold feet and needed to think. I finally decided that marrying John was great. It was my chance to grab love. I told Joel that I'm all in. I couldn't wait for this trip to interview witnesses, then when I returned, I was jumping into this wedding planning. I had called my mom this morning and everything. Joel was surprised; he thought I had fallen down the rabbit hole on Saturday and wasn't coming back. I told him that I was excited. Finally, I thought I just needed time to realize that John was great and wonderful, and I was lucky to have him.

Joel was happy for me, especially since he went home on Saturday unexpectedly and heard his wife having phone sex. I told him he probably just misunderstood. He said she was very secretive for the rest of the day and totally jumped his bones that night. He said he thinks she is having an affair with another man, and the days she can't see him are the days Joel is getting laid. I feel bad for Joel. He is a great guy, and his wife is nice, too. I never totally liked her. I thought he could find someone a little less materialistic, but he loved her, and that was all that mattered. I think he liked how beautiful she was and the attention she got when they were together. She could be a model or actress if she wasn't so dense. She came from a high society family, too, which is another reason their families were so happy when they were married last year. They only dated for three months, which I told Joel was too quick, but he insisted that Sarah was the one for him. He was head over heels for her.

I loved Joel, so I shut up and supported his decision. The wedding was the most glamorous I have ever seen. They spared no expense with gold-rimmed glasses and plates, roses everywhere, and the location was the Plaza. My wedding would be totally different. I didn't think John would agree to the Plaza. I thought he was more of the park kind of guy. I thought John would want something simple and classic.

I finally felt like I was getting excited to plan my wedding. I was thinking about the location and guests. I couldn't wait to go to John's tonight and talk about the wedding.

I arrived at John's apartment and kissed him so hard. He was surprised. I told him I missed him all day. I had wedding magazines and ideas to discuss. He was stunned. He told me he thought I was having second thoughts, since I left early on Saturday. I told him no, I was really preoccupied with work, and I said I was sorry and am totally excited about the wedding and can't wait. I kissed him, hoping he would take the hint and take me like he had never before. John kissed me and suggested some wine and wedding details. We started planning a simple and classic wedding next June, just as I thought. That would give me plenty of time to find a dress and plan. I suggested the beach at sunset. John suggested a church, even though neither of us had been to church since college.

I told John I would be heading out of town on Wednesday with Joel to interview witnesses for the case I'd been working on. John said he would miss me, then he suggested we discuss our living arrangements. John said we should start looking for a house, as he would want kids almost right away. I think my face said more than my mouth did, because John stopped and said, "You do want kids, right?" I looked at him and said that I hadn't thought about kids. I was still working on my career and trying to prove myself.

I said to John, "How soon are you planning on kids, and how many?"

John looked at me and said, "I was hoping for two or three kids and a house with a yard." John said, "You know, if we pick a small house, you can stay home and be with the kids. I've spent my life saving money so my wife can be a mom."

I was shocked. I had never thought of being a stay-at-home mom. I always wanted to work. I told John I hadn't planned on being a stay-at-home mom, and John said that was okay—we could have a nanny, but he wanted me to really think about if I wanted someone else raising my kids. I kind of felt like that was a dig at me for wanting to work.

I agreed with John that we needed to think about the kids, but I told him that for now, let's just concentrate on getting married and where we would live. He agreed, but I could see his face. He was disappointed that I didn't want to stay home with the kids—which was great, except I wasn't sure I even wanted kids. I had never thought about it until John decided we needed to move. I was all on board with this wedding and really starting to get into the planning until John started discussing having a family. Now, I was right back to where I started: scared and unsure of what I got myself into.

CHAPTER 2

JULIE

Wednesday finally got here, and I was so ready to get on a plane and get away for a while. Joel would be there to keep me grounded. My life had been doing flip-flops all week. I couldn't decide if I was in or out, getting married or not. I was so confused. Work was the best thing to keep me focused. Joel kept telling me that it would all work out in the end.

Joel and I boarded the plane and were seated in first class. Joel tried to take my mind off of John by telling me about his wife and how he thinks she is having an affair. She was all of a sudden busy shopping and working out all the time, but she was totally not into him at all. Joel hired a detective to follow her and report, and he was waiting for a call. I think he is totally crazy; his wife has no reason to cheat, and he is a great guy. He's faithful and loving and always takes her calls at work. Joel was the perfect husband. Good-looking and sweet, Joel had the most beautiful deep green eyes, and with his blond hair, he was totally hot. He worked out all the time and tried to keep himself in shape. His wife would be crazy or stupid to cheat. Not only was he great-looking, but the prenup they signed had a cheating clause, so if either of them ever was to cheat, they would get nothing from the marriage. I knew she was from a society family, but Joel's family was much more well-off and kept her spoiled beyond belief.

Joel and I spent the entire flight going over questions for potential witnesses. I was happy for the distraction. I couldn't handle thinking about my personal life right now.

Our flight finally landed, and we grabbed a cab and headed to our hotel. We had separate rooms that were right next door, which made it very convenient for us to work. My eyes were so tired from reading on the plane. I just wanted to curl up on the couch and do nothing, but we had one hour before we need to be downstairs in a conference room we had reserved to complete all our witness statements. I went to the bathroom to freshen up and make sure my makeup and hair were presentable.

I arrived at the downstairs conference room, which Joel was already setting up. Joel was wearing a dark-gray three-piece suit. I decided to go with a simple dark-blue pant suit. I knew Joel thought I looked like a librarian, but I just needed something familiar. Blue was a power color that made me feel strong. Today, I needed to concentrate on work and forget my personal issues.

Joel and I started interviewing witnesses. We had 20 people scheduled to interview as potential witnesses. One by one, we interviewed people, asking question after question. My last interview was with a nice, simple woman named Susan. We were just finishing up when her husband walked up. He had dark hair and dark eyes. I looked up and saw his eyes. I would know them anywhere.

"David," I said out loud. He looked at me and said, "Julie." I was shocked. I hadn't seen David in years. Just the sight of him made my heart stop. I didn't know what to say, and next thing I knew, David and I were hugging. David said he missed me. His wife looked a little stunned to see that we knew each other. I don't think Susan knew what to make of our relationship, but then again, I didn't know what to make of it either. In a split second, all those feelings I had in high school came rushing back.

I asked David where he had been living. He said he had been all over the place, since his dad was in the military. They moved at least four times after he said goodbye to me. But he had been in Washington for the last two years and married for just over a year. David was a Marine on leave, and he was stationed in Washington. He joined right after high school. I told him I was working in New York and was just here to interview his wife. David asked how long I was in town for, and I told him I was leaving Friday and was just here for a couple of days. David suggested we get together and catch up over drinks. I told him that would be great. I gave him my cell and told him to call me.

Joel and I wrapped up all our interviews for the day, but after seeing David, all I could think about was him. David was the love of my life, and I never got over him. He was the reason I stopped looking for love. I had found it and let it get away.

Joel stopped me and told me to stop dreaming, David was married, and I needed to remember that. He clearly moved on after me, and I needed to keep my life moving forward, too. And most important, I needed to remember that I was engaged to John.

In my heart, I knew Joel as right, but I couldn't stop thinking about David and hoping he called. My phone rang, and my heart skipped. I started digging in my purse for it. Finally I saw the incoming call: it's John. I knew he could hear the disappointment in my voice.

I heard him say, "Hi, Honey, tough day?" I responded with a simple, "Yeah, it's been a little draining today. Interviewing people is always a long, boring process." I of course left out the part about seeing the love of my life.

I felt guilty for wishing David would call, especially since I was engaged to a great guy. I should be happy and full of joy while planning my happily ever after. I just couldn't stop thinking about the past. David and I were so close that we talked every day, and it was such pure, innocent love. We never even had sex. The love we shared was just a true first love, deeper than I have ever felt. I think when David moved away, he took a piece of me with him. I never got over him leaving, and I felt like it was unfinished. Maybe that was all this was: unfinished business. Maybe once I talked to David and heard him tell me he loved his wife and was happy, I could move on with John.

Joel and I decided to have dinner and talk. I couldn't stop thinking about David and Joel could tell. He kept telling me to get my head back on Earth. Joel and I talked for hours about David, John, and of course, Joel's wife, Sarah. I asked him if he heard back from the PI he hired to follow her, but he said there was no word yet. We both seemed to have way too much drama in our lives right now. I wasn't sure what to do about John. I just didn't want to hurt him.

I woke up in the middle of the night. I had dreamed of David all night. He and I walked along the beach, holding hands watching the sun come up. It was my perfect romantic night that I always wished for. I tried to sleep, but every time I closed my eyes, I saw David. His dark hair and dark eyes stared at me, telling me I was the one he wanted to be with.

Joel and I spent the next day interviewing more possible witnesses. My head was totally not there. I tried to concentrate on work, but I couldn't get David out of my mind. He was all I could think of. I didn't sleep much and I couldn't think straight. I felt like I was a total mess. These people I was interviewing must have thought I was a first-year student or something.

Joel reminded me when the interviews were over that our flight would leave first thing Friday morning. We had to be at the airport early. He looked at me and said, "Jules, are you listening?" and I just said, "Yeah, I'm here." He gave me that look that told me I wasn't listening. Joel asked if I wanted to have dinner and talk. I told him I was hoping to have a drink date but haven't heard yet. Joel shook his head in disapproval. Joel said, "Look you need to pull your shit together. You go home to John like this, and he will run like hell."

Joel was right. I needed to pull my shit together. David hadn't called anyway. I needed to take that as a sign. I called Joel and made dinner plans. Joel and I met downstairs at the hotel restaurant. I apologized for having my head up my ass all day. Joel looked at me and said, "Did you finally pull it out?" I looked at him and said, "I'm working on it. Seeing David just really threw me for a loop. I didn't expect to see him, and I didn't expect all those feelings to come rushing back like they did. I feel like a total teenager. Just like in high school, the walls I had built so high came down like the pouring rain." I just looked at Joel and said, "How pathetic am I?" He laughed and said, "Pretty pathetic. You acted like a lost puppy. It was really bad." I can always count on Joel to be brutally honest and incredibly sarcastic.

Joel and I had drinks and dinner. We talked for hours, mainly about what a sad, pathetic sap I was over the last couple of days. We also talked about his wife. He finally heard from his PI. His wife was meeting up with some guy, but he couldn't tell if they were having an affair yet. He was going to keep tracking her for a few days and see what he finds. She went to the gym and was there for hours, followed by a visit to some doctor. She was at the doctor for hours, too, so it's possible she was cheating, but maybe she was just working out and getting way too much Botox again. For Joel's sake, I hoped she was being faithful; he really didn't need this in his life, especially since he wanted a family. Joel has dreamed of having a family for as long as I have known him. He always wanted kids and a dog. The real white-picket-fence deal.

Joel and I got on our flight home. All I could think about was that David didn't call, and I needed to move on. I needed to plan a wedding and start my life with John. I needed to get out of my head and live life.

Our flight landed in New York. Joel and I had to head to the office to drop off all this paperwork. We had a quick meeting to update the members of our team, then Joel and I headed out for the day. Joel stopped me and asked, "You back, or are you still in Washington with him?" I looked at him and told him that I had thought about this the whole way home, and I was here with John. I got this. I decided that since David didn't call me, I was here where I should be. I needed to put David out of my mind and start planning a future with John.

After our office meeting, I stood outside the building, wondering if I should see John or go home. I felt like I should really want to go see John, but I just felt like going home and crashing. I finally decided that I needed to go see John. I needed to start my life with John. I would put David and the past behind me and start moving forward.

I got to John's apartment, and he was waiting for me with a nice glass of wine. We caught up on the last couple of days, minus the ex showing up at work. John ordered Chinese for us for dinner. It was nice to just talk. We started talking about the wedding, trying to decide dates and where to get married. My head started spinning. I just didn't know where to start or how to start. There is so much involved in getting married. John could tell I was overwhelmed. He suggested I call my mom and ask her to help. I looked at John and asked why we didn't hire a wedding planner. John looked a little surprised, but he said we could check into it.

My cell phone rang, and I jumped, expecting it to be David or Joel. It was my friend Jody from high school. Jody was a married mother of two. Jody got pregnant in high school, married her high school sweetheart right after graduation, and promptly had 2 kids. She is a stay-at-home mom who adores her children, but once a month, Jody calls to vent and talk to a girlfriend who understands her life. Every year Jody gets spring fever and can't stand being a housewife and just needs to spend the weekend being single and free.

Jody usually traveled to New York to hang with me and crash at my apartment. Her husband thinks it is just a weekend with no kids and girl talk. But I don't think he knows she usually crashes at some random guy's apartment for a weekend of hot, no-strings-attached sex. Jody says it's how she sows her wild oats that she didn't get to sow after high school. Her husband is an accountant. Jody skipped college to take care of their sons. After high school, they had no money, so her husband worked during the day and did online and night classes to get a degree. Now they just get by with two kids and one income. They barely make it, and they live in Jersey and commute everywhere.

With spring in the air and a beautiful weekend coming around, I expected this was Jody's spring fling time. Jody and I talked for about an hour about the kids and her husband, Greg. She loved her family, but they tended to get on her nerves. Greg had been busy with work, and Jody had been running the kids to soccer, baseball, and all sorts of activities. This weekend was the only weekend there are no activities, except a birthday party for the boy down the road. Greg could handle driving their son to one event. Jody said, "If you don't mind, can I hang out with you this weekend? It's a welcome distraction for me." I told Jody I was ready to go out this weekend. Jody said she would be over in the morning, and we could spend the day catching up and go out on Saturday night to enjoy single life before mine ends, too.

I spent the rest of the night with John, talking about the wedding. We couldn't decide on a date or location. I told John, "Let's pick the location first. That may determine the date. If it's not available, then we may have to change it." John and I spent a quiet night at home, watching a movie and drinking a bottle of wine. We tried to talk about the wedding, but we would get frustrated not making any decisions. Finally, we just went to bed. John laid next to me and fell asleep in moments. I thought that with me being gone for a few days, he would want to have sex, but he was too tired. I couldn't help but feel like this would be our marriage, with no excitement or spontaneity. I wondered if this was why Jody had her spring flings. Would I need to have spring flings, too? Could I live like this for the rest of my life?

I found myself excited to see Jody, since I had so many questions about marriage. Jody was my only friend who was still married and had been married a long time. I jumped out of bed and headed home to meet Jody. John was up having his morning coffee, and he could tell I was anxious to see Jody. I grabbed my purse, kissed John, and told him I would see him Sunday. He said 'I love you' to me, and I said 'I love you' back. I'm pretty sure I meant it.

I grabbed a cab and went home. I knew Jody would be there soon. She usually came in the morning to get as much time as possible away from her family. I know she loved them, but sometimes she really needed a break. I don't know how she does it. I only have John, and sometimes I need to hide in my apartment just to have alone time.

Jody got here a little after 10:00 am. Here was my bestie from high school: she has dark hair, dark eyes, and still looks great, even after two kids and being married. Jody says it's the yoga she does while the kids are in school. We hugged like it had been years since we saw each other. I listened to her tell me all the great things going on. The kids were great. Greg was great; he just got a raise at work. She seemed happy. So I told her about John and I getting engaged.

She looked at me and said, "You don't look excited or happy, so spill. What's up?" Jody was my only friend who knew David and I and what we had together. So I told her about running into David in Washington. She looked at me and knew before I said a word.

She said, "You still love him don't you?" How could I tell her no? I knew I never got over him. I told her how I could still love him. It had been forever, and I loved John.

She looked at me and said, "You can't hide anything from me. I know you better than anyone, and I know you never gave up hoping David would come back. You have loved him since you saw him in high school." Jody was the one friend I could tell anything to and know she would know if I was lying.

Jody listened to me whine about David for hours, then she looked at me and said, "If there is one thing I have learned about being married, it's that you need to be certain before you walk down the aisle. Once you make the walk, there is no turning back."

Jody said she loved her family, but she wished she would have waited to get married and start a family. She never got the chance to be wild and free and experience life—which I know is part of the reason she has her spring flings. I asked her why she cheats and what drives her to leave her family and be with another man. Jody told me her husband is great, but their sex life has become so plain and boring that she needs something exciting to keep her going. So she goes out and has a hot night every now and then to keep her marriage going. If she didn't have great sex, she would be bored and unfulfilled. I asked her if Greg knew what she did, and she said she tried to tell him several times. But every time it would turn into an argument about their boring sex life, and Greg would feel inadequate and like he was not sexually satisfying. B.O.B. (battery operated boyfriend) can only work for so long. She just needed a fix.

I told Jody my issue with John, how he is so vanilla and our sex life is just plain missionary. She told me to call it off and run like hell. Jody stopped me and said, "You're still in love with another man, and you're not getting fucked. All women need a good fucking now and then. If John can't do it, you will never be sexually satisfied, and you will end up like me: out looking for a good lay."

Then she reminded me of Jake, my cheating ex. Jody said, "I remember you telling me about all the sex you had and all the different places.

You were satisfied by him. You need to find the love you have for David combined with the sex from Jake. That would be the ideal marriage."

Jody and I ordered lunch and kept catching up. Jody said she was thinking about getting a job, something fun to do while the kids are in school. She gets bored sitting home just cleaning. Jody said that some days, she just wants to jump on the UPS man and ride him in his truck. I listened to Jody and realized she was right. If I couldn't get John out of his sexual shell, then I would have to let him go. I didn't want a marriage like Jody's. I wanted a commitment, and I wanted to be the only woman for my husband, and I wanted him to be the only man for me.

As Jody and I were eating, my cell rang, and I looked at the caller ID. It was unknown. I answered, expecting a phone solicitor. It was David. I looked at Jody, and she could see from my face that it was David. She listened while I talked to David. He apologized for not calling: his wife was ill, and he had to take care of her. He wanted to meet and catch up before I left, but with his wife being ill, he couldn't call. I told David I was glad to hear from him. I was hoping to get together, too. He said he was in New York this weekend. His wife was home, and he had to go to New York to take care of some personal business. He wanted to know if I was free tonight for dinner. I told him that Jody was here, and we were planning on going out tonight. David asked if that was the same Jody from high school. I told him it was the same Jody, and he laughed and said he hadn't seen anyone in years. He offered dinner tonight with Jody and I. We could catch up on old times. I looked at Jody, and she giggled and nodded yes. I told David we would meet him at 7:00 for dinner at the bar down the street from his hotel. I hung up the phone, looked at Jody, and said, "I am in trouble."

Jody laughed and said, "Maybe he will be great in bed, and you can solve your wedding problem."

I threw a pillow at her and said, "We need to shower and get ready. You have to help me pick something out to wear."

CHAPTER 3

JULIE

Jody and I were finally ready for dinner with David. I looked at her, and she said, "God, you look so nervous. You're as pale as a ghost."

I didn't know what to do. I felt like I was betraying my fiancé just for meeting David. I haven't done anything wrong—well unless you count the naughty dreams and fantasies in my head. Maybe it was wrong, but I put my engagement ring on the dresser and opted for some less notice-able jewelry. I saw Jody looking at me, and she said, "I see how you're playing tonight."

I looked at her, gave her a dirty look, and said, "Shut up, you cheat-ing whore."

She laughed and said, "I bet I can say that to you in the morning." She had no idea how much I hoped that was true.

Jody and I arrived at the bar. David was already there waiting. He got up and kissed us both on the cheek. We began exchanging pleasant-ries. I listened to Jody tell David about her husband and kids. David asked about my life and if I was seeing anyone. I told him I was seeing someone, but it wasn't serious. Jody giggled and said, "Really?"

David could read us both just like old times. He looked at me and said, "What are you not telling me?" I looked at him, and before I knew what I was saying, I just spilled everything.

I said, "I never got over you, so any relationship I have ever had has not meant much. I never let anyone in."

Jody laughed and said, "Boy, is that the truth. Finally!"

David laughed and said, "I never got over you, either. I learned to love my wife, Susan. We had been together for over a year, and when she got ill, I felt I needed to marry her. I never was totally in love. I just couldn't let her go through this illness alone. She has breast cancer and isn't expected to make it. She is actually the reason I am here this weekend. After we ran into each other at the deposition, she asked me about how we knew each other. I told her everything about how I was dragged from school to school and you were the only girlfriend I had truly loved. She told me I had to promise to find you again. She insisted that if she dies, I remarry and find my love. She knows I married her to take care of her and be supportive. She is great, and we have a love that is based on mutual respect and friendship. Susan was ill last weekend, so I stayed with her, but she insisted that I call a nurse and family to stay with her and come to New York and find you."

I was shocked to hear David's story, and it only made me love him more, since he had married his friend to take care of her knowing he may have to watch her die. We talked for hours. Jody tried to stick with us, but finally her spring fever hit again. She caught the eye of some cute guy at the bar. Jody said she was going to the bar for a drink and let us chat. I could see the look in her eye that she wasn't coming back. I looked at David, and he was just as cute as I remembered. Our eyes locked, and he said, "Jody hasn't changed, has she?"

I laughed and said, "No, she is still wild and can't be tamed."

David looked at me and said, "What is the real story? I can tell you're not telling me something."

I just looked at him and said, "Do you want the truth?"

David said as he grabbed my hand, "You have never lied to me. I don't expect anything to change."

I took a deep breath and told him about John. I told him how I said yes to the proposal, but I thought it was a mistake. I didn't know how to tell John I couldn't marry him. I was still in love with the past and couldn't let go. David looked at me. I could tell from his eyes he still loved me, too. Jody came by and said she was going home with Mr. Cutie, and she would check in later. Jody had a lot to drink and was definitely primed for a fun night. David looked at her and asked if she was sure that this is what she wanted. She looked at him and said, "I am positive I am doing this, and you should do that," as she pointed to me.

I blushed and got totally embarrassed by Jody. David laughed and said, "If you change your mind, you call, and I'll come get you." She kissed his cheek goodbye and took off.

David and I left. I invited him back to my place for coffee. He was hesitant, but he agreed. We got to my apartment. It was still a little early and too late for coffee, so I offered him wine. We had a glass while we talked. We talked for hours. It was late, and David said he should head back to the hotel. I told him it was too late, and he should crash here. There was plenty of room, and Jody was obviously not coming back. Besides, I told him, he had too much to drink, and I would feel better if he stayed. He hesitantly agreed. So I opened another bottle, which had to have been at least bottle number three or four. I lost count a few hours ago.

I sat down next to David, and we started talking. He held my hand. It was just like it was in high school. He leaned in and kissed me. My heart pounded. I had never felt that kind of a rush. My body burned for his touch. David's kiss was so gentle, and I wanted to devour him. He pulled away and asked if I was sure that I didn't want John. I looked at David and said, "I am sure John is not who I want. I want you."

With that, David picked me up and carried me into the bedroom. I wanted David so badly. I wanted to make love to him.

David laid me on the bed, then kissed me and said goodnight.

I tried to stop him and asked where he was going. He looked at me and said, "I'm sleeping on the couch. You are engaged, and I am still married. I do not want to come between you, no matter how much I want you right now."

David left and shut the door behind him. I fell asleep moments later and started dreaming of David and what could be our life together.

When I woke, David was gone. He left a note that said, "I missed you." He left his phone number and address and said, "Call when you're available."

I hated that he was so honorable. I knew he didn't want to come between John and I, but he wasn't: John and I were done, and I should have never said yes. Now I needed to figure out how to break it off with John so I could have David back.

My cell rang, and I hoped it was David, but it was Jody. She had no idea where she was and needed a ride. I laughed at her and said, "Look outside to see if you see any landmarks or street signs so I can find your trampy ass."

She finally found some street markers, and I told her, "Give me 20 minutes, and I'll be there to get you."

I arrived to pick up Jody. She looked like hell. I drove her back to my apartment, and Jody showered while I made coffee. Jody came out of the bathroom in a robe and smiled and said, "Well?"

I looked at her and said, "Well, what?"

She said, "Spill. Is David good in bed?"

I looked at her and said, "I wouldn't know. He left last night. We kissed and made out a little." She laughed and said, "You two are still in high school."

I told her that David said he couldn't be with me until I was single.

Jody said, "Oh my god, he is the last honorable man on Earth."

Then she looked at me and said, "Why did you tell him about John?" I just said that he knew I was hiding something, and I had to tell him because I could never hide things from David.

Now how was I going to break John's heart? Jody still looked like hell, but I asked her how her spring fling was. Jody started all the sordid details.

"His name was Rod, I think. He was great young and hung. He tore me up. We had sex in so many positions and so many times. I swear he must have been on Viagra. I think we started in his living room, then we did it on the dining room table. It was great. He has magic hands. I wish I could have stayed longer, but I couldn't take the chance of him wanting to date or make this more than a one-time thing. But man, he was so cute and made me cum so many times. I won't be able to have sex with my husband for a week."

I just looked at her and said, "I'm jealous."

It was after noon, and Jody said she needed to start packing up and head out so she could make dinner for her family. I stopped her and said, "Before you go, do you have any idea how I can break it off with John?"

Jody looked at me and said, "Honey, I'm sorry, but you have to figure that out on your own. John will be hurt, but it will hurt less than if you marry him and cheat, like I do."

Jody left, and I sat around for hours, trying to think of the best way to tell John I had to break it off. Finally, I picked up the phone and called David. I needed to hear his voice. When David answered, I said, "Hey, I just wanted to make sure you made it home safe."

He laughed and said, "Really, is that all you want to know?"

I smiled and said, "No, I guess I missed you. You were gone when I got up, and I never got to say goodbye." He apologized and said he was afraid he couldn't leave if he had to say goodbye again. I asked how his wife was doing. He said that she's okay, and it's probably not going to be long before she is gone. She seemed to be declining a little every day, so he planned on not leaving her side until she passed. She insisted he go this weekend, but now he hoped she would let him stay because she knew he had someone waiting. At least, he hoped I was waiting. I told him not to worry. I was here when he needed me, and in the meantime,

I was working to be single. I told him to call when he needed to talk. We said goodbye. He was right: I don't think I could have let him leave this morning.

I headed out to go see John. I had to end this before we ended up married and before I chickened out. When I arrived at John's apartment, I should have called first, but I was afraid of chickening out and letting him talk me into a wedding.

I knocked on the door when I arrived, but there was no answer. I thought maybe he was in the bedroom and couldn't hear me knocking. I checked, and the door was unlocked, which was unusual, but he must have forgotten to lock it when he came in. I heard noises coming from the bathroom. It sounded like the shower. I walked back there and heard a man's voice. Then, I peeked in the bathroom and saw that John was in the shower with another man. They seemed to be lovers. I stood there dumbfounded and didn't realize that I was staring when they saw me. I must have been beet red.

They stopped, and John said, "Julie."

I turned to leave as quickly as I could. John was behind me, soaking wet. John grabbed me and said, "Wait, it's not what you think."

I looked at him and said, "I think you're gay."

John said, "No, I'm in love with you, and yes, I am bisexual. I want you to be my wife. I swear I decided that this weekend while you were with Jody was my last fling. I swear I am all yours. I want nothing but to marry you and start a family."

I just started to cry. I looked at John and said, "No, I can't do this. I can't marry you. Obviously, I am not enough, and I don't want to do that to you."

I handed John the ring and ran out. I was crying so hard I couldn't breathe, let alone drive. I called Joel crying. Joel came to pick me up and talk me down. We went back to Joel's, and I told him everything that happened with David and John. I was so confused, and I couldn't believe I didn't see that John was bisexual.

Joel said, "That's why he was so vanilla with you. He was cherry covering his boyfriend."

Joel took me home. I called Jody crying, and she was surprised and kind of jealous. She suggested I try a threesome with John and his friend. I just said, "I'm so glad I called. You always know how to cheer me up."

She said look at the bright side: "You can totally fuck David now." She was right: this may have been exactly what I needed. I could be with David. I was so worried about how to break up with John, and now it was over. He did it for me.

I looked at my phone, and it had four voicemails on it. I bet they were from John. Then the doorbell rang. I went to get the door, and it was John. He came to beg for me to forgive him and to take him back. I just couldn't deal with this. I looked at him and said, "I can't do this now, John. I just can't deal with any of this. I don't want you to have any regrets, and I don't want to be the one you resent for making you choose."

John looked at me and said, "I love you, and you are who I want. I would never resent you. I just needed to get it out of my system one more time. I should have told you."

I looked at John and said, "No, I can't. I won't be Mrs. Vanilla." John looked at me, and his face was trying to figure out what I meant.

I looked at him and just said, "Forget it. I just can't and won't do this. Please just go."

John refused to leave before we settled this. He looked at me and said, "What is vanilla? What are you trying to get away from?"

I didn't know what to say, so I just said, "It's our sex life. It's vanilla, and then I see you with another man. Clearly you're more comfortable with a man than with me, and you have sex in the shower, and we have never done it other than in the bed in missionary."

John looked surprised. He said, "I thought that was what you liked. I just did what I thought pleased you. If I thought you wanted something else, I would have done it."

I just shouted, "Clearly, you would do it with a man." I was just being hurtful now, and I know it, but I was hurt. I just wanted this over with. I looked at John and could see he meant what he said, but would he really be done with the men, or would he be like Jody and have flings? I couldn't take the chance.

I looked at John and said, "It's over. Just leave now."

I walked toward the bedroom. I hoped he would leave, but as I turned to close my bedroom door, he was standing there. He pushed in and shut the door behind him. He looked at me in a way I had never seen before. He said, "I love you, and you will marry me. I will prove that you are mine."

He threw me on the bed and started kissing me. I tried to push him off. He was so strong and just kept pushing. He grabbed my hands and pinned them behind me. He ripped my shirt open, pushed my bra up, and started kissing my breasts. It felt so good, but I wanted him to stop. I asked him to stop. I told him it was over, and he pulled my pants off and then pulled his pants off. I tried to get up, and he pulled me back and threw me back on the bed. He rolled me over so my back faced him, then I felt him enter me. He was fucking me like I had always wanted. My body was enjoying this fucking, but my head and heart knew it was wrong. I came so hard, I didn't know what to do. My body was sending all the wrong signals. John pulled out. I think he was done. I had never felt such sexual satisfaction. But I felt violated at the same time. I didn't know what to do. I just started crying. John grabbed his clothes, kissed me goodbye, and said, "I love you. I'm not vanilla. I was trying to please you all this time, and now that I know what you like, I will give it to you. Please think about it and call me when you're ready." I just rolled over and started crying. I didn't know what else to do but cry.

I was crying when I called Jody. I told her everything, and she first said, "You lucky bitch."

I told her to stop, that I think I was just raped by my ex-boyfriend. She said, "Yeah, you're right, he overstepped, but he did it to show you he isn't vanilla and that he loves you."

I couldn't stop crying. Jody asked if I was okay or if I needed her to come over. I told her no, I was okay. I locked the door and locked myself in the bedroom. I just needed to figure out what to do. Jody said, "You have two options: one, take him back and fuck him every day, or run like hell.

I laughed and said, "I can't marry him. I love David, and even if John is no longer vanilla, I feel violated and like I can't trust him anymore."

Monday morning came quickly. Joel could tell I wasn't right. He asked if I needed to go to lunch, and I told him, "Yeah."

Joel and I went to a bistro around the corner. I filled him in on what happened. Joel said, "You need to go to the police and make a report of the rape."

I just said, "I can't, I just want it over. And I really enjoyed it, so I feel bad, like I misled him. I was moaning, and my body was really into it. I came so many times. I have never come so hard before, not even with Jake. John did things to me that, if he had done them before I found him in the shower, I would have loved and enjoyed and asked for more. I just felt like he was trying to show me he could be what I needed."

Joel said, "I get that, but he violated you and took advantage of you." "I just want it over with. I will call and tell him it's over." Joel said, "NO, you will not call. I will call and tell him it's over and to stay away. No mixed messages, it's done."

Joel grabbed his phone, and I heard John answer. Joel said, "John, it's Joel. We need to be clear: you and Jules are over. Do not contact her or try to see her. If you need anything, you deal with me. You are not to speak to her again. Have I made myself clear?"

John said, "I love her, and you cannot stop our love. I will have her again."

Joel insisted I stay with him tonight just to be safe. He called a locksmith and had an additional deadbolt installed on my apartment door and the locks changed. I thought he was going overboard. John was harmless. I think last night was just him trying to prove his love. I know he did it the wrong way, but I think he truly felt he was proving he could be what I want.

I called David, and he could tell I was upset. I told him I broke up with John. He felt relieved, and he asked how he took it. I didn't answer. He could tell I was hiding something again, and then I started to cry. David said, "You need to tell me if you're okay." He kept saying, "Tell me what happened."

I finally broke and told him everything. He got really upset and said he was lucky I live in another state. I told him I stayed with Joel last night. David sounded relieved. I told him that Joel had new locks installed and was picking me up for work all week and bringing me home. I told him it was too much, but Joel insisted just in case. David agreed. John seemed like he was dead set on getting me back and proving himself, so who knew what he was capable of.

CHAPTER 4

J U L I E

David's wife was in and out of the hospital last week, and he said that when this was over, he would see about being stationed in New York so we could try again. I felt such relief that he would be closer and maybe this would work out—especially since my breakup with John didn't go as I had hoped.

There was a knock on the door. I told David to hang on a sec. Someone was at the door, and he told me to take the phone with him and ask who it was first. I asked, and I heard John's voice say, "It's me, Julie." I answered, "John you need to leave, we are over, please just go."

I could hear David on the phone saying, "Julie, is everything okay?"

I put the phone to my ear and said, "David, it's fine. I'm not opening the door."

I heard John try to use his key and say, "Julie, the key isn't working. Let me in."

"John, the lock has been changed. You need to leave. I don't want to see you anymore."

David was telling me to call the police. I heard John leave, then I peeked through the peephole. I could see his face, and suddenly his eyes were peering into the hole like they could see right through me. I had never been so afraid of John before. He looked pissed, and had I let him in, I think I would have been treated like I was the night before. David

38

asked if I was okay. I said I could see John leaving, and I promised I wouldn't open the door until Joel came by to pick me up for work. David told me to make sure the doors and windows were locked and to stay inside. He made me promise to call every morning and every night, just to be safe.

Just hearing that David wanted me to call him every night and every morning made me feel loved. I really thought David was my soulmate. It has taken us years to find each other, and it could be years before we could be together, but I didn't care. I would wait this time. I was not going to make the same mistake twice.

After hanging up with David, I called Joel and made sure he was picking me up. I told him about John. He wanted me to come stay with him and Sarah for a while, but I said I was okay. I was on the phone with David when he called, and I promised I would call every night and every morning to check in. As long as I stayed in, I should be fine. Joel said he would come to the door and get me in the morning. He said I should pack an overnight bag just in case I changed my mind. I told him I would think about it.

I had trouble sleeping all night. I just kept thinking about John and how he had changed since I saw him with that man. He changed after I saw him. The real him came out, the violent John. A John I had never known existed. I tossed and turned all night, and I couldn't sleep. Finally, I got up and got ready for work. I was going to head out early, but I remembered my promise to David. I called him and said I was okay. I had a rough night of sleep, but Joel was on his way to pick me up, so I would be fine. He still said he wanted to talk to me until Joel arrived. There was a knock at the door, and I went to open it. David said to check the door first. Ugh. I looked through the peephole. It was John again.

"Oh my god, David, it's John. What do I do?"

He said, "Call the police. He can't keep doing this." John was yelling, "Julie, let me talk to you. Please let me make this right."

Then I heard Joel yelling for him to get out. He told John to never come back. We were done. John left, then Joel said, "It's clear, let me in."

39

I was still on the phone with David when Joel came in. He asked if David was on the phone. I nodded, and he said, "Let me have the phone."

Joel talked to David, and they agreed it would be best if I stayed with Joel for a few days. David made him promise to keep an eye on me and to let him know if I needed anything. They hung up, Joel said, "Grab your bag and a few days of clothes. You're staying with me."

We made it out of the apartment; there was no sign of John. Joel had the cab driver take us to the police station. I just looked at him and said, "No, I don't want that."

Joel said, "Jules, you're an attorney. What would you tell your client to do in this case?"

I looked at Joel. I knew he was right, but putting on paper what John did to me was going to be hard. I went into the police station. Joel never left my side. I told the officer everything John did: the rape, the stalking, everything. Joel told him how he was at the apartment when he arrived. I had documented everything that I told the officer. I just wanted to make it part of the record in case anything happened. I didn't want to file charges, I just wanted to have documentation. Joel thought we should press charges, but I told him I didn't want to deal with this. I just wanted it over.

When we got to work, Joel went to security, told them about the incident at my apartment, and gave them a picture of John. He said, "If he enters the building, call the police."

I was so lucky to have Joel and good friends who take care of me. And now that I had David, my life was complete. Even if David was still married to someone else and living in another state.

Joel and I ordered lunch in, just in case John was waiting for me. I spent the whole day afraid to go home. I never thought John was so violent and angry. I guess I dodged a bullet when I found him with that man.

Joel and I left work and we made it to his house without any issues. I called David when I got to Joel's. It was good to hear his voice. He sounded upset. I asked if Susan was okay, and he said no, she was in the hospital, and he was not sure she would make it. I told him, "I'm sorry to hear that. Is there is anything I can do?"

He said, "No, I'm glad you're okay. I'm glad you have Joel to take care of you." I told David to go be with Susan, hold her hand, and take care of her, and I would call him tomorrow. I could tell he was upset, but he said he needed to go.

Joel, Sarah, and I ordered Chinese takeout. I told Sarah I appreciated her letting me crash with them. She said she wouldn't have it any other way. She said that we were family, and when the crazy comes out, the family sticks together. She said that she never really liked John; he always seemed perfect. I had never thought about it, but she was right. He was so perfect that there had to be something wrong with him. I couldn't believe it took two years to figure out that he wasn't the right guy. How could I have been so blind?

I called Jody just to let her know I was staying with Joel. She couldn't believe everything that had been going on. She said I was turning into my own soap opera.

It had been days, and I hadn't heard from John. I told Joel that I was low on clothes. It was time to go home and start living my life again. It had been three days. Joel said that he would take me home to get clothes. I told him that I would be fine. He said no, that he didn't trust John. I made a deal with him: "How about I run home for lunch and grab a few things?"

John would still be at work. Joel agreed, but I could tell he didn't want to. I grabbed a cab and went home. I told the cab to keep the meter running. I ran upstairs and went into my apartment. I started packing another bag. I grabbed a few days worth of clothes and some personal items. I watered my plants.

I started to leave, and there was a knock on the door. "Julie, I know you're in there. Please let me in so we can talk."

"It was John. How did he know I was home? He never went far from the office for lunch. He must have had my phone traced or had me tracked somehow. I called Joel on the phone and told him that I was trapped in my apartment. John was outside. Joel told me to keep quiet and not to open the door, no matter what. He was on his way. Joel would be at least 20 minutes out, and during lunch it would take longer. New York lunch traffic is crazy. John was pounding on the door.

"Julie, I'm really sorry. I just want to apologize. I swear I won't hurt you."

I was scared. I didn't know what to do. John left. I waited and called Joel. I told him he had left. I was going to get in the cab I had waiting downstairs. I told him I would be back to the office in 20 minutes. I hung up and took the elevator down. My cab was waiting. I jumped in, and John was in the cab, waiting for me. I started to cry. He told the cab driver to go.

John started to tell me how sorry he was and how he would never hurt me on purpose. He said, "I just need a few minutes to clear everything up." He never meant for me to see him with Sam. That was over. He just wanted me. He promised he could be a great husband, and I could do whatever I wanted for work. He wouldn't make me stay home. He promised we would have a great life together. I told John that I didn't want to be with him anymore. I didn't love him, and I just wanted to move on with my life. John gave the cab driver the address to his apartment.

He said, "Take us there so we can talk."

I said, "No, I need to go to work." I told the cab to take me back to my office. My phone rang. John grabbed it out of my hand.

He said, "You need to listen to me. I love you, and I will win you back." John had the cab stop, and he got out. I told the cab to take me to work.

Joel was waiting outside. He asked what took me so long. He saw I was upset and crying. I told him that John was waiting in the cab. He had me, but he let me go unharmed, so hopefully the worst was over.

Joel said, "It's time to find a new apartment. You're not going back there. John can't be trusted, and you can't let your guard down."

Joel called David after we got back to work. He told David that he wasn't letting me go back to that apartment. I would be staying with him until they found me a new apartment. David thanked him and told him he appreciated him calling and letting him know what happened. David said that he would call me later to check on me.

Joel and I finished a long day of work. We went straight to the police department to update the detective on John, and then we went back to his house. Joel had already called a realtor to find me a new apartment and list my current apartment. Joel was taking care of everything. Sarah and I were talking at the house. She was making dinner while I cut vegetables for the salad. We were discussing my screwed-up love life and her and Joel's relationship. Sarah really did love Joel. I didn't know why he thought she was cheating. I think he was just paranoid. I asked Sarah if she and Joel planned on having kids, and she said she thought so, but right now Joel was so focused on work that he was too preoccupied to have kids. Sarah said that was why she went to work out so much, and she has been working with doctors to do volunteer work so she has something to do all day. She has been spending time with cancer patients, holding their hands while they get chemo.

That explained all the time she had been missing while Joel thought she was having an affair. She was just trying to keep busy while Joel was working. Joel had been worried about nothing. Joel was so lucky to have a great woman who loved him and wasn't batshit crazy.

I spent the next couple of weeks at Joel's while he worked with a realtor to find me a new place. It seemed like forever since I had been to my own place. I tried to tell Joel I needed to go home and pack, but he said that's what movers were for. Joel was worried John had my place staked out. I thought the worst was over. I hadn't seen John in weeks, and he hadn't called. Joel thought this was the calm before the storm.

Finally, I convinced Joel to go out for lunch. It had been weeks, and we needed to stop living in fear of John. We went to a nearby bistro. I finally had a chance to talk to Joel about his wife, Sarah. I told him I thought he was paranoid about her cheating. He said his PI confirmed that he was paranoid. I told him about my conversation with her and how she was just filling time until he was ready for kids. Joel said he was ready; he just kept himself busy since he thought she wasn't ready. I told him, "It sounds to me like you need to have a conversation and really talk and get on the same page."

Joel asked how things were with David, and I told him they were good, but his wife wasn't doing well, and I felt bad for him. It has to be hard to watch your wife slowly slip away, knowing there is nothing you can do. I told him I wanted to go see him and try to be there for him. His wife had been in the hospital for the last week. David wasn't sure if she would come back home. I was thinking it would be a good idea to get out of the city for the weekend and give Joel and Sarah some time to talk. Besides, I missed David and just wanted to see his eyes looking at me. Joel replied with his usual smartass comment of, "Man, you got it bad for this dude, and you haven't even had sex with him yet."

I smacked his arm and stuck out my tongue at him. I loved Joel, but he was right. I had it bad. I never totally got over David, and now that he was back in my life, I felt I had a chance at true love.

I still hadn't told my mom about David. I told her about John and I breaking up. I left out the details of our breakup, but I told her I called off the wedding, and we were no longer seeing each other. My mother felt that I was being a spoiled brat and wishing for something that would never be when I had a great man who wanted to be with me. I hated to tell her that the great man she thought I should marry raped me and stalked me for weeks. I didn't want to worry her, but most of all, I didn't want to hear her tell me how I keep making the wrong decisions in my life. I just couldn't take another lecture on what I did wrong with my life and how she would have made completely different decisions. I couldn't imagine what she would say about David, especially since he was married. I knew his wife is ill, and he promised her he would move on, but I couldn't help but feel bad.

CHAPTER 5

JULIE

My flight landed in Washington, D.C. I had been waiting for this weekend for days. I hadn't seen David in weeks. David met me at the airport since it was late on Friday night, and he wasn't planning on staying at the hospital with his wife. Our eyes met, and David hugged me so tight. We were so happy to see each other.

I told David I was happy to stay at a hotel, but he insisted I stay with him, especially since all the issues with my ex. When we arrived at David's house, it was different than I expected. It was a quiet two-bedroom house outside of town. It had a small yard with a garage, and it looked like a great place to have a family. I could only imagine that David and Susan planned on starting a family in this house.

David and I spent hours on the couch talking about Susan and how she was doing. He said that he thinks she gave up, especially since he has been talking to me. Susan has taken solace knowing that we have been talking, and she thinks that us talking is making losing her a little easier for David. She insists he call me all the time and tell her all about our conversations. I asked David how he was really doing with all of this. He said he was just numb, and he didn't know how to feel anymore. He loved Susan, but he knew she wasn't coming home. Having me to talk to had made things easier, but I wondered if I was complicating everything by being here. Is me being here with David fair to Susan? Even though she knew about us, I still felt a little bad, like I was betraying some marital vows.

I had so many feelings going on. I felt bad for moving in on her man, but I couldn't help being totally smitten with David. I had been waiting to find him since high school, and I couldn't help but want to spend every moment with him.

I finally asked David, "Are you really okay with me being here? I don't want to complicate things for you and Susan."

David looked at me and said he was glad I was here. He needed someone to talk to, and Susan was happy that he had someone to confide in. Susan wanted him to find someone he could talk to and spend time with. She was worried that if he didn't have someone, he would run back to the military and go on another mission, and he would possibly just keep burying his feelings in his work. She was afraid he would never find happiness or love again and would just live to work.

David told me that when Susan found out our history, she was happy that we had found each other. She thought it was the universe sending her a sign that it was okay to start to let go. She made David promise he would move on and find love again. She insisted he call me and try to move on. After talking with David, I had to ask if he only called me because Susan insisted. Was he really interested in being with me like I was with him? He said he was glad he called, but the look on his face told me it was mostly Susan. I had to wonder if this is a good idea.

It was late, and David and I decided to go to bed. I slept in the spare room, but I mostly just tossed and turned all night. I couldn't help but think that I pushed my way into David's life. I wanted to be with him so badly, I didn't think about how this affected him and Susan. I was questioning everything I had done. Coming out here was a mistake. I wasn't sure David was ready for me in his life. I wasn't even sure he wanted me in his life. He said he did, but did he say that to make me happy or to make Susan happy? Did I read too much into this relationship? Did David just want a friend while I was looking for the love of my life? I thought he still loved me, but maybe I was wrong. Maybe he was just lonely and needed a companion. After all, Susan was his best friend, and she was dying. Maybe he just needed a friend. I hadn't been able to sleep all night. It was early, and David wasn't up yet. I grabbed my bag and wrote David a note.

My dearest David,

I have loved you longer than I can remember, but I can never replace Susan. I want you to spend every possible moment with Susan. Cherish this time and these moments while you can. Know that when the time comes, you did everything you could. I hope that someday our paths cross again. Please know I have come to cherish your friendship and will be there when and if you need me. Right now Susan needs you, please be there for her. I hope someday we can have a relationship, even if it is just a friendship.

Yours forever,
Julie

I left David's house crying, knowing I may never see him again. I wanted to give him a way out just in case I read too much into this relationship. I felt like I tried too hard to relive the past. I knew it was what my heart wanted, but I couldn't do that to David. I needed to know he wanted to be with me and that I was not just a filler for Susan. I wanted to be there for him, but I didn't think I could and not fall in love with him even more. I didn't want to fall in love deeper and find out he only wanted a friend. That would kill me.

I arrived back in New York. Joel came to meet me at the airport. I texted him when my plane took off. He said David had already called him and asked what he did wrong. David had called and left me a voicemail. I hadn't listened to it yet. I was too scared to hear what he said. I think it would be best if I just took a break from men completely. Clearly, I had no idea what I was doing.

I sat with Joel and Sarah through dinner, and I knew we talked, but I had no idea what we said. My mind as so preoccupied with David. I finally caved and listened to his voicemail:

"Julie, I'm sorry I made you feel like you had to leave. I wanted to be with you. I know this is hard. I'm sorry I put you in this position. Please call me when you are ready to talk. I am always here for you."

I cried myself to sleep thinking about David and how I had screwed up my love life so incredibly bad.

I couldn't get it out of my head. When I woke in the morning, I called the realtor to see how the apartment hunting was. She said she had a new listing, but it was $500 more a month than my budget. However, it did have security and a doorman as Joel had requested. I told her I would take it. I hadn't even seen it, but she assured me it was great and perfect for one person. I needed to move on. I told Joel over breakfast that the apartment would be ready next week, and I would be out of his hair. Joel said I needed to look at the place and be sure. He assured me that my staying here wasn't a problem.

I looked at Joel and told him, "I need to move on and forget my past. I need to start over and forget about David and John. A fresh start, new apartment, new life."

I told him I needed to be single for a while, too, and remember what life was like without living it for someone else.

Joel called the moving company and had my apartment packed up for me. I wanted to do it myself, but he insisted this was safer for me. I assured him I hadn't heard from John in weeks. I think he got that it was over.

I spent the rest of the week buried in work and thinking about what a mess I had made of my life. The only thing I had going for me was work. At least I had that to keep me sane. I finally got the call from my realtor that my apartment was ready, and I could move in this weekend. Joel had the movers coming, and everything was ready. I couldn't wait to start over and give Joel and Sarah back their privacy.

I told Joel I would be leaving in the morning, and this would be our last dinner. He looked at me and said, "This may be our last dinner as roommates, but this is far from our last dinner. We are best friends. We share everything."

"By the way, Jules, David called me," he said, "You haven't called him back since you left. He is worried about you. I told him I got you a new place, and you are moving this weekend. That only worried him more. Jules, you can't run from everyone. David seems like a good guy. What other guy would stand by someone and watch them slowly slip away? He stood by his wife and their vows. I think he genuinely cares for you. Just talk to him. He said Susan passed last night, too, so you may want to call and check on him."

"I know, Joel, but my life is so screwed up, I just can't do that to him. Not after losing Susan. I don't want to do that to him. I don't want to burden him with my problems. I need to get my shit together before I jump into anything, and I need to make sure he wants to be with me, and not just because Susan pushed him to me. I feel like it's all one-sided. David only called me because Susan told him she wanted to make sure he had someone to be there for him."

"All the more reason for you to be there for him, Jules. She just passed, maybe just call and make sure he is okay. Just be a friend, everyone needs friends. Just call him."

"You're right, Joel. I'll call him. I should be a good friend at least, especially after the way I left."

Joel and I arrived at my new place. It was everything I hoped for: secure and John-free, nice and close to work. It was a little more than my other place, but it was definitely more secure, which was worth it. It only had one bedroom. I really wanted a two-bedroom for Jody to have a place to crash for her spring flings—not that she actually sleeps at my place.

The moving company had everything unpacked and set up except for a few boxes, but my bed and couch were all set up. I felt like I was home already. I just had to put my dishes and silverware away. There was not really much to unpack. I thought I could get it all done in a weekend. I would need to go out and get groceries. Joel said we would go together—of course he still doesn't want me going anywhere alone. This complex had a gym downstairs, so no need to leave to go there, either. I only needed to leave the building for groceries or work.

I looked at Joel and laughed and said, "Well, how about fresh air, would that be okay? Should I consider a dog, or would I need to walk him, and that would be against the rules?"

Joel looked puzzled, and he said, "Hmm, I'll think about that. A dog is a good idea. However, it would need to be walked." He just laughed, and I punched him in the arm. The doorbell rang.

I looked at Joel and said, "No one knows where I live." Joel said, "Well, it could be the groceries I ordered." I punched him again.

"Seriously, Joel, you won't even let me go out and get groceries?"

He said, "Why would you? When they get delivered, there's no need to leave the apartment if you don't need to."

"You know, you're making me more of a prisoner than John."

"But I am doing it in a good way, and I just want to make sure you're safe."

"Joel, at some point you need to let me go back to living my life. I can't be afraid anymore. I have to go on. Besides, John has no idea where I live anymore. I changed my phone number and my address and made all my social media private. Everyone knows we broke up badly and not to tell him anything, and I told everyone at work not to give out any info about me."

"So what are you saying, Jules? I'm being too overprotective of my best friend?"

"Well, yeah, kinda. Joel, you can't protect me 24/7. You are married. Remember, you have a beautiful wife at home waiting for you."

"You're right, Jules, and she is amazing and understanding, and she knows you are my best friend, and that right now, your safety is my priority, and that I will be home tonight to rock her world."

"Nope, too far, Joel." Joel just started laughing and started putting groceries away. "Let's finish unpacking," he said. "I ordered a pizza for dinner, so no worries on that, either."

"So you literally handled everything so I can't go out today."

"No, Jules, I literally made your life easier so you can stay home and unpack and relax."

"Joel, you need to stop handling me. I need to move on and get past John. I can't do that if I don't live my life."

After Joel left, I called David to let him know how sorry I was to hear about Susan.

"Julie, thank God. I thought I would never talk to you again."

33"I'm sorry, David, I just needed to clear my head. I should have talked to you before I left."

"Julie, I should have been clear about my feelings and my intentions. This whole situation with Susan passing and finding you again threw me for a loop. I never got over you, I never stopped loving you."

"David, I can't do this. I have to spend some time alone trying to get over this mess of a life I have. I want to make sure that if you and I do end up together that it's right and for the right reasons—that we're not together because Susan died, and she didn't want you to be alone. I want to make sure you're not rebounding or just lonely. I don't want to get you caught up in my drama, either. I don't think John is part of my life anymore, but I don't want to take the chance that he is still out there and put you in the middle of this mess. I just think it's best that we take a break and be alone for a bit and see what happens. I love you too much to hurt you."

"Julie, I understand, but I assure you, my feelings for you are real. I am not rebounding or doing this because Susan wanted this. I genuinely love and care for you, but I understand if you need time. Promise me you will keep in touch this time, even if it's just a text every now and then. I'm putting the house up for sale and moving on. I was hoping for a fresh start with you in New York, but I understand that you need time. I will always be here for you. I can't lose you again, even if it means we will only be friends."

Chapter 6

JULIE

It had been a couple weeks at my new apartment. I was finally starting to feel like myself, and Joel was finally starting to let me go outside. He was really starting to drive me crazy with the grocery delivery and food delivery. He brought menus to work for me and delivery places for me to try. He even downloaded Grubhub on my phone. With the secure building, everything gets left at the counter unless they are approved to come to the door, and only select vendors and approved grocery deliveries could come to the door. Grubhub was not approved, so I had to go down and pick up at the desk. This was why Joel loved the secure building where no one came to my door without prior knowledge. Visitors had to sign in to come up, and then I would get a phone call when they were on the way up.

I felt safe here, so it was great, they also had surveillance cameras on every floor and in every elevator. There was no way John would be able to get to me. Each apartment also had an emergency button to send help. The front desk sent security up to check each apartment, and police would be notified immediately. It was also coded: just to get into the building, you had to have an apartment code and a building code, and visitors were signed into a log. I felt safer here than anywhere I had ever lived. I had to put my building code in my phone so I could remember it.

Joel left to go home and made me promise to dead bolt and chain lock the door. It was a little overkill, but I promised. I sat on the couch, then I picked up my phone and fulfilled my other promise to call David back. He answered on the first ring.

I was finally getting back to myself. Joel and I were doing dinner out, since I finally convinced him it was okay to go out to dinner. He was hesitant, but he agreed. I hadn't heard from John in weeks, so hopefully that meant he finally gave up.

Joel and I had a great dinner. We talked about him and his wife. He had finally given up the PI pursuit and agreed that she wasn't having an affair; she was just bored and filling her time with volunteer work, like she said. I told Joel he had the perfect life. He just needed to learn to live it and like it now. And when I am going to be an aunt, I need someone to spoil, since I am not having kids any time soon since the engagement is off and my dating life is so screwed up. Of course, Joel reminded me I had a perfectly good opportunity with David, and I had pushed him away to be single and alone. So I had no one to blame except myself.

I hated it when Joel was right. But my life was so screwed up right now, and I didn't want to screw up anyone else's.

I was sitting in my nice new apartment, but I still felt uneasy. It was weird; I still had that feeling that John was right outside the door yelling for me, but I knew he had no idea where I lived now. I left no forwarding address, and I had everything sent to Joel's just in case John found out anything. No one knew where I live but Joel, David, and work. I should have felt safe and secure, but John was still in my head.

I spent all day at work, but my mind was just not in it. This case had been really tough, especially whenever I saw Susan's name on it. We had to use her deposition since she passed. I kept reading the same pages over and over. I was not sure why I couldn't get my head together today.

Joel popped into my office, and he said I looked tired. I just laughed and said, "Yeah, I didn't sleep well. Not sure why, but I feel off."

Joel said he talked to David last night. David didn't want to bother me, but he wanted me to know the house was sold, and he was moving. His dad left him a place in Connecticut, so he was going to stay there for a while, in case I was curious.

"Thanks for letting me know, Joel. I can't talk to David right now. I'm just in a weird place. I can't get my head on straight. I need to just focus on work and get over John and David and the mess I made of my life."

"Jules, just go home and take a hot bath tonight and relax, order a pizza. I know it's your favorite food. You just need to relax and let go. John is gone and never coming back. I think he got the message when you changed your number and address. Besides, he has no idea where you live. You're perfectly safe at the apartment, it's Joel approved. But we could revisit the dog conversation."

I just laughed and said, "Joel, you really know how to make me laugh. But I'm not getting a dog. I would have to walk it and take it out."

"Jules, they have dog walkers to do that for you."

"God, Joel, you need to stop. I swear Sarah is going to think you're losing it, too. Don't make me call her and tell her how crazy you are."

"Jules, she knows how crazy I am, and she still married me."

I laughed and said, "That just makes her as crazy as you. Your kids will be wonderful if you ever have any."

Joel laughed about that. "Um, remember how I told you Sarah was all over the place with her mood swings?" he asked.

"Yeah, I remember. Why, is she okay?"

"Yeah, turns out she was pregnant. She told me over dinner last night."

"OMG, and you didn't call and tell me I was going to be an aunt?"

"Well, I was going to, but I spent the night with Sarah, talking and just being a family. Sarah did suggest that you being an aunt wasn't enough. She thought you would be a good godmother to our child."

I just started crying and smiling. I hugged Joel so hard, I just couldn't stop crying. "I'm so happy for both of you."

Joel smiled. "I'm glad, because I would like to reserve you for baby-sitting on date night and diaper duty whenever possible."

I said, "Yes, of course I am babysitting, and I can't wait to plan a huge baby shower."

CHAPTER 7

JULIE

It had been a couple weeks. I felt pretty safe here in my apartment, but every once in a while, I still felt like someone was watching me. I think it was just residual fear of John returning. But I hadn't heard from him in over a month. My life had finally calmed down. I had been going to work and had really been able to concentrate on my cases for a change. I had made great progress with Joel on our current caseload. Joel even let me go out for a walk this week alone. I still had to call when I made it back home, but it was nice to get out and not feel fear. Now I just need to concentrate on moving on with my life starting over without a man. I needed to learn to live on my own and not rely on anyone else.

There was a knock on the door.

Who could that be? Joel would call first, and I didn't order groceries. I peeked through the eye hole in the door. It was a man I didn't know. I opened the door but left the chain on. "Can I help you?"

He said, "HI, you must be Julie. I am the building manager, and I wanted to invite you to our events of the month."

"Oh," I say, "Hold on." I unchained the door and said, "I'm so sorry, I'm still learning who everyone is."

He said, "No need to apologize. This is a secure facility, and we take extra precautions, so I totally understand. I just wanted to drop off this flier for the monthly meetings personally and introduce myself since

I didn't get the opportunity to meet you when your realtor toured our facility. My name is Tom, I am so happy to meet new tenants since we do not get many new people in our building. The turnover here is low since we are a secure facility. We do have you and one other tenant on the fourth floor who just moved in last week. I just want to assure you that we take safety here very seriously, and we have meetings and fun mixers if you're interested. Every meeting is held on the first floor in our main meeting room. The dates are on the flier, and on the back is a list of our safety-approved vendors. Each vendor has been fully vetted by our security and had background checks completed for anyone who will be going up to apartments."

I must have looked scared. Tom said, "There is no need to ever worry in this building." I thanked Tom for the flier and said, "I will try to make some of the meetings." Off he went. He seemed very nice.

I read in the flier that there was a mixer on Friday night, and the tenants' monthly meeting was next Wednesday. I guess I should try to make the tenants meeting at least—not sure about the mixer. This calendar had lots of events for security and domestic violence, even a demonstration on self-defense. Tom wasn't joking when he said this building took security seriously.

I spent the next couple days working on my cases and going through some boxes that I stuck in the closet and said I would do later. Of course, I keep putting it off, but I can't find a few things still, so now it's time to get the boxes unpacked. I'm missing my favorite slippers—not a big deal, but they were so comfy. They were perfect in case I needed to run downstairs for food to the lobby. It was odd that they were not in my clothes boxes. My favorite earrings were missing, too. They must have been in some box together. I wondered if they got lost. I found a coffee cup that John gave me that could go in the trash. I was still find-ing a few items John left or gave me. Anything of value, I had shipped to John (from Joel, of course—I wouldn't call or go to see him ever). He had finally stopped calling and coming around. I hadn't seen him at work either, so that had been wonderful. I was finally starting to close this chapter of heartbreak and move on.

It was Wednesday, and I thought I really should go to the tenants meeting to meet my neighbors and all. I got downstairs, and everyone was in the meeting room. There were hors d'oeuvres and everything. I took a seat and waited for Tom to start the meeting.

Tom stood up and started talking as he introduced himself. "Hello tenants, I am Tom, your manager, of course. You all know me. We have two new tenants in our building. Julie is on the third floor. Please stand up, Julie, and say hi."

I didn't want to, but I stood up and waved hi to everyone.

Tom started again. "And on the fourth floor, we have Sam, who I do not see here tonight. He must have had a prior engagement, no big deal. Hopefully we meet in person at the next meeting."

He continued, "Just to go over some basics for Julie and reminders for all of us who need it: this building is specifically built for security, and we take it very seriously. On your flier, you will see our approved vendors. Only those vendors will be allowed up to your floor, and only those who have passed a background check will be allowed into your apartments. For example, our wonderful dog walker has completed background checks and can get to your apartment to walk your dog if you are not home. He will be escorted to your apartment if you request it. Groceries can be ordered and placed in your apartment, and of course, if you request it, the delivery man will also be escorted. We have tons of security cameras everywhere and do not anticipate any issues in this building, but as the majority of us are violence survivors, we know you can't go too far with security. Keeping that in mind, I have set up a few demonstrations this month for self-defense. We do at least one full training a year and a few small talks throughout the rest of the year, especially before the holidays, as there are upticks in violence around the holidays."

He went on, "If you ever have any suggestions on demonstrations you would like to see, please feel free to let me know. I am always open to suggestions. Your safety is always our first priority—followed by your rent payment to pay for the hors d'oeuvres." Everyone laughed. Tom seemed very well liked. I got the feeling he made these meetings fun and educational.

"Just FYI, we will be doing some maintenance painting in a few hallways, so if you smell fresh paint, it is your rent money working hard. The painters have all been vetted and completed background checks to be in the hallway unescorted. They will not have access to any apartment; this is for hallways and stairways only."

Someone raised a hand, and Tom said, "Yes, George, you have a question?"

"Yes, what if I want my apartment painted pink?"

Tom said, "Well, George, first we will have your vision checked. Second, we will ask your wife, who is currently giving you a dirty look, and then we will fill out paperwork to get your apartment painted pink."

Everyone laughed, and George's wife gave him a nudge. Tom said, "There is an opportunity to get apartments painted if needed. If you are interested, I have request forms available in my office, and for a small fee, George will come and give you a color suggestion." Everyone laughed again.

This tenant group seemed really fun and relaxed. It was kind of nice to get out of my own head. Tom adjourned the meeting and said, "Please, stay, eat, and mingle. Don't forget, Friday is self-defense night, if you are interested."

Tom comes over, reintroduces himself, and introduces me to a couple of neighbors. I was a little curious. "I didn't realize this building was for violence survivors," I said to Tom.

Tom said, "Oh, yes, just about everyone who lives here has suffered some sort of violence. I myself was in a violent relationship that ended. We have survivors of domestic abuse, elderly abuse. A few people that were mugged. Most people look for a secure facility only after something bad has happened in their life. Since I myself was a victim of violence, I want to make sure this facility is proactive against violence, which is why we do some seminars and training to help our tenants stay safe. You should try to join us and meet a few more of the tenants. Knowing everyone in the building is a great way to help someone feel safe. Knowing your surroundings and the people around you helps you feel safe. Besides, the more people you know, the more this place feels like home, and we have some wonderful tenants. Judy over there is on your floor, and she bakes the best cookies, especially at Christmas. Her apartment smells like a gingerbread house around Christmas. I walk by every day just to smell what she's baking. She owns the bakery down the street if you're interested in baked goods. Joshua over there also lives on the third floor. He is an assistant at city hall, and he makes sure we always have extra patrols in our neighborhood if crime starts to uptick. Our tenants in this building all take care of each other. We are a large extended crazy family. We also look out for one another, so don't be afraid to say hi when you see your new crazy family in the elevator."

I laughed. Tom was really nice and a great manager. He was very funny, too.

I left the meeting and called Joel on my way back up to my apartment. "Joel, did you know this building is specifically for violence survivors and stuff?" Joel said, "I may have read something about it in the description from the realtor."

"Seriously, and you didn't think to tell me? We have seminars on violence. Joel, don't you think that should have been discussed?"

"Well, I thought it would be good for you to be around others and you don't have to tell them anything. But I do think you should do some of the seminars. You might learn something."

"I thought this was just a really secure facility."

"It is," Joel said, "With a few extra perks. Look. I know it isn't what you really wanted, but I want to know you're safe, and if they do classes to give you tools to be safe, then that is a perk. And it makes me feel better that everyone there is on the lookout for violence, and they are less likely to be weirdos in that building. So yeah, I picked it, but I did it out of love."

I laughed and said, "I love you, but next time, tell me. I do like the building. Tom, the manager, is really nice, and apparently the lady down the hall has a bakery and makes wonderful cookies. So you should know I feel very safe. Thank you."

Joel said, "Finally, and you're welcome. Now next time you question my decision, please refer to this as exhibit A."

I laughed and said, "Goodbye, you lunatic."

I finally got back into my apartment. I needed a little snack to go with the hors d'oeuvres I had at the meeting. Then, a bath and bed would be in order. But maybe a little wine and TV before I hit the bath. I could use some me time. It had been a long day. *Let's see what's on Netflix to go with my wine,* I thought. Maybe I could find a romcom to watch or something.

Yeah, my apartment was too quiet. Maybe Joel was right—maybe I needed a dog or a cat, someone to keep me company. Maybe I just needed a roommate. Nope, no way Joel would approve of that. Maybe a fish to talk to. I wouldn't have to walk a fish, I just had to remember to feed it. Maybe a cat was a better idea—then I would be able to pet it and feed it. I could have great conversations, and she would always take my side. I wondered what the pet policy was for this building.

You know what? I needed a nice warm bath, and I was going to bring my wine with me and think about a cat. Maybe it would come to me in the tub. But if I got a cat, then I would have to change its litter, and ugh, that is not fun. But a dog needs walks outside; however, they do bark when strangers are around. Maybe a dog was the way to go. A fish was definitely not going to let me pet it or bark when there was trouble.

Maybe a hamster. I could play with a hamster.

Jeez, I was totally crazy. Who was I kidding? I was not getting a pet. I was never home. I was always working. I would be crazy to get a pet. I just needed to give up and go to bed.

I woke suddenly and jumped. I just felt like someone was staring at me. I knew no one could get into my apartment. Joel and I were the only ones with a key to my apartment. I just had this uneasy feeling. I couldn't explain why it came on. I knew I was safe. I got up and showered. I still had this uneasy feeling, and I was hoping it would pass. I got dressed and went to work early. I told Joel about my feelings. He said it was probably just from finding out that the building was a secure facility, and most people there were people who had survived violence. He was probably right. My brain was probably just catching up with the information it collected at the meeting.

I was just going to put everything out of my mind, go about my usual day, and get my work done. That would keep my brain occupied and keep me busy. Hopefully, if I exhausted my brain, it would sleep well and not work so hard to freak me out. I still wondered how I could have been so wrong about John. Did I totally miss all the signs? Did he hide it that well? Why was I still letting John in my head? He was gone. I needed to focus on work. That part of my life was over. I was all moved into a new apartment and a new life.

I was wrapping up my work day. It sucked—this case was draining. I was still working on the case that led me to David, and still I couldn't call him and talk to him. I knew I should call David and talk to him. I just didn't want to lead him on. I also didn't want to drag him into any drama. Hopefully all my drama was over. Why was I so crazy about this?

Joel popped into my office on his way home. "Hey, you headed out soon, or are you working late?"

"No, I'm headed home. I'm just in my head again, as always."

"About what today?" Joel said.

"This case, David, the same old stuff."

"Wanna talk about it?" Joel asks.

"I just want to call him, but I don't know what to say."

Joel said, "Start with hello, ask him how he is doing since Susan passed. The conversation will come. Try just being a good friend. I think it would be a good idea to call him. You did promise to keep in touch."

"I know, you're right. I'm a terrible friend."

Joel said, "Go home, order takeout, have a glass of wine, and call him. You will feel better. You might sleep better, too."

"Joel, I hate it when you're right."

CHAPTER 8

JULIE

I arrived home and did what Joel suggested: poured myself a glass of wine, ordered takeout, and decided I needed to be a good friend and call David. I just didn't know what to say. I didn't know if he would even answer.

Well, here goes nothing. The phone rang.

David answers, "Julie, hi, how are you?"

"David, hi. I am good. I just wanted to check in and see how you are doing and see how the move went. I'm so sorry about Susan. Are you okay?"

"I'm good, Julie. The move went well. I guess it was harder than I expected. Packing up a lifetime of memories is never easy. Susan's family came and helped. There were some family heirlooms they wanted, so I had to go through all her things and my things as I packed everything. It was a lot harder than I expected. But I'm doing good now. It's a little weird being back home at my dad's place. How are you?"

"I'm good, things have been good. Joel has been great taking care of me. My new apartment is great. I finally feel safe. I haven't heard from John, either, so I'm hoping the nightmare is over. I think I am finally in a good place. I'm trying to move on."

The doorbell rang. "Oh, David, hang on, that is my dinner. I ordered in—as you know, Joel prefers I do not leave my apartment for any reason."

I shut the door. "David, you still there?"

"Yes, of course, Julie. So, what is for dinner?"

"I ordered Italian. Meatballs with some rigatoni. And, of course, some garlic bread."

"Sounds amazing. Too bad you have to eat alone."

"Well, it is my new lifestyle. I do everything safely. No men allowed in my life, according to Joel. I can have a dog, but I must have an approved dog walker."

"Joel isn't being a little too overprotective, is he?"

"Well, I think so, but if you ask Joel, he says no. If I go for a walk, I have to call and talk to him while I walk. So I suppose I could get a dog and call him while I walk the dog. But I honestly don't want to pick up dog poop. I just like driving Joel nuts. It's kinda fun. And right now, driving Joel nuts is all the fun I get. I might send him some pics of poodles or wiener dogs at the rescue and ask if that is acceptable for a dog."

"You know he is going to call and have a fit. He went through a lot of trouble to get you set up in a nice, safe apartment, and you want to get an ankle biter dog to protect you?"

"David, I wouldn't actually get the dog. I just want to send him the pics of a cute one with ribbons in his hair or something. Oh, I didn't tell you—Joel and Sarah are expecting. I'm going to be an aunt."

"Wow, that is great news. I'm sure Joel is excited."

"He is super excited, and he asked me to be the godmother. They just found out, so Joel is still getting used to the idea. I'm glad I moved out when I did so they could have alone time and start getting ready for the baby."

"Julie, I really am happy that everything seems to be going well for you. You sound like you're in a good place. At the risk of overstepping, I want you to know I care about you. I always will. I hope we can be friends, if not something more. I still love you. I know you need time to sort through everything. And I am more than willing to wait for you forever if that is what you need. But I just want you to know I am here whenever you are ready."

"David, I honestly don't know what to say. I'm still so confused about my life. I just don't want to drag you into anything. I don't want to lose you, but I don't want to hurt you, either."

"Julie, I understand, and I don't want to force you to decide. I just want you to know how I feel about you. I am always here for you. Even if it's just to talk. Besides, right now, I don't have anything else going on in my life. I'm off work for a while and just going through everything from my dad's house. This house needed a lot of work, so I'm working on a lot of small projects before I decide what to do with this place. So if you need to talk, I have lots of time. If you need dinner, I have time for that, too."

"Thank you, David. Thank you for understanding and for not pushing. I really don't deserve you. I would understand if you moved on with your life while you're waiting for me to get my life together."

"Julie, that is not going to happen. I am here for you. My heart has always been yours. Even being married to Susan, I knew who had my heart. Yes, I loved my wife, and yes, I was always faithful to Susan, but Susan knew you had my heart. That is why she made me promise to reach out to you. She knew who you were and what you meant to me before we met in Washington. She knew from me telling her about our past. When she found out you were the same Julie from my past, she thought it was fate that brought us back together. She made me promise to go to New York and fight to be with you, no matter what."

"David, I really want us to work, but I don't want to jump into a relationship and have it blow up. I don't want to put you in a bad position, either. This mess with John is over, I hope, but it's only been a few months, and honestly, I'm not ready. I just don't trust myself or anyone yet. I'm such a mess, and my life is a mess. John was just a mistake that I don't want to repeat. I just need time to get my head straight and make sure that we're both doing this for the right reasons and are both clear-headed and not rebounding or jumping into this too quickly. David,

I still love you, too. I just don't want to ruin a great thing by jumping into this. I don't know what to do. This is so weird to me, wanting to be with someone but not being able to. I'm afraid of hurting you."

"Julie, the only way you're going to hurt me is if you don't let me in. If you cut me out of your life, that will hurt me. I can handle taking it slow and being friends. I can handle distance. I can handle anything you throw at me, but don't cut me off. Don't push me away; that I can't handle. Not after losing Susan. She was my best friend. Right now, I have no one. If Joel hadn't called and kept me in the loop about you, I wouldn't even know you moved. Joel has kept me in the loop cause he knows I care about you. I think he knows how much you care about me. This isn't a mistake, and it isn't wrong. It might have been bad timing, but that is all. I don't think we need to hide our feelings for each other. If you want to take it slow, I totally understand. I agree that taking it slow is a good idea. I just lost Susan, and I am not ready for a serious relationship, but I am ready to have you in my life. And I don't blame you, dealing with that mess with John was a lot, and it took a physical and emotional toll on you. But hiding yourself away from the world won't change what happened, and it won't help you heal."

"I know you're right, I just need to put my past behind me and move on. I really need to rebuild and start to forget my past. You're right, David, holding on to the past is not going to help. Thanks for the insight. I should let you get back to your work. But I promise to call more and keep in touch."

"Julie, I am always here if you need me."

"Thanks, David."

David was right. I just needed to get out of my head and move on, forget John and what he did to me. Ugh, I needed a relaxing bath. And more wine. I decided to take a nice hot bath and have a glass of wine.

I must have dozed off a little in the tub, because the water got cold. I finished my wine and got out of the tub. I felt a lot better. I'm not sure if it was the wine, the talk with David, or the bath, but I felt more relaxed.

I dried off and got ready for bed. I finally felt like I could sleep. I was relaxed. I slept better than I did the night before, no waking up suddenly. I got ready for work and headed out. There was someone new in the elevator. I said, "Good morning." He said, "Good morning." I looked at him. He looked familiar, but I couldn't place him. Maybe I had seen him in the building before. I asked if he was new to the complex. He said he was, and he just moved in on the fourth floor.

I said, "Oh, you must be Sam. Tom, the manager, said we had a new tenant on the fourth floor."

"Yes, I just moved in a couple weeks ago. I'm still bringing in boxes, so I haven't spent much time in the apartment yet. But I'm getting there."

We arrived on the first floor. "Well, I am Julie, on floor three. It was nice meeting you."

"You too, Julie. Have a nice day," Sam replied.

I still swore I had seen him before. He looked so familiar. It had to be from the building.

I went on my way to work. When I got to work, I told Joel about Sam. I told him how I thought I had seen him before. He just looked so familiar. I couldn't figure out where I had seen him before, but as soon as I saw him in the elevator, I swear I recognized him.

It was just one of those things that was going to bug me all day, like a song that gets stuck in your head. Forget it, I needed to focus on work. I was so preoccupied that I couldn't get anything done. I needed to focus. Okay, no more thinking about Sam, just work.

Case notes. I needed to go over this case again and make sure I had everything I need.

Joel said, "Jules, how about we have a breakout session. You look like you need a coffee and something to eat."

I just looked at Joel. "Well, you're right about the coffee."

Joel and I headed to the cafe down the street, and I grabbed a muffin and a coffee. Joel and I tried to talk about work, but I just couldn't think. I was so preoccupied by Sam and how I knew him. Joel kept telling me, "You probably saw him in the building or at a coffee shop or something. You have been more alert lately, so it only stands to reason that you would have noticed people. You may have seen him in the building or at a store, or possibly grabbing takeout. I think you're just on edge still. You know you're safe in that apartment."

"Joel, I know I am safe. I just hate it when I can't place someone, especially now. It makes me uneasy. If I could place him, I would be fine. If I knew he worked at my favorite restaurant, I would be fine. It's just the fear of the unknown that is driving me nuts. I'll be fine, I just need to get something else in my mind. Joel, we need to head back to the office. I need to get some work done on this case. We are behind on the case. I'm not getting much accomplished."

"Yeah, we will, but first, tell me: how did your call with David go?"

"It was good. We cleared the air, and I told him how I felt. I was honest with him. He was honest and told me how much he still cared about me. Said he would wait for me."

"Well, that's good. So you didn't totally screw that relationship up."

"Joel I swear, if you weren't my best friend—"

"What, Jules, I'm just being honest. You tend to mess up your relationships. You put up walls and run when things are good. I mean, look at John—who, granted, was a total piece of shit. But you never were totally honest with him. You never told him how you really felt. You accepted a marriage proposal and hoped you would be happy someday. You thought you could make it work. You thought he was a good guy, but you never were honest and told him you weren't sexually satisfied. You never gave him your total heart, not like you did with David. But with David, you gave your heart to him back in high school. I think after David left in high school, you were afraid to let anyone else in, so you never really let the walls around your heart completely down. I think that is also why you left David's house that night and came back home. You're afraid of getting your heart broken again. You know that if you don't let anyone in, you will never find love. Then you will be stuck with me calling you crazy Aunt Jules."

"Joel, I get it, I will end up single alone with lots of cats. Don't worry, Joel. I will get a cat for your kid, too. Now we really need to head back to work."

After work, I decided to take a bath. That seemed to really relax me last night, so I thought, why not try it again? I was hoping to get a good night's sleep. I had been on edge lately for some odd reason. A glass of wine and a bath always seem to help. Maybe it was this case bringing up the past and the breakup. Maybe after I got through this case, everything would go back to normal.

I felt so much better after my wine and my bath. Bed was screaming my name. I finally crawled in and dozed off.

I woke up. Oh My God! I jumped out of bed, grabbed my shoes and keys, ran out of the apartment, and hit the button for the elevator while putting on my shoes. I called Joel. No answer. I didn't expect him to answer at 5 a.m. He was probably sound asleep and didn't hear the phone. Now what? I went downstairs to the security in the lobby. I used my app to get an Uber. I guessed that my next option was to go to the office. I was still in my PJ's. I must have looked insane. I told security I was going to the office, just in case something happened. Work emergency. I called David. I didn't want to get in an Uber without someone on the phone and someone knowing where I was going. I was so freaked out.

"Julie, are you okay?"

"David, thank God you answered. I'm getting into an Uber, and I'm freaking out. Sam is the guy from the shower."

"Julie, I have no idea what that means, but I am sure it's important, so just stay on the phone and talk to me while you're in the Uber. Where are you headed?"

"I'm going to the office. Joel didn't answer his phone. I have nowhere else to go that I can think of. I'm scared, David. It just came to me when I was sleeping. Sam is the guy from the shower."

"Okay, Julie. I'm going to call Joel from my landline while I'm on the phone with you. Just hold on. Stay with me. Try to calm down. It's going to be okay."

"Uh, no answer," he said. "Let me try again."

"Hello?" Joel said.

"Joel, thank God. It's David. I have Julie on my other phone. She's crying and upset about Sam being the guy from the shower. She's in an Uber on the way to the office."

"What? Sam is the guy from the shower?"

"Joel, I have no idea what is going on, but she is really upset."

"David, can you have her change her drop-off to my house and stay on the phone with her till she gets here? I will meet her outside."

"Yeah, sure, no problem. Julie, can you change your drop-off and go to Joel? He will meet you outside."

"Yes, I can do that," I said.

"Julie, it's going to be okay. Joel is going to meet you. You're not alone. I'm staying with you on the phone the whole time. We will figure everything out together. I promise Joel and I will figure this whole mess out. You're not alone, and you're safe. How far until you're at Joel's?"

"About seven minutes."

"Okay, so we can talk for seven minutes. Tell me, did you even get dressed on your way out of the apartment, or do you have slippers on?"

"No, I grabbed my tennis shoes, but I'm still in my PJ's."

"Okay, well, that's a nice look. I'm sure Joel has an app to get your clothes delivered for you."

I laughed.

"Okay, that sounds better. You know Joel is going to be right there when your Uber stops. And I am right here until Joel hugs you tight. You're totally safe."

"I don't know what I would do without you and Joel."

"Well, it's a good thing you will never have to find out, because we will always be here for you. You can try, but you're not getting rid of either of us. I know Joel loves his early morning calls, and they will keep him on his toes. Besides, he needs practice for fatherhood. So you're really doing him a big favor by getting him ready."

I laughed again. "David, thanks. I really needed you."

My Uber arrived at Joel's house. I got out and hugged Joel.

"Jules, are you okay?" Joel asked.

I was crying. "Sam is the guy John was in the shower with."

"It's okay, we are going to figure everything out, okay? Let's get you in the house. Let me have your phone so I can let David know you're okay."

I gave him my phone. "David, I have Jules. She's safe. I'm not letting her out of my sight unless I know she is safe."

"Joel, what is she talking about? Who is Sam, the guy from the shower?"

"She met some guy at the apartment building named Sam. She kept saying she recognized him but couldn't place him. Apparently, in her sleep, she remembered he was the guy she caught John in the shower with. This can't be a coincidence."

David said, "Joel I'm coming down there. I can't sit here when Julie needs me."

"Honestly, David, I think that is a great idea. How about we plan on going to my house for dinner tonight and make some plans on what to do. Then we can discuss what I find out. I'm going to get more details from Jules, then I am headed to the police station to see what I can get done. Also, I need to go to her apartment manager. She is not going back to that apartment until this is over. I'll text you my address."

"Sounds good. Let me know if you need anything."

"Will do, see you tonight."

I asked, "Joel what am I going to do? Sam is the guy from the shower."

"Don't worry, Jules, I am going to go to your apartment manager and talk to him and the police and find out our options. In the meantime, since we're up, how about some breakfast? Sarah has already started making pancakes."

"Pancakes sound great, Joel. I don't know what I would do without you."

"Good thing you don't have to ever find out."

"That's exactly what David told me on the way over here. He said I never have to be without either of you. He also said these early mornings were great practice for fatherhood."

"Well, he is probably right about that, but let's not make a habit of it. Just so you're not surprised tonight, David is on his way. He's coming to dinner tonight. He was worried about you, and I thought it was a good idea. Now come, breakfast is ready, and we've got a big day ahead of us."

"Wait, why is it a big day?"

"Well, I've got a lot of work first at the police station and your apartment building, and David is coming, which means I also need to pull your head out of your butt and make you realize he is the man of your dreams."

"Seriously, you're worried about my love life right now?"

"Yes, I am not having my kids have cats at your house. That is just way beyond pathetic, Jules."

"Joel, I think you are a little too worried about my love life."

"No, I am not. I need you to find someone. I need you to be happy. I need to know you are taken care of. I am going to have kids in a few months. They will take over my life, and it may kill me. Then who will take care of you?"

"Joel, you are blowing that a little out of proportion."

"Okay, maybe I am, but what is wrong with wanting my best friend to be happy? I know David is the guy for you. I saw it in your eyes. I hear it in your voice. I see it, you just keep denying it. You are running away from it, and I totally get it—you're scared because of John. But instead of running away from him, why not run to him? Let him be there for you, Jules. Let him take care of you. Let him be your strength. Jules, you can't push him away."

"Joel, what if he gets hurt trying to protect me?"

"That's why you're pushing him away? Jules, David is a Marine. I think he can protect himself and you. Besides, he has made it very clear he wants to be with you and help protect you. He hasn't gone back into service yet, either. He's still on leave. Maybe just start by talking to him. Stop pushing him away."

"You're right, Joel. I need all the friends and help I can get, and I know I can trust him. David is a good guy."

"Finally, I've been trying to pull your head out of your ass for weeks. So I'm thinking of a destination wedding. What do you think?"

"Oh my God, Joel, I think you're moving way too fast. Maybe we could have a first date."

"Fine, date first, then wedding plans. But you're not getting any younger, Jules."

"OMG, Joel, you sound like my mother."

"Well, is it so wrong that I want my kids to have cousins to play with and not cats?"

"Joel, can we please go have breakfast and discuss my imaginary wedding and kids later."

"Fine, can you have an imaginary boy named Thompson and girl named Trixie. Sarah nixed both those names already, and I really liked them."

"Oh my God, Joel, stop it."

CHAPTER 9

JULIE

Joel and I finally made it to work. Joel stopped at the reception desk and told them there were to be no visitors for me and no deliveries under any circumstances. Joel also went to security and let them know there was an issue and to make sure no one was allowed to see me. He also showed them John and Sam's pictures just in case either show up, so security knew not to allow them in.

I was back at work now, and I couldn't think about work again. I knew I was safe here. I had security downstairs and lots of people around my office, but I was struggling to get my mind on the case. I was totally preoccupied with Sam. How did he find out where I moved to? Did he tell John? Were they working together?

Joel didn't stick around long; he headed right out to the police station. He said he would call and keep me updated.

JOEL

I arrived at the police station and said, "I need to see the detective in charge of the case for Julie Marks."

After waiting for what seemed like forever, a detective finally came out to meet with me.

"You're here for the Julie Marks case?" A dark haired man, about 6'2" with glasses, came down wearing a gray suit. "Do you have new information?"

"Yes, I do. I am Joel Canton, Julie's best friend."

"I am Detective Jordan. Good to meet you."

"Julie moved to a new building, and the neighbor who lives upstairs from her happens to be the man who she walked in on showering with her ex, John. That can't be a coincidence. Somehow John found her new apartment and had his partner move there and has been spying on her. Julie has felt uncomfortable for the last couple weeks. She felt like someone was watching her. She just never knew why until she saw Sam in the elevator. Is there anything you can do to this Sam person or to prove John is behind this and protect Julie?"

"First things first. Sam moving to this building could be a coincidence. Maybe John and him are not even together anymore. We can check Julie's apartment and make sure no one is spying on her just to set her mind at ease. I can check into this Sam and make sure he is on the up and up. But I can't just go snooping on this Sam person because he slept with someone who was bothering Julie. I can check into him, but without probable cause, I can't go much further. So I can do some checking, but if it leads nowhere, then we're stuck. So let's start with the apartment manager and check out Julie's apartment to see where that leads."

"Let me grab a couple things, then we can head over to the apartment."

We arrived at the apartment building and went to find the manager, Tom. I had a key to Julie's place, so no need to get permission to enter. I just wanted the manager to answer questions about Sam.

Detective Jordan and I started in Jules's apartment.

Detective Jordan didn't see any obvious signs that anyone was spying on Jules. He started to look in the vents and behind the mirror. I was asking the manager about Sam without trying to alarm him that Sam was in on this.

"So ,Tom, Jules told me Sam, the new neighbor, reminded her of someone she couldn't place. You happen to know where he works by chance? I'm thinking she knows him from wherever he works."

Detective Jordan pulled the vent covers off and pointed flashlights in the vents. "So far, nothing in the living room. Let's check the kitchen. I'm not finding anything so far."

I kept trying to get information out of the manager. He wasn't very helpful. He either didn't know a lot about Sam or didn't want to tell me about Sam. Maybe once we found something, he would be a little more cooperative. Not that I was hoping we found something. But I would like to know that Jules wasn't having these feelings that someone was watching her for nothing.

Detective Jordan headed to the bedroom to start looking. He didn't seem to be finding anything out of the ordinary—at least nothing that would lead to John spying on Jules. I had no idea what he was looking for, though. Detective Jordan came out from the bedroom.

"Okay, guys, pack it up, we have to leave. I found something in the closet. I have to get a tech team in here to do a full sweep and see what we are dealing with exactly. Until they come and verify everything, we cannot touch anything. So until they arrive, let's lock up the apartment, and we can meet downstairs and I can get some information about this Sam person who lives upstairs."

Tom started to ask what Sam had to do with this. "He seems like a nice person."

Detective Jordan answers, "Well, Tom the wire looks like it is fed from the apartment above this one, which would be the apartment Sam lives in. Is that correct?"

Tom responded, "Yes, that would be correct."

Detective Jordan said, "Well then, that would make him our lead suspect in planting the device I found in the apartment, which gives me probable cause to search the apartment above this unit. I need information from you about the tenant who occupies the apartment."

Detective Jordan grabbed his cell phone, called the station, and requested a tech team to his location to do a detailed search of both apartments.

I couldn't believe Jules was right, someone was spying on her. Was John using Sam to keep tabs on her?

She was never going to feel safe again, not until John was behind bars. I just hoped this was enough to get him arrested. I hoped they could catch him.

I couldn't believe this was happening. I really thought this was over. I thought John was done and over.

How was I going to tell Jules that John was still around? How was I going to protect her?

Detective Jordan said, "Okay, let's go discuss this Sam person. The tech team is going to do a full sweep of both units. They will let me know their findings. Once I know exactly what we are dealing with, I will know how to proceed. Tom, I need to know everything you know about this Sam. His previous address, current employment, any info you have."

"Honestly, I don't have much info on him. I have his application and background check. But he has only lived here a few weeks, and I haven't had much interaction with him, so there isn't much to tell. I will print copies of everything I have in his file for you. He did apply with a co-applicant, so we did run both backgrounds. However, his partner hasn't moved in yet. I haven't met him, either, since he emailed his application over. My understanding from Sam is that they had separate apartments and were waiting for them to be rented or sold before they moved. Sam's went really quick, but John's hasn't been rented yet, so he hasn't moved in yet. The realtor is having issues getting a renter in his place, from what Sam said."

Detective Jordan said, "Okay, if I am right about my feelings for this John guy, I think he is watching every move Julie makes: leaving for work, coming home, listening to her phone conversations. Joel, where is Julie now?

"She is at our law firm."

"Okay, that is perfect. Later I am going to have a uniform unit pick her up and bring her to the station. I will get her statement then, and we can figure out how to protect her. I honestly think he has been watching her from afar this whole time. You may have given him the slip while she moved apartments, but it sounds like he found her pretty quickly, and he isn't giving up. We need to make a plan to catch him. Let me get with the tech team to see what they find, and I will meet up with them later at the precinct to figure this out. Until then, do not tell Sam or anyone what we found. We still have the element of surprise. If Sam tells John, then he might go after her sooner, and we can't risk that.

Joel, you head to the office to let Julie know the plan, and I will call you from the precinct with any updates. I am headed there now to hopefully start digging into Sam and John and find out what the tech team found."

I headed out to the office, and I had to update Jules. I didn't know what to tell her. How could I tell her it's not over? How would I keep her safe?

How did John find her? We were so careful about changing phone numbers and her address. He must have followed her home from work. That was the only thing I couldn't change.

Hopefully the police would take this a little more seriously than they did previously. John had definitely shown that he was stalking Jules. How did Sam fit in? Was he John's partner in this, or was he unaware of what John was doing?

I finally got to the office. Jules was worried. I could tell by her face.

"Joel, what did you find out? Tell me everything. Don't keep anything from me to keep me safe. I need to know everything."

"Jules, I don't have a lot of info yet. We need to go to the police station in a little bit to go over what they found in your apartment."

"What did they find, Joel?"

"Honestly, I'm not sure yet. I know they found something, but as soon as the detective found it, he had us clear out so some tech team could come in and go over everything. The tech team is there now, going through your apartment and Sam's apartment."

"Sam? Why would they go through his apartment?"

"Jules, it looks like whatever they found was tied somehow to Sam's apartment. No idea if Sam knew or if he is part of this. Tom said Sam's partner is named John, but he hadn't met him. He just ran his paperwork, and nothing showed up on his application. Honestly, Jules, I'm not sure what is happening. I'm hoping we find out a lot more when we get to the police station. In the meantime, David is on his way. I don't think it's a good idea to meet at the house. I'm going to call him and have him meet us here."

"At least here, he looks like a client. If John is still out there, I'm worried he might be watching my house as well as yours."

"David might be our only ally John doesn't know about. I want to keep it that way."

"Okay, so when do we head to the station? I need to know what is happening."

"I will call David, then I will call the detective and see when we can meet up and find out what is happening."

Chapter 10

JOEL

"David, this is Joel. I know you're on your way to meet us, but we need to change the location. Can you meet us at the office?"

"Yeah, of course. Is everything okay? Is Julie okay?"

"Yeah, Jules is fine. We had some new information come out, and I'm taking Jules to meet the detective shortly, so I'm hoping by the time you arrive we will be able to update you on everything and know a lot more. We're getting bits and pieces of information right now, so nothing is making much sense. I'm keeping Jules at the office for safety just in case."

"Good idea. I'll plan on meeting you at the office. I'll text you when I arrive."

"David, when you arrive, make it look like you're a client coming into the reception area and everything, just in case we're being watched. We can't be too safe right now."

"Yeah, good idea. I'll make sure I look client-like and play it safe. Good thing I left Maddie at home."

"Maddie? Who is Maddie?"

"Maddie is the dog I adopted a couple weeks ago. The house got too quiet, so I got a dog."

"Oh, that makes sense. Anyway, I gotta go. I let Jules know you're coming. I'll let you tell her about Maddie."

"Was that David on the phone?" asked Julie.

"Yeah, he is coming to the office to meet us," I said.

"What was that about someone named Maddie?"

"Well, I said I would let him tell you about Maddie."

"Joel, who is Maddie?"

"Jules, it's not my place."

"Joel, don't do that. Who is Maddie?"

"Jules, don't put me in this position."

"Joel, spill now."

"All I know is that he said they have been together for a couple of weeks. He was planning on telling you everything when he saw you later. I swear that is all I know."

"Oh my God, Joel, are you kidding me? He met someone else? I'm losing David, too. I can't do this anymore. I can't keep losing everyone and everything. John has cost me my entire life. Now I'm losing David. I thought he would be there for me. I thought I would have him to turn to. He said he loved me."

"Jules, I know you love David, but you keep pushing him away, and if you keep doing that, you will lose him. He will look elsewhere for love. You need to realize that. Apparently he already may have. You can't keep pushing the man you love away and expect him to just wait until you decide you're ready. Maybe Maddie isn't pushing him away. Maybe she is giving him exactly what he needs."

"I know you're right, Joel. I just need to get through this mess. If Maddie makes David happy, then I want him to be happy, even if it's not with me. I pushed him away. I guess I need to live with those consequences. But if there is any chance for us, then I'm taking it."

"Great, I'm glad you see the light now. Let's go to the police station. We need to see what the detective found out."

CHAPTER 11

JOEL

"Detective Jordan, please. Julie Marks and Joel Canton. He's expecting us."

Detective Jordan said, "Joel and Julie, come on, let's grab this conference room and go over what the techs found. Okay, I talked to Sam while the techs went over your apartment and Sam's apartment. Sam knew nothing about what we found. He seemed genuinely surprised about everything, and honestly, I didn't tell him what I found. I thought the less he knew, the better. I did show him a picture of John, and he confirmed that he is his current roommate. I also asked him not to tell him that we searched the apartment or asked any questions. The less John knows, the better for us. Sam seemed to be shocked to find out John is being investigated. I might have misled him a little and told him we were looking at him for small infractions, not stalking. I told him it was an active investigation, and I couldn't discuss any information. I did present him with the search warrant for his apartment, so he knows we searched his place, but I did ask him to keep it quiet. I'm not sure what John will do if he knows we are on to him.

"Now for the apartment. We found listening devices in your closet, so John has been listening to your conversations. Not sure how long he has had them planted in there. They are gone now. We removed everything. It looks like he ran them from his apartment upstairs down to your closet. It looks like there was only one. So that is good. It means he had limited access, he didn't get to every room, and he wasn't in every aspect of your life. I would also like to have our techs do a sweep of your office just to be sure there are no issues there. Joel, I think it may be a good idea to also have them check your home just to be safe, since Julie stays there a lot.

"I would also suggest that for the time being, you do not go anywhere alone. If possible, take time off, or if you must work, work virtually and stay in a secure location. Is there anywhere you can stay that John has no idea about? Any family or friends that John has not met?"

I said, "How about David's?"

"Joel, I can't ask him to do that," Julie said.

"Well, Jules, he is the only one John has no idea about, and he thinks you pushed him away. He is the only one that John wouldn't know about, and he just moved where no one knows about, not even me. It might be your only choice. David is coming later today, so maybe we can see what he says, Jules. Just keep an open mind."

"Joel, what about Maddie? I'm sure she will not be happy about him bringing me home."

"Jules, just wait and see what David says. You're jumping to conclusions again."

"Let's head back to the office and see what David says."

Detective Jordan said, "I will have an officer escort you back to your office. Please keep in mind what I said about security, and don't go anywhere alone. Joel if I could have a moment with you. I wanted to keep this between us. I don't want to worry Julie, but John has not let up, and he doesn't seem to be stopping. I don't think this is over. I'm not really sure how far John will take this to get what he wants, but I have a bad feeling about this guy. I just want to make sure you keep an eye on Julie. I will keep you in the loop about whatever I find."

"Thanks, Detective. I will make sure to keep an extra eye on Julie. Please let me know if you find anything else out, even if it's small."

David finally arrived in a red pickup truck.

"Hi, I have a meeting with Joel Canton," David said.

"I will let him know you are waiting," the receptionist said.

"Thank you."

I came into the reception.

"Mr. Canton is right this way to the conference room. Hey never mind we're going to my office just did that for show. Jules is in my office."

I told David, "We already had it checked for bugs."

"Bugs? Seriously, what the hell is going on?"

"Okay, so here is the quick version. John is dating the guy, Sam, from upstairs in Jules's building, and he planted spyware in her apartment. So the police suggest that she not stay there; they suggest she stay somewhere that John doesn't know about and not alone. So any ideas, David?"

"Well, she can stay at my place. It's out of state, and no one knows where it is."

"No, I can't ask you to do that, David," said Julie.

"Julie, you didn't ask, I offered."

"What about Maddie?"

"Maddie? Joel, I thought you were going to let me tell her about Maddie."

Joel said, "Sorry, Jules overheard and made me talk."

"Maddie won't mind; she is very sweet and loving, and she enjoys when people come to visit. We get lonely in that big house alone."

"You guys live together?"

"Of course we do, Julie. Anyway, you are welcome to stay with us for as long as you need."

"Perfect, it's settled," I said. "You will stay with David, starting tonight. I will go get a bag from my house and bring it here, and we can have someone take you to the police station and have the detective escort you to a meeting location to meet up with David. I will leave here and head home so that hopefully John follows me, hoping I'll lead him to you. Just in case he is watching us."

"Great, I will stay with David and Maddie," Julie said.

"Great, I am going to head out and drive around until you text me and let me know where to meet up to pick you up. Then, we'll will head home. Maybe I will go get some groceries. I need to pick up some of Maddie's favorites. Is there anything you would like while I am out, Julie?" asked David.

"No, David, putting me up is more than enough."

"Are you sure? Not even those chocolate cookies you ate an entire box of while we were on the phone one night?"

"Okay, maybe cookies are good, if you find them."

I said to Julie, "Jules, I'm headed to my house to get your stuff. Anything else you need while I'm out? Personal items or anything?"

"Could you get me some tampons? I don't want to have to ask David for them, just in case. And my favorite blanket from my apartment? Thanks, Joel. And tell Sarah thank you for everything."

"I'm also getting you a burner phone so you don't get anything traced, just in case. No one will have the number except me and the detective. I want you to tell no one. We can't trust anyone, not even work people. I am going to call you from a burner phone, too, so no one can trace me, either. Just to be safe. We will limit our contact, too. Maybe we need a code, too."

"Code? Seriously, Joel? For what?"

"Yeah, Jules, a code for trouble. Or a weekly check-in so I can know if you're safe, and so I don't worry."

"Joel, I think you are being a little overdramatic."

"Jules, John is crazy, and who knows what he will do? I am just trying to protect you. Maybe it's overboard. I hope it is. Better safe than sorry. So pick a code word for safety and a code for needing help."

"How about 'margaritas' for safety and 'Heather' for needing help?"

"Seriously, you are going to use my ex-girlfriend as the code word for trouble?"

"Well, she was trouble, Joel, and no one else will know that code."

"Fine, Jules, whatever. Hopefully you won't need the code anyways. I do expect margaritas every week."

"That I can promise you."

Chapter 12

JOEL

I returned with bags for Jules.

"Jules, I don't think it's a good idea for you to walk out with bags. It is screaming for John to follow you. So I'm thinking I'll send these bags over by courier to the police department, then you can pick them up there. I'll send them in file boxes so it looks like they are for a case. Detective Jordan can double check them for bugs just in case, too.

"I'm going to call him and set it up. Oh, and before I forget, here are two burner phones, one for you and one for David, just in case. If David goes to town and you need to reach him, you call his burner phone. Never use regular phones, only burners. I programmed in each number for each burner phone and Detective Jordan's number. I also programmed in the code for help just in case. No one knows our codes, not even David. That is just between you and I. Don't tell anyone. Now I'm sending your bags over to the detective, and then we are sending you over, so anything you want to say before we have to go? It might be a long time before we see each other."

"Yeah, you're not allowed to have that baby until this is over. I need to be present at the birth. No exceptions."

"I'll try, but that is up to Sarah. I make no promises. Now get ready to go. I'm calling Detective Jordan, and I will drop you off at the station. He should have your stuff by now, then you can have him call David and let him know where to meet. Let's head to the station."

CHAPTER 13

JOEL

"Joel Canton and Julie Marks for Detective Jordan."

"Joel and Julie, come right this way. I went through all of Julie's things and had tech go through everything, and no bugs were found. So the plan is, I have an officer who is going to change into Julie's clothes, walk out with Joel, get into his car, and go back to the office with Joel. Then, she will uber back to the station. While that is happening, David and Julie will actually be downstairs, getting into his vehicle and heading out undetected from our parking garage. Just in case John tries to take Julie, the officer will try to lure him out. Hopefully he tries something so she can catch him, and this will all be over. But if not, then Julie and David are safe and on their way. No one will know where they are except for me. I am the only one who has access to David's address. It is not electronically anywhere. I left it out of the system on purpose, just in case John has computer skills or access to anyone here. I am playing this extremely safe. Julie will be safe.

"Let's get the female officer and get started. I am going to call David from a secure line and have him pick up in the garage. We should be all set, so say your goodbyes. I'll give you guys a couple minutes while I go make those calls."

"Okay, Jules, this is it. No more calls, no more contact," I said.

"Oh my god, Joel, how am I going to get through this without talking to you every day?"

"Jules, you will be fine. You will have David to take care of you. I am sure he will not let anything happen to you. He loves you, he said so himself."

"Yeah, and now he loves Maddie, so how am I supposed to navigate him and Maddie?"

"Jules, just trust me. As soon as you are with him, it will all fall into place again. You will see that you still have his heart. Maddie will just be a friend, not his love. Besides, we will still have margaritas every week. And I expect one as soon as you arrive safe at Davids."

"Yeah, and when this is all over, we are having real margaritas and celebrating for a month. I love you Joel. You are my best friend." He hugged me tight.

"I love you, too, Jules. This isn't goodbye, this is see you soon. Besides, you're going to be a godmother soon, so you have to be safe and take care of yourself. I am going to need a sitter and a lot of help raising this kid. Sarah is going to need help, too. God knows we have no idea what we're doing."

Detective Jordan returned.

"Okay, guys, this is Detective Lacey. She will be playing the part of Julie and riding back to the firm with Joel. So, Ms. Marks, if you want to go change clothes, then I will escort you downstairs to our parking structure. I have been informed that David has arrived to pick you up. He is waiting with a couple of uniformed officers. This is standard for prisoner exchange and release, so it looks like he is waiting on a prisoner release. We have taken every precaution to make sure John has no idea that Ms. Marks is going with David, and he will not be able to follow her."

• • •

Joel left with detective Lacey. They headed back to the office and walked into the building. About 10 minutes later, detective Lacey got into an Uber and headed back to the police station. She watched to see if she was being followed. She noticed a car following her. It was a gray four-door sedan. She asked the driver to make a couple extra turns just to be sure it is following her. She called Detective Jordan and let him know she had a tail. Detective Jordan had an officer in the vicinity try to catch up to the Uber and follow the car.

"Keep away from the station until we get Ms. Marks away from here just in case it is John following you. Keep him on your tail. I'll call you when she is safely away, then you can lead him this way, unless our officers catch him before that."

Detective Jordan took Julie downstairs to the parking garage. "We need to get you on your way. Detective Lacey has a tail, so I assume it's John, which means he isn't watching you. It's a good time to get you away from here. So let's get you out of here before John finds out we have a decoy out there. David head straight out of town, no stops. No contact at all. I will contact you on your burner phone if needed. As soon as it is safe, I will contact you. No one knows your address, so no one but me will contact you. Remember that. Be safe."

David and Julie headed out.

Detective Jordan headed back up the stairs and called detective Lacey.

"Detective Lacey, we're clear here. You still have a tail?"

"Yes, sir, three cars back. Officers have caught up to him, and they are following him and are about to attempt to pull him over. Let's see if he follows you to the precinct. If not, we can have the officers grab him."

"Got it. I'm heading back to the precinct. I'll have the driver drop me off a block away to see if he tries to grab me. Have plain clothes waiting at the station."

Detective Lacey exited the Uber. John kept driving, and the officers kept following him. John must have known they were watching him. John got on the freeway and sped up. He lost the officers following him.

"We had him, and now he's gone again. We're going to have to try to catch him at his apartment or work to see if we can catch him there. Hopefully we haven't totally spooked him."

CHAPTER 14

J U L I E

David and Julie were heading to David's house.

"So, David, when did you get this truck? I thought you had a car."

"Oh, I did. This is actually my dad's truck. It was at the house he left me. When I talked to Joel, I thought it might be a good idea to take this so no one knew anything. No one knows about this truck. It's still registered to my dad, so it's not traceable to me. So I figured it wouldn't be traceable to you or Joel, either. Just being extra cautious. I grabbed your cookies. They are in that bag there if you're hungry. Grabbed a couple extra things too, some wine and fresh fruits and vegetables. Got lots of supplies in the back, so we don't have to go to town for a while. Might be stuck with canned goods and boxed stuff, but we can make do. I also picked up some security cameras to connect when we get there to make sure you're safe."

"You didn't need to go through all this trouble for me, David."

"It's no trouble, Julie. I told you I care about you. I would do anything to keep you safe. Besides, Joel told me John is a lot more crazy than we thought. And I think this will give us a chance to really see what is between us."

"So, chocolate cookies. Let's see what else you got in this bag. Dog biscuits. Did you get a dog?"

"I thought Joel told you."

"No, Joel didn't mention a dog."

"Yeah, her name is Maddie."

"Wait, what? Maddie is your dog? I am going to kill Joel."

"Why, what did Joel tell you?"

"Joel led me to believe you were living with someone named Maddie. He left out the dog part."

David started laughing.

"Yeah, that sounds like Joel," he said.

"I thought I was going to be a third wheel. I thought you had moved on."

"Julie, I told you I could never move on from you. I love you. I told you that."

"I know, but I pushed you away, and I thought you met Maddie and maybe she stole your heart."

"Well, she sort of did, but she is my dog. She will love you as much as I do. She is also very protective, so she will help take care of you."

"Joel did this on purpose. He did this to make me realize my feelings. I am so going to kill him when I see him. I would call and yell at him if I could."

"Well, let me ask you: did you realize any feelings when you thought Maddie was my girlfriend?"

"Maybe. I just am such a mess with this John crap. I don't want to drag you down, and here I am, dragging you into my mess. I love you, I honestly do. I know that I love you more than I have ever loved anyone. Maybe being trapped in a car makes me say things I want to say to you. But I don't want to drag you down. John is crazy. I thought he was a normal, good guy, and it turns out he is a crazy psycho. Clearly, I have no clue about dating or relationships."

"Look, Julie. From what Joel said, he had everyone fooled—you, Joel, and even your whole family. He played everyone. He looked good on paper, and he played the role right. For all you know, he was a good guy, and when you broke up with him, that is what made him snap. Speaking from experience, you can drive a man crazy."

"Funny, David, funny. And the gay lover in the shower was just a one-time thing, I'm sure."

"Yeah, that one I can't really explain. Midlife crisis?"

"David, I am just a crazy magnet. I swear, if there is a man out there that is bad at relationships, I will find him."

"Well, you know you could solve all your problems and stop dating. Or you could just be with one person for the rest of your life and let him be your only issue. Like me. You know I'm not crazy. I passed my background check."

"Well, maybe it's me that drives men crazy. Maybe I am the problem. Maybe if I stay with you, then I will drive you crazy."

"Well, then I guess we will find out after you have been living with me for a while. So if after us being confined together for a while, I go nuts, then we will know you are the problem. But if I stay sane, then we will know it's just the guys you date, and you're just a crazy magnet."

Julie started laughing, "God, I hate when you make sense. You and Joel both do that to me."

"Look, Julie, you know it's not you. You're a good person. You know you can't control people any more than you can control the weather. You know you just need to feel how you feel. The problem is, you keep running from feelings. You're afraid. I get it. I didn't want to feel how I felt about you while I was married. I hid my feelings. Now, I don't have to. I can be honest, and I want to. I'm not going to hide how I feel about you. I'm not going to let you go without telling you how I feel. If you leave after I tell you, fine, at least I tried. But if I didn't tell you, then I would risk losing you. I'm not losing you without a fight. So yes, when Joel called, I jumped at the opportunity to help. Especially since I get to lock you in my house with me."

"See, right there. Now I have turned you crazy."

David started laughing. "Let me ask you this: how long have you known Joel?"

"I don't know. Years. As long as I can remember."

"Okay, and is he crazy?"

"Yes, he is definitely crazy. David, he made me think your dog was another woman."

David started laughing again. "Okay, maybe Joel isn't the perfect example. He isn't stalker crazy, though. He is best friend crazy, but not stalker crazy. I think Joel just wanted you to realize your feelings, and making you jealous was an easy way to do it. And he probably wanted to have a little fun, too."

"David, I hate it when you're right. And I really hate it when I am trapped in a car with no way to get away from my feelings."

"Yup, you have to face it, but I did bring you cookies so you can eat your feelings if you want. We can sit here in silence if you want."

"I'm not sure what is worse, silence or talking about my feelings. You know what? Let's change the subject. Tell me about Maddie. What kind of dog is she?"

"Maddie is a mix. She is a pitbull and I think maybe a bulldog. She definitely drools like a bulldog. She is really sweet. She is very protective and barks at every noise. She snores a little, too. Loves belly rubs. She is black and white. She is going to love having company. I think she gets bored with just me."

"You really do love Maddie, don't you?"

"Of course. I always wanted a dog, but with Susan being sick, I couldn't take care of a dog, and when I was in the service, it wasn't an option because I was traveling so much. But now I was home alone, and I had no one to talk to, so I thought this was the perfect time to get a dog. Maddie looked so sad at the shelter. When I first saw her, our eyes met, and we just connected. She looked so hopeless. Then she saw me, and I think she thought I looked more hopeless. When I brought her home, she perked up, and when I took her for walks, she really perked up. When we started to play fetch, she just looked at me funny. But she saw I genuinely had an interest in having her around. I pet her and gave her dinner when I had dinner. She watches movies with me and loves her treats. She got excited when I took her to the stores with me. I let her pick out her own toys. I even let her pick out her own bed. Not that she uses it—she mainly sleeps on the bed with me. And, of course, she gets first dibs on the couch. I think she just wanted a family like me. Honestly, though, I think she wanted a family with kids to play with. She loves when we go to town. She lets everyone pet her. Wait till you meet her. She is going to love having someone else to play with. Especially since you have her favorite treats with you."

"So, since your life is off-limits, tell me: has Joel picked any baby names yet? Do they know the sex yet?"

"No, he hasn't told me anything. It's driving me nuts. They want the sex to be a surprise, so they have to pick a boy and a girl's name or a gender-neutral name. Sarah has started getting some baby clothes and furniture for the baby room. I think Joel said she started painting. But they can't decide on any names. Joel did name my kids. Apparently, I am having a boy and girl, Thompson and Trixie. Those were Joel's picks, and Sarah nixed them. I offered to name a couple of cats that, but the look I got from Joel, geez."

"Thompson and Trixie, huh? Well, we are almost home. Any suggestions for dinner tonight? I have tons of groceries in the back, so we can have anything you want.

Chicken, steak, pasta. What do you feel like?"

"How about we go simple tonight and just do some spaghetti? I'm sure there are a lot of groceries to put away, and honestly, I am exhausted. A good bottle of wine to go with it would be greatly appreciated, though."

"I think I can handle that. Maybe some garlic bread, too, and a small salad?"

"Mmm, sounds perfect. I swear, David, you know how to make a simple dinner amazing. Oh, I have to text Joel before I forget to let him know we made it, or he will send out a search party. There, 'margarita' with a pissed puppy."

"Why the puppy?"

"He will know what it means."

CHAPTER 15

J O E L

It was starting to get dark out. I headed home from work to see Sarah after saying goodbye to Jules. I just needed my wife and some normalcy. I grabbed my phone and called Sarah on my way home.

"Hey, Sweetie, I'm on my way. Do you need anything?"

"I'm good. How did things go today with the police?"

"Everything went well, I guess. I really just need this mess to be over with before the baby comes."

I needed my best friend. I hoped Jules made it to David's okay. I had never been so worried, and I couldn't call her or anything. I just had to wait and hope. I shouldn't have worried; I knew David would keep her safe. He was a Marine, for God's sake. If anyone could protect her, it would be him. Besides, I knew he loved her, so he would do everything he could to keep her safe. Honestly, I didn't know why I was so worried.

"You're worried because she's your best friend, and you love her," said Sarah. "I'm sure David will take care of her."

"You're right. Besides, I think I'm the one she wants to kill now anyway after what I did to her."

"What did you do?"

"I may have let her think David's dog was his girlfriend."

"Oh my God, Joel, you didn't. What were you thinking?"

"I was thinking that she would realize how much she loved David, and she would get jealous and realize her feelings. Besides, she can't exactly call and yell at me, so I figured I was pretty safe."

"Joel, women don't like to be lied to or manipulated like that. You shouldn't have done that. She is totally going to kill you when she sees you again, and I am going to let her. You ever do that to me, and you will be sleeping on the couch."

"You're right, it was a shitty thing to do. I should have corrected her. But I didn't know how else to make her realize she was losing David by pushing him away. She can be so stubborn, especially with her love life, since it's a total mess. I didn't want her to lose the only good thing she had going. But you're right, I shouldn't have done that, and I promise I will never do it to you. I will apologize when she comes home. I should be home in about 10 minutes, are you sure you don't need anything? Craving anything for dinner tonight?"

"No, I'm good, but I reserve the right to change my mind at any second."

"I'll see you in a few, then. Bye, Sweetie."

CHAPTER 16

JOHN

I went to the apartment to see Sam. I caught him outside the building in the car garage.

"John, dear, I didn't expect you tonight. Would you like to have dinner?"

"No, I didn't plan on dinner, but I wanted to check the closet sizes. I was starting to pack, and the realtor called. She has a very interested client who toured the apartment today and loved it, so I am hoping an offer is coming, and I need to get everything packed to move. I realized I have no idea how much closet space we have, so I wasn't sure if I needed to pack, toss, or put stuff in storage. I was hoping to measure the closet real quick, then I'm headed back home to pack. So, hopefully by the end of the month, we will be together finally."

"Honestly, our closets are actually very nicely sized, but I think measuring and maybe taking a couple pics so you know the shelving is a great idea. We can take a look together and figure out what space we have."

"It's alright, I can measure myself. You go ahead and relax. I'm sure work was exhausting."

Sam and I reached the apartment and headed inside. He turned off the alarm system.

"You go ahead and measure," Sam said. "There is a tape measure in the kitchen drawer if you need it. I am going to get changed out of my work clothes. Let me know if you change your mind and want to stay for dinner. We can order takeout if you like."

I frantically searched the closet, looking for the devices I had hidden in the closet. Nothing was there; someone found my setup. Was it Sam, or did Sam let the police in the apartment? How much did the police know? They saw me following Julie earlier, so she obviously went to the police. I expected her to go to the police eventually, but I didn't think she saw me. She couldn't have found the devices I planted, but someone did, so now what? How much did they know? Did Sam know? How did Julie find out I was following her today? Where did I slip up? Maybe dinner was a good idea. I could get Sam to talk and see what he knew.

"Sam, I was thinking, we haven't gone out in a long time. How about we hit our favorite restaurant tonight? We can discuss the apartment and furniture we need or don't need so I know what to get rid of. What do you say?"

"Yeah, sure, dinner would be great. We haven't been out in months. I was starting to think you found someone else or changed your mind."

"Never, you are my everything. I'm sorry this move hasn't gone as smoothly as we planned. I really was hoping my apartment would have sold as quickly as yours. Between work and packing and trying to get my realtor to sell my apartment, I have just been really busy. I'm sorry I have been neglecting you. Let me make it up to you, and let's go to dinner. We can talk and have a few drinks."

"Will you be staying the night?"

I wish I could, but I do need to pack. But being with you is more important tonight, and soon we'll be together every night. So let's start with dinner tonight and packing later, followed by us together forever." I leaned in and kissed Sam.

"Let's go. I really need a drink. It's been a long day," I said.

"So, tell me: how was your day? Did anything special happen today?"

"Special like what? I work for the IRS. I deal with taxes and accounting. It's especially boring."

"I'm just checking. You never know. Maybe you had some really odd, cool case."

"Nope, no such luck, pretty boring day. How was your day? Anything awesome happen to you at work?"

"No, same old clients, same old investments. Market went down a bit, which had us worried as to how long it's going to trend down. Few clients called asking what to do. This market and economy has everyone on edge."

"Hey, I was going to ask: did you move anything out of my closet? I thought I left a bag in there from last time I stayed over. I didn't see it tonight."

"Nope, I haven't seen anything and haven't been in that closet at all. Maintenance was in to change some light bulbs last week, but not in the closets."

"It's probably at my apartment, lost in the boxes. I keep misplacing things with this move. I am really scatterbrained. I keep packing and putting boxes in the basement storage. I need to start bringing them over to our place."

"I agree, you should bring the boxes over. Then you would have a reason to stay the night with me. I miss you sleeping next to me. I miss our morning showers, too. Are you sure you can't stay the night?"

"No, I can't tonight. I want to pack a few boxes, and I have an early morning meeting. I wish I could. On Friday, I will bring some boxes over and plan on spending the night. We can have a nice romantic dinner at home. How does that sound?"

"Perfect, we haven't had a nice night together in a long time. And I am sure that after moving boxes on Friday, you will want a nice relaxing dinner. I will cook—and by cook, I mean order takeout."

Sam thought to himself, *I hope John doesn't see through me and know I talked to the police. How can I keep this from him? He is my world, and I am not telling him our apartment was searched by the police. I know the police asked me not to, but what did he do? Is this related to his work? I'm freaking out. He has to be on to me. I hope he doesn't want to come home tonight. I can't keep this from him all night.*

After a nice dinner, Sam said, "We should head back home. It's getting late, and you have packing to do. I have a book on my nightstand that I have been trying to read all week. I keep falling asleep. Either it's not a good book, or I am just exhausted lately."

"I don't know why you bother. You always fall asleep reading. Do you know how many times I have come to bed and you have a book on your chest?"

"Reading helps me unwind and relax. I like my horror novels. A good Stephen King thriller helps me sleep better."

"You are the only person I know who sleeps better after a horror movie or book. I really don't know how you do it."

"Anyway, let's grab the check and head home. I will drop you off and head back to my apartment. Hopefully the realtor sells my place soon, and then we can just go home together. This dating is getting old. I'm ready for living together."

I pulled up to the building and let Sam out. He leaned over and kissed me goodbye before stepping out of the car. "Hopefully, I will see you tomorrow. If not, for sure on Friday. I love you. Sleep well."

"I love you, too. Call me tomorrow so we can figure out some plans soon. I want you to move in before winter comes."

Sam headed into the building and up to his apartment. He locked the door behind him and set the alarm.

I headed home to my apartment. I wondered if the police were watching my place. Maybe I needed to go to a hotel tonight. I didn't see them at our other place, which was why I didn't go in. But if they followed me earlier, they could be looking to arrest me or something.

Maybe I needed to play it safe tonight and go to a hotel. I needed to check my recordings and see what they caught. I needed WiFi for that. Maybe I could hit the coffee shop and check it on my laptop. I needed to see how long Julie had been out of her apartment. She wasn't at Joel's. Where would she go? Did the police have her? Did she go to her friend's or her mom's? No, she wouldn't leave work. She must be working remotely somewhere. Sleeping at her office—is that possible? The police don't know much, if anything. She only went in today. I needed to see my videos. I would go to a coffee shop and see if I could access it on my laptop.

Perfect, this coffee shop was nearly empty. I wouldn't be bothered too much. I just got a muffin and a cup of decaf so the barista would leave me alone.

I could set up my laptop and see what the last footage showed.

Here was the recording from Julie's. It sounded like a cop. Hmm, now I heard them leaving. Odd. Now, nothing. Did they leave or what? I fast forwarded. Now I heard voices again. Multiple people were talking, and they sounded like technicians. I heard a warrant. Now it was dead.

They definitely found my bug. That meant they went into my apartment, too. Sam didn't say anything. They had to serve him with a warrant to get in. He had to know, damn it. They must have told him something, what did they tell him? He must have known something. I needed to know what they knew. I couldn't go home now. They were definitely on to me. They probably searched my apartment and had been looking for me. I couldn't go to work, either. They would be looking for me at my place and work. *Shit, what do I do? I need cash. I need to switch to plan B,* I thought.

Time to go off the grid and find out where they took Julie. I headed back to my car, put my laptop and phone in the trunk, and grabbed my go bag. Now it was time to switch cars. I left one in a long-term lot. I could drop this one off and pick up my spare car. I had money and clothes in that car, so I would be good for a while. I had a spare cell in my go bag and some cash.

It was time to find out: what Sam did not tell me? I had to go back to Sam tonight and find out what he knew. What did he tell the police?

Finally, I arrived at the long-term lot. I dropped off my car, grabbed my bags, and got in my new car. Well, a new old car. I bought one of the most common vehicles in America. It was a Chevy malibu, black so it wouldn't stand out and couldn't be seen at night. I tinted the windows, too. No one even knew about this vehicle. I registered it in Julie's name. They would never think to look for a car registered to Julie. Julie didn't own a vehicle, so they would never look for it. I used her old address so no one would be the wiser.

Now it was time to find out what Sam knew. I really wished I didn't need to bring him into this. Things were so much easier when I was dating both him and Julie. Julie was my everything; she was going to be my wife. Sam was always going to be my lover. I never planned on Julie finding out about Sam. I told Sam I wasn't ready for a relationship. I just liked dating and spending time with him. After Julie walked in on us, I told Sam that Julie was my ex who was trying to win me back. Yeah, I lied to him, but what was I supposed to do? Tell him the truth? I was in love with Julie, and I enjoyed having sex with men. I wanted both Julie and Sam. I loved Julie. She was an amazing woman. But I enjoyed sex with men.

Sam was a great lover and a nice guy. I also could access his IRS laptop and keep tabs on Julie. That was how I found her new apartment: the change of address she filed with the government. The IRS knew everything. You have to update your work and W-2 info, and the IRS gets copies of everything. So Sam was perfect to help me keep tabs on Julie.

I parked in the garage and headed up the back elevator. I had to be quiet and turn off the alarm before it woke Sam, unless he was still awake reading. I doubted it. He usually fell asleep within 20 minutes of reading.

The apartment's dark lights were all off. Sam must have been asleep. I turned off the alarm, closed the door, and locked it behind me.

Sam must have been in the bedroom. I headed that way. He was asleep with a book on his chest, as always.

I went over and kissed him, waking him up.

"Hey, I need to ask you something," I said.

"Now? It's late, John. What's wrong? Is everything okay? I didn't expect you back tonight."

"Yeah, everything is fine. I need to know what happened today."

"What are you talking about? Nothing happened."

"Sam, I know the police were here, and you didn't tell me about it. Tell me what they wanted and why they were here."

"John, I don't know what you're talking about. No one was here today. I was at work all day."

"Sam, don't lie to me. Don't make me do something neither of us wants."

"John, I was at work. I never saw anyone here today. I got home when you saw me tonight. No one was here."

"Sam, don't make me do this. Wake up and tell me what the police told you and what you told them. I need to know what is happening."

"John, I have no idea what you're talking about. Can we discuss this tomorrow? I'm really tired."

"Damn it, Sam, I tried to be nice. I'm done playing. Tell me everything, now." I grabbed Sam and pulled him out of bed.

"John, what is wrong with you?"

I punched Sam in the face.

"John, stop! I don't know anything."

I punched Sam again and threw him on the floor. "That's for lying to me earlier."

Sam had a bloody nose and a split lip. I went after him, hit him again, and kicked him in the stomach. I kicked him so hard that I knocked the wind out of Sam. He was gasping for air, trying to crawl away.

Sam finally said, "Okay, the police came by and asked me not to tell you. They said they found wires in the closet, that's all I know. They said they were investigating you, that's all I know. I swear. I'm sorry I didn't tell you."

I picked up Sam and hit him again. Sam fell to the floor, bleeding and barely conscious.

I headed to the door and left the apartment. I headed downstairs and used a key to get into Julie's apartment to see if she was there.

I didn't see her anywhere. Her bathroom was missing her usual items, too. She must have been gone—staying with Joel, maybe—but I didn't see her leave with him. Where could she have been hiding? I realized I had better go because they had cameras and could easily find out I was here.

I headed out the back entrance. I got into my car and drove to a motel, checked in, and paid in cash. It was a run-down motel, but it would do. There was a shower and clean linens. I needed to find where they had Julie at. Maybe she went to her mother's place. I would call her mother in the morning and check in. She wouldn't go far due to work. She had to have another new place. Maybe if I got to her work early, I could see her go in and follow her home. That would be the easiest way to find her. If I didn't find her, I would follow Joel. He never went more than a couple days without seeing her, so he would lead me to her at some point.

Sam started to crawl to the door to reach the help button. He finally reached the help button.

Tom came into the apartment.

"Sam, are you okay?" Tom came in and saw Sam, beaten and bloody. He grabbed his radio and told them to call the police and an ambulance.

"Oh my God, Sam, who did this to you? How did they get in?"

"John," Sam said. "It was John. Call the detective."

"Sam, don't worry. the police are on the way, and so is an ambulance. I'll stay with you." Tom grabbed his radio. "How long on that ambulance? I need help up here."

The ambulance finally arrived and took Sam to the hospital.

"Sam, don't worry. I am coming with you to the hospital." Tom grabbed his cell phone and called Detective Jordan.

"Detective Jordan, this is Tom. Sam was attacked in his apartment. He said it was John. We are on the way to the hospital now. Can you please come meet us?"

"I am on my way."

Detective Jordan arrived at the hospital.

"Tom, thanks for calling. What happened?

"I'm not sure. Sam pushed the emergency button in the apartment. I went up to check on him and found him beaten. He said it was John. That's all he said."

"Thanks, Tom. I'll talk to Sam as soon as doctors clear me to talk to him. I have a unit going to his apartment to pull forensics and see what else we can find. Do you have cameras in the halls or anything that would show someone entering or leaving the apartment and the building?"

"Yeah, we have cameras on all floors and all exits. I can have someone send the files to you. Does this have anything to do with Julie?"

"I'm not sure yet, but I would bet John found out we were looking for him, and he lost it.

Tom, I will need to speak with all your employees and tenants to see if anyone saw anything. In the meantime, you may want to let people know to be extra cautious. I will also increase police presence outside the building. I'll have more cars on the road driving by to keep an eye out for John. Now that he has attacked Sam, I don't think he will be easy to find. He has to know we are on to him.

"I will contact a judge and have a warrant for his arrest issued. I already have people looking for his car. We're also trying to track his phone, but he must have turned it off. I have a feeling he is going after Julie. But I have nothing to base it on. But now that he has done this, I can get a warrant for his other apartment and see what I can find there. Tom, you may want to increase security for a while just to make everyone feel secure. At least do more walk-arounds in the halls. Make sure all your cameras are functioning and being watched 24/7. I can't guarantee John won't come back looking for Julie or Sam."

"Excuse me, Detective," said a nurse. Sam is awake if you would like a couple minutes. Please be brief. He has been given pain meds and will fall asleep soon."

"Sam, it's Detective Jordan. Can you tell me what happened?"

"John. It was John. He wanted to know what I told you and what you told me. I didn't tell him earlier, and he was mad I didn't tell him about searching the apartment. I tried to not tell him, but he kept hitting me until I told him. He left after I told him you searched the apartment and found wires in the closet. I told him you were investigating him."

"Thanks, Sam. You get some rest. I will have an officer posted outside your room, just in case. You don't need to worry. We will arrest John for attacking you."

"Detective, what is this all about? What is John mixed up in?"

"Sam, don't worry about that right now. I will explain everything once you are better. Right now, you just rest and get better."

JOHN

I arrived early to Julie's work as planned and watched the entrance to see if she came in. I watched closely, but I never saw Julie.

This was odd. I didn't see Julie yet. I wondered if she was sleeping here. Maybe she never left last night. That would explain how I missed her leaving and coming in. She could be working from Joel's house, too. I needed to get into Joel's house and check it out, and I needed to see if she was living at the office. How would I get into the office without being noticed? Joel's house was easy. I could break in while his wife was out. Maybe I would call first and see if I could get patched through. If she was taking calls, I'd know she was there. If not, then she was most likely at Joel's.

I called, and the receptionist answered. "Julie Marks, please," I said.

"Ms. Marks is unavailable currently. Would you like her assistant?"

"No. When will she return?"

"I do not have information for Ms. Marks. I am just informed she is unavailable currently."

"Is she out of the office or on a call?"

"Sir, she is out of the office."

Okay, so she is not at the office, or they are lying to everyone who calls. I doubt that if she were there, she would be taking calls. So she must have been at Joel's. Or Joel hid her somewhere, so I needed to break into Joel's and see if she was there. I needed to follow Joel and see if he leads me to her. Maybe I would follow Joel. If he only went to work and home, then she must be with him. He would never let her out of his realm for long. Those two couldn't go a day without talking. I was just going to keep following Joel. He would lead me to Julie.

CHAPTER 17

DAVID

"Good morning. How did you sleep last night?"

"Honestly, David I slept better than I have in a long time. I thought being in a different place would be an issue. But knowing that John has no idea where I am I think gave me a weird sense of comfort. How did you sleep?"

"Good, but actually, I have been up for hours installing the new camera system around the property to make sure we are safe and have lots of eyes in case John does come looking for you. And Maddie has been on guard dog patrol. She is actually a very good guard dog, given the right treats. For breakfast this morning, I was thinking about pancakes. How does that sound?"

"Sounds perfect with a side of bacon."

"Yes, you read my mind. I have some fresh orange juice, too. After breakfast, I can finish the camera system. I have to tie it into the house system. I have an app on my phone so I can check it whenever we need to."

"David, is all this really necessary? I mean, I appreciate everything, but isn't this a little extreme?"

"Well, let me ask you this: would Joel approve of all this?"

"No, Joel would say we need guards at the door. Probably armed guards. Maybe Dobermans, too, and gates with a moat."

David laughed. "Well then, I guess this isn't overdoing it. Joel would think I'm slacking. Anyway, just in case John does find you, I want to make sure we are covered. I have cameras all over the property and on the doors and windows, so we will see where he is. The cameras are all motion-activated, and as soon as they are triggered, I get a notification on my phone.

"Just in case he does get into the house and I am not here, you need to head outside to the barn. There is a tornado shelter in the barn floor for emergencies. It locks from the inside. I also put a loaded gun in there with extra bullets and some water and protein bars in a metal box, so you can hide for a couple days, if needed. There is also a disposable cell in that lock box to call for help in case I don't come right away. But if you are ever not in this house, then you should be there. You can't leave this house without me or Maddie. Honestly, you shouldn't even go outside, just in case John does find the house.

"If he sees you, he may come after you, but if he doesn't see you, he won't be sure you're here. Right now, he has no idea where you are. I'm betting he thinks you're with Joel. Until he figures out you're not, he won't start looking. Once he figures out you're not with Joel, he will start to look for you and turn over every rock to find you. Hopefully the police find him before he figures out you're with me, but just in case, I want to be ready. John isn't stupid, I'm afraid. He will hide from the police and eventually find us. So when he does, we need to be prepared.

"I go to town once a week to get groceries, so I'm going to keep that schedule. When I go, I will talk to the sheriff and let him know that if I ever don't come to town on my scheduled day, then he needs to come to the property and check on us. I am not going to tell him why. I'm just telling him I'm doing house repairs, so if something happens and I break my leg, he should come check. I just want to make sure someone notices something if we don't go to town. I'm taking every precaution to make sure we have backup."

"David this sounds crazy. Do you honestly think John will come here looking for me?" I asked.

"Honestly, Julie, yes. Nothing John has done has been normal so far. He has been stalking you. He's not stopping, not even after you moved. He raped you, Julie. He won't stop until he kills you or is put in jail. Something in John broke when you broke up with him. He can't let you go, and he won't stop looking for you until he finds you. He didn't kill you before because he thought he could win you back. Now he knows you're not coming back to him, so now if he can't have you, no one can.

"Julie, I hope I am wrong, and John never comes here and just gives up and moves on, but I'm playing it extra safe. Maybe I am going overboard—not Joel overboard, but a little overboard. It's only because I love you, and I promised Joel I would do everything to take care of you. And if I don't do everything I can to protect you, Joel will hunt me down, and I know he will find us."

I laughed. "Yeah, you are right about that. Joel will definitely find us. He would call the national guard, and honestly, I wouldn't be surprised if he put a tracker in my stuff. You didn't give him access to the video feeds, did you?"

David laughed. "No, no one has access to the video feeds except me. I can send him a link if you want."

"Oh, that's not even funny. Can we go back to breakfast? I'm starving."

"Yes, I'm making the batter up and frying bacon, too. Breakfast will be ready in a couple minutes. After breakfast, I was thinking I would finish tying in the security system. Then our afternoon should be free, if you have any ideas on what to do to kill time. I'm not going to lie, it gets a little boring here with just me and Maddie. So if you have any ideas , I'm all ears. TV can only entertain us so much, and I hate to tell you, but we have very limited TV options, too. Usually we go fishing and do home projects, but I don't think fishing is a good idea for you, and I don't think you want to paint and redo the bathroom."

"Wait, you're redoing the bathroom? Does that mean we will not have plumbing at any point in time?"

"Well, yes, for a bit, but we can turn the water off for a couple hours, then install things and turn it back on. It won't be that bad. But I understand your concern, since this is a one-bathroom home. I would never leave you without a bathroom."

"David, I was just concerned. I can't exactly go outside like you can."

"Fair point. I promise I will let you know before I turn the water off. Besides, it's not a full gutting and redo; it's more of an update. Changing out the faucets and stuff, painting. Retiling the shower. The faucets I can do in a day, and paint I can do with water on. Tile I should be able to do with water, unless I run into an issue."

"So why are you updating the bathroom?"

"Honestly, I was thinking I would get this place ready to sell. I thought about selling it as is, but then I thought I have time and nothing to do, so why not update the place a bit, then sell it? I thought it would keep me busy. I needed a distraction. I didn't plan on you needing a place to hide."

"Yeah, I'm really sorry about invading your place."

"No, that is not what I meant at all. Here, sit down and eat before it gets cold. Julie, I'm happy you're here. I finally feel like we can talk and clear up our feelings. Now that John is not part of the equation, I'm hoping you being here will allow you to open up to me and tell me how you feel and how I can help you move on."

"David, I love you. I know that much, but until this mess with John is over—and I mean John in jail and me free to work and live at my place again—then I don't want to drag you into my crazy world."

"I hate to break this to you, but I am in your crazy world already. Honestly, I wouldn't have it any other way. I want to be here for you, crazy or not. And I guess you technically brought your crazy to my door. So if I didn't want it in my life, I wouldn't have opened the door. So we're in this crazy world together, like it or not."

"You're right. I brought my crazy to you. And I am sorry. And just so we're clear, anytime you want the crazy to leave, you just have to say the word, and I am gone. I promise to pack my crazy and take it back home. But I must say, if you keep making me breakfast that tastes this good, you're only feeding the crazy, and it may not want to go. Ever."

"Ah, well, you have figured out my master plan: keep you happy and filled with good food so you will never want to leave."

"I knew you had ulterior motives for letting me stay here."

"Yes, that, and Maddie needs a friend to play with. I don't throw the ball enough, so she is happy to play whenever you want. Especially when I am working on projects. She seems to want to play when I am busy."

"Honestly, I'm hoping you can occupy Maddie so I can get some work done around this place. She's still in her playful stage, and once in a while I catch her nibbling on something she shouldn't nibble on. But she is a great dog. And I adore her, and I think she uses that against me for more treats."

"David, I would love to hang out with Maddie while you work in the bathroom. Maybe we can trade secrets about you. I bet she knows everything about you."

"Um, yes, she does, but I have sworn her to secrecy. She will not divulge any secrets."

"I bet that with the right treats, she'll talk."

"Okay, well, maybe after breakfast. Here you go. If you want syrup for your pancakes, it's on the counter. Maddie gets all the leftovers, unless she spills the beans."

"Hey, don't you threaten her. She is my new bestie."

"Oh, I see how this is going to go. You girls are going to gang up on me. So, I am going to get started on the bathroom. Last call to use it."

"Ooh, I need a shower before you turn the water off and start, just in case."

CHAPTER 18

DAVID

"Oh my gosh, that shower felt so great. So I was thinking, how far is town from here?"

"It's about 15 miles away. We're outside of town, in that perfect area where few people live."

"Well, I'm just wondering how long it would take to get help if we were to call. Is it a big town or small town?"

"It's small, one officer and a small grocery store. It has basics there, but if we need major things, there is a larger town about 30 miles away. It will take time for anyone to get here, but you don't need to worry about that. I know this area better than anyone. I grew up here, so I know all the hiding spots. I also know the best place to fish. So no matter what, we will not ever starve. Maddie has also been getting to know the property, so she can take care of you. Maddie goes out with me every morning, and we walk the property to get her used to her area. You don't need to worry. The police can be here within 20 minutes. I don't think we will need them, so don't worry.

"Look, I'm not trying to scare you with everything, but I also want you to be safe. We are safe here. I am making sure of it. I really hope I am being overprotective, and you don't need it. But just in case, I want to be prepared. Better safe than sorry. Besides, I'm not afraid of John. Joel, however, is another story."

"I get it, David. I'm just in my head again. Joel tells me all the time to get out of my head. I'm overthinking everything. It's great for being an attorney; however, it's not so helpful in relationships."

"So, about this barn. You said there is a door in the floor. How will I find it?"

"Well, I'm glad you asked. Maddie and I are going to take you out and show you so you know exactly where to go. I thought that would be a good idea before I turn the water off. I wanted to put a couple more things down there just in case. Maddie needs dog treats just in case."

"I don't know how I am going to get through this. I can't work or call anyone. My caseload is already behind . I don't know how I will ever catch up."

"Joel has that covered, I'm sure. He probably called in a substitute to pitch in. He knows you have to stay off the grid as much as possible. We have a landline for emergencies, and our cells are throwaways that can't be traced. Your regular cell we left at the office, so if John tracks that, he will see you at work. Julie, you are safe here."

"David, I know I'm safe with you. I'm just worried about my life falling apart while I'm hiding from John. I spent years building my career, and now I feel like I'm just walking away from everything. I'm hoping the police find John, and this is just a vacation. I hate to lose everything because of a bad relationship."

"Julie, don't think about it. Think this is a short vacation, and you will be back to work in no time. Besides, when is the last time you actually took time off?"

"It's been a while. You're right. I was working so hard to make my mark, I hardly took time off. I only took time for family weddings and funerals."

"That is not taking time off, so it sounds like the company owes you a little vacation. Besides, I am sure Joel explained the circumstances to your boss, and they would want your safety above anything else."

"You're right. Joel said he talked with the partners and explained the situation. I'm sure he handled everything. Besides, they can ask the detective, and he will verify he sent me away. This was part of their plan. I think I'm just having a hard time with being off the grid. I'm used to checking my phone and my laptop constantly. It just feels weird."

"So you're having anxiety about not using your devices. Well, that tells me it has been way too long since you have been on a vacation. Seriously, out here, I go days without even looking at my phone. I leave it on the counter. If it rings, I answer. Other than that, I have no use for it out here. We don't have great WIFI. I did run a stronger signal for the cameras, but they are tied in directly to the system here. I put a booster in the highest tree so we could get a better signal. It makes it way easier to watch Netflix. But your phone will work, just slowly. Honestly, you can't do anything with that phone Joel gave you, either. It's a basic dumb phone, no games or fun stuff. So we are going primitive while you're here. If you really want to go back in time, I found my dad's DVD player. I can hook that up."

"OMG, seriously? You found a DVD player?"

"I bet if I look, he has VHS, too."

"OMG, I'm seriously lost in the woods out here."

"Oh, come on, it's going to be fun. If you want, I can try to get a deer, and we can really go primitive."

"No, fishing is more than enough. I prefer to eat my meats from the grocery store. I can't be totally primitive. Going without the bathroom for a couple hours is more than enough."

"So, get your tennis shoes on, and we will show you the barn. Just in case you need it.

So, when you leave the house, head back behind it. You should see the barn from here. Follow this path through the trees. Dad planted a lot of these trees to keep the barn from being noticed. He wanted the house to be cabin-like, but he wanted a barn to keep things in, like his old truck and lots of tools and fishing equipment. His boat is out here, too.

"See there? It blends in with the trees, so if you don't know the property, you won't know it's here. And if it's night, you can't see it unless the lights are on. Anyway, go straight in this door. You can see the boat is straight ahead. Behind the boat is a hidden door in the floor. I moved the boat in the way so that it would hide the trap door.

"So, if you come right behind the boat, you will see: here is the door. You pull this rope handle, and then below it the shelter. Now when you get in, there are flashlights and food in this box, along with the cell phone. I left blankets down here in case it's cold. But you and Maddie can sit down here. No one will see you unless you have the flashlight on. The floor is old, and the light will show, so when you come down here, turn the light off. Just to be safe. I know it will seem scary, but you will be safe. Here is a gun and extra ammo. It is loaded. You just point and squeeze the trigger. There is a slide lock right here on the door, so once you're in here, no one can come in behind you. If you need to use the phone or you hear someone, cover it with the blanket to make sure no light shines through."

"David this is a lot. I really hope I never need to use this shelter."

"Me too, Julie, but just in case, it's here. We can use it as a tornado shelter, too, if needed. There's no basement in the main house, just a crawl space. So this doubles as our storm shelter. There is a crank radio, too, but I don't suggest you use that unless there is a storm.

"Hey, I know it's a lot, but don't worry. Everything will be fine. Now let's head back to the house. Maddie earned treats, she led us right to the barn. And now she is going to lead us back home."

"Okay, but I get to give her the treats," I said. "We're still bonding, and us girls gotta stick together."

"Deal, but I'm taking my time turning the water back on."

"You're playing dirty. I never realized you had such a mean streak in you."

CHAPTER 19

J O H N

Back in New York, I was sitting outside of Joel and Julie's workplace, waiting to see if Julie went home with Joel.

Joel left and watched to see if he was followed.

I kept waiting to see if Julie came out alone. She never came out. I was getting angry.

How did I miss her? I saw Joel leave alone. I know she wasn't with him. How did I miss her? Was she sleeping in her office? How could I find out where she was? Maybe she was staying at Joels' and working from home. I needed to find out if she was at Joel's. I would park out at Joel's early and see if she left with Joel. If not, then I would wait for his wife to leave and check his place.

I had to find Julie. She couldn't stay hidden long. She wasn't at her apartment. So that left Joel's and work. I hadn't seen her leave work, so I was betting she was sleeping at the office.

I was sure Sam told the police what I did to him, so I couldn't go back there. I was sure they were looking for me. I couldn't go to work either, They would be looking for me there, too. I needed to stay off grid and lay low until I found Julie.

Then, when I found her, I would show her how much I had missed her and prove that I love her. I knew that after that, she would marry me. She just had cold feet.

Now, first things first: was she with Joel or staying at the office?

I needed sleep, then I would be up early and be out in front of Joel's to see if Julie left with him.

CHAPTER 20

JOHN

Finally, Joel was leaving his house. Now I needed to see if his wife left so I could search his place. If Julie wasn't there, then that only left the office. So how would I search the office?

Maybe I would just stake it out. She would have to leave at some point for clothes or food. Joel couldn't keep getting her stuff for her.

I wondered if she had any cases she had to appear in court for. That would get her out of her office.

I'd been sitting there for hours. Sarah needed to leave soon; she must have appointments or something. I needed to get in there and find Julie.

Finally, she was leaving. I would wait a few minutes, then go in and search the place. I'd find Julie, and we could run away and start our lives together. Maybe in Florida or someplace warm. It will be like being on vacation every day.

Now, I was going in through the back in case anyone is watching. I would do a quick search, look for Julie or her stuff. Seriously, where was she?

There was no one there. The place was empty. The spare room was a baby room now, and nothing in the living room, no sheets or pillows. Joel's room looked normal. No luggage or bags anywhere. Damn it, she must be at the office.

I needed to head there and watch for her to come out. What if the police had her in a safe house? Was that possible? Could they be ahead of me on this? I saw Joel take her back to the office. They got in his car and went to the office. He dropped her off in front. I saw her walk in. She had to be there.

Julie must have been sleeping at the office. I would have seen her leave. I just needed to keep watching there. She would come out, she had too. No one could live in the office, especially not on the weekends. And if she was there, Joel would come in to see her on the weekends. There was no way he wouldn't check on her or bring her food. She couldn't live on vending machines. Worst case, I would wait until the weekend. If she didn't come out then, I would find a way in to check her office.

CHAPTER 21

JOHN

It was Saturday, and there was no sign of Julie. She had to be sleeping at the office. Now I had to find a way in. There was way less security on the weekends. It had to be easy to get in. There was no receptionist on the weekends, so I wondered if there was any security, or if the building was just locked.

I needed to find a way in. So I would just try to walk in and see who is there or if the building is locked; if so, then I would use the back door. There had to be a fire escape or back entrance.

The front door is locked. I didn't see any security at the desk, but they could be walking around. I'd better check the back door.

This is better, way less people and cameras. Now, how to pick the lock or break in. You know what, this couldn't be that hard. They did it on TV all the time. Seriously, how hard could it be? I needed something sharp to stick in the lock. I thought I had a knife in here. That should work. The back door should be easier to open.

Finally, just a little bit more to turn, There it goes.

Now, to start searching for Julie. I would start with her office. I would be able to tell if she was living in it at least. I thought she was on the second floor.

There should have been a guard on the doors or somewhere. I needed to be quiet in case there was security wandering around.

I would take the stairs in case they could hear the elevator. Let me start with her office.

Finally, here it was. It was dark, no lights, nothing in it. No blankets, pillows, nothing. Maybe there was a clue to where she was in her desk.

I heard someone coming. I better hide.

There was nothing in her office. Maybe she was in Joel's office. Or maybe there was a clue there.

I needed to check his office and search for anything. If I didn't find Julie, then I was betting I could find a clue to where he had her hiding.

There had to be something in this office—a phone number, address, anything. Damn it, I wasn't finding anything, including Julie.

Maybe his caller ID on his phone had something. Nothing, I couldn't find anything. Julie wasn't here. There was no sign of her in her office or Joel's. I would check the rest of the building to double check, but he must have hidden her somewhere. She had to be here. She wasn't at his house. I saw her come into this building. I knew she was here somewhere.

CHAPTER 22

DAVID

"Good morning, beautiful. How did you sleep?"

"Good morning, I slept great. How about you?"

"Well, I slept like a rock, but I think it had a lot to do with last night's late-night activities."

"Oh, I see. I wore you out and helped you sleep well, and you're complaining?"

"Oh, no, I am not complaining one bit. As a matter of fact, we can do that every night, as long as I can sleep that well after."

"So I was thinking: since the bathroom is done, how about we remodel the kitchen next?"

"The kitchen? Really? I think it looks nice."

"Yeah, but I was thinking about new cabinets, or maybe just repainting the current ones. They aren't in that bad of shape. New appliances, how about stainless steel instead of the white? Change it up a bit. Maybe a new backsplash. The island could use some work too, maybe put a sink in."

"If you put a sink in the island, you will lose all that counter space. I like the extra space when I cook."

"But a sink would give us both space when we're in there together, and we could put a cutting board over the sink to make it multi-use."

"I see your point, but I'm not sure about the sink."

"Okay, let's start with cabinets and colors. How about I paint a couple options, and we look at it and see?"

"I think I have some white paint in the garage. We can paint some boards and see what it would look like. Maybe put a new light over the island, change it to LED, brighten up the room. These fixtures are old. Dad didn't change anything in years. I don't think anything in this cabin is energy efficient. But I like it. It feels cozy and homey like a cabin should. If you update everything, it won't be like a cabin. It would be a house in the woods. Then I would feel like a hipster."

"Okay, I get your point. let's keep the cabin feel but make a few updates. Is the remodeled bathroom to your liking?"

"Yeah, actually, I like the shower the most. The tile you did is beautiful."

"Just so you know, I changed the lights to LED, and it brightened up the space."

"Okay, but a bathroom needs to be bright so women can do their makeup and men can see their face when they are shaving. It's totally different. The kitchen should also be nice and bright, so LED, is fine, but can we keep the fixtures to keep the character of the space?"

"But the fixtures are old and need work. A new one would be easier."

"Yes, but if we threw away everything that is old and needs work for something new, then relationships would never last, because they also need work."

"Point taken. You're right. You don't just throw things away because they need a little attention or are old."

"Okay, so repaint the current cabinets and change the light to LED, but keep the fixture. So how about the island—do we change that?"

"Can I think about that for a bit? I'm still on the fence about the sink."

"Of course. We don't need to make all the decisions today. We can start with the cabinet color, and I can pull that fixture down and give it some love, maybe some touch-ups and new bulbs."

"I am going to go out and find the paint in the barn. You start looking for a new backsplash and colors you think might look good. Think about the sink. I think it would be nice to have two sinks in the kitchen. I could do vegetables in one and rinse dirty dishes in the other."

CHAPTER 23

JULIE

"Hey, there you are. I was wondering what happened to you. You have been gone for a while."

"I went into the attic of the barn and found these old fixtures. I was cleaning them up to bring them into the garage to show you. I think we can repurpose these in the house. They'll look really good after a little love."

"Oh, so now you want to put the effort into the fixtures?"

"Okay, I think you were right about the fixtures. It will keep the character of the cabin. Now can I show you what I have in the garage? I painted some wood to show the colors I am thinking of for the cabinets, and I cleaned up the fixtures I found. So we have a couple options."

"Yeah, let me finish cleaning up the kitchen. I started prepping dinner. I got some fish out of the freezer. I have it defrosting in the sink. And I am washing potatoes on the other side. I see your point on the sink. I had to move the dirty cups in the sink so I could wash the potatoes. So I am thinking the sink is a good idea with a garbage disposal."

"Deal, I can put a garbage disposal in, no problem. Actually, that is a good idea. I'm not sure why I didn't think about that sooner."

David wraps his arms around me and started kissing my neck.

"David, I am trying to wash potatoes."

David spun me around and began kissing me. David lifted me up on the island. David slowly undressed me, kissing and caressing my body. David slowly made love to me.

David said, "I see your point about the counter space on the island."

I laughed. "God, you're awful. Show me the fixtures. Before we get sidetracked again."

"Yeah, I could use a shower. If you want to join me."

"Later. We need to go to the garage. You're so distractible."

"So, what do you think? I painted some wood white and another one blue that I found in the barn. It might be too dark for the kitchen, but we could offset it with a light backsplash and maybe keeping the white appliances. What do you think?"

"I like the colors, but I'm not sure how they will look in the kitchen. Can we bring the wood in and look at it next to the cabinets and fridge? I want to see how the blue would look next to the white fridge."

"Yeah, we can do that. Let's bring them in, and we can lean them on the counter and see."

"What do you think?"

"Honestly, I kinda like the blue. I didn't think I would, but I think you're right. If we offset the darker color with a light backsplash, it would work. But I think I like it with the stainless steel appliances. Look at it against the toaster. It looks nice."

"Okay, so blue cabinets, stainless steel appliances, and a new small sink in the island so we can keep some of our counter space."

"With a disposal. Don't forget my disposal."

"Right, I promised you we'd get the disposal."

"Now let me put this stuff back in the garage, and we can cook dinner. After dinner, we can look at the fixtures I found and see where we want to put those."

"Fish tonight. Huh, we haven't had that in a while."

"That's what I thought. It's been a while, so I thought, why not? I found some salmon in the freezer, and with some potatoes and a vegetable, it sounded good."

"Can you hand me the scissors so I can cut this bag open and wash the fish?"

"Sure, here you go."

I cut open the bag of fish, then took off running for the bathroom.

David followed and heard me throwing up in the bathroom.

"Julie, are you okay?"

David went in and held my hair back. "Hey, what's wrong?"

"I don't know, I just smelled the fish, and it made me nauseous."

"Maybe the fish went bad. I'll check before you go in the kitchen. You wash your face and take a couple minutes."

Later, David asked, "Hey, how ya feeling?"

"I'm fine. I think it passed. Not sure what that was."

"Well, I checked, and the fish isn't bad. Smelled just like salmon. It's in the sink, but if you want to have something else tonight, I can get some chicken or something else out."

"No, I think it was just a one-time thing. I'm fine, really."

"Okay, well, I can cook the fish if you want, or I can throw it away and cook chicken."

"No, it's fine, it was just a one-time thing. Maybe I stood up too fast or ate something earlier that my stomach did not agree with. It could be anything. I'm fine. Now, let me season the fish, and let's have dinner."

I started to season the fish, then ran to the bathroom again.

"Julie, are you okay?"

"Yeah, I'm fine. I just guess it hasn't passed yet."

"Take your time. I threw the fish out in the garbage, and I took the garbage into the garage. I have chicken thawing in the sink. You sure you're okay?"

"Yeah, I'm fine, David. I don't know what this is. I just got nauseous again. Maybe I caught a bug."

"Okay, well, can I ask you a question?"

"Of course, David, you can ask me anything."

"Is it possible you're pregnant?"

"No, I take the depo shot every three months like clockwork. We're covered."

"Um, Sweetheart, we have been here for a couple months now. When did you have it before we came here?"

"Um, I don't know. I have a reminder set up on my phone to tell me when I'm due."

"Sweetie, I don't want to push here, but we left your phone at the office. Is there any chance you missed the notification?"

"OMG, David, I don't know I don't remember what month I got it last. Everything has just been so crazy. I didn't even think about it. I had reminders set up so I didn't have to think about it. David, what if I'm pregnant?"

"Julie, don't worry. If you are, then we will change that extra bedroom into a baby room."

"David, I can't have a baby. I have a crazy ex and a career. This is not the time to have a baby."

"Okay, well, let's first calm down and not get too upset. This could still be a bug. But tomorrow, when I go to town, I will pick up a pregnancy test or two, and then we can worry about it. But don't worry. No matter what, I will be here for you, and nothing will change how I feel about you. We are in this together. I am concerned about something. Joel. He will be upset if we don't tell him. And honestly, I do not want to get on his bad side."

"OMG, Joel! I can't have a baby without him. I have missed him so much. Just sending him 'margaritas' all the time isn't enough. Do you think there is any way I can talk to him just for a few minutes? I really need him. Joel would know what to do about this. He's having a baby, and he would know if this was pregnancy related or not. Joel would talk me down, too. I need him so much. He is my best friend and my rock."

"Okay, let's stop worrying about what might be and focus on what is. We don't know anything for sure, so let's keep calm, and we can make a plan."

"Tomorrow I will go into town and get a test. While I am there, I will also go to the police station and call the detective and see if there is any update on John. I will ask him if there is any way to talk to Joel. I check in with him every couple weeks, so I'm sure there has to be some way to talk to Joel."

"Why can't I just go with you, and Joel can be at the police station? Then we could talk."

"Julie, no one knows you're here. Including the people in town. We have to keep it that way. Detective Jordan said the less people that know where you are, the better. If people in town know you're with me, and John finds this town, then there are more people to ask and more chances of him finding you. We have to keep you a secret."

"So what are we going to do if I'm pregnant? I will need doctors and stuff."

"Okay, let's not worry. First of all, you might not be pregnant. But if you are, I will talk to the doctor in town and have him make a house call, and since you're his patient, he can't talk to anyone about you. It would be safe. But Honey, let's not worry about anything else. For now, let's worry about dinner. Come on, let's get dinner started. You have to be hungry. And since there is a possibility of you carrying my child, you get extra vegetables with your dinner."

"Seriously, you're gonna start that crap with me? Really, David?"

"Hey, I'm just making sure you're eating healthy. If it's a bug, it won't hurt, and if you're pregnant, then it will be beneficial."

"Are you one of those guys?"

"What are you talking about?"

"You know, one of those guys that thinks he put a baby in me, so he gets to tell me what to eat and when."

"No, I am not one of those guys, but I am a guy who worries about the health of the women he loves. And if you are carrying my child, then I have twice as much to worry about. And if anything were to happen to you, Joel would have my head, so yes, I am going to take extra good care of you."

"OMG, David, how did I let this happen?"

"Would you stop blaming yourself? You forgot something that you had in your phone. It happens. Besides, we don't know if you're pregnant."

"David, this isn't a bug. You know it. I'm pregnant and trapped by my ex. I can't have a baby here. David, this is all wrong. I can't do this here in the woods. I need a big hospital and a doctor's care. I need vitamins and extra fruits and vegetables. Not to mention, I need clothes. This can't be how this happens."

"Okay, you're right. This isn't ideal. But were not destitute or living in a cave. I will go to town tomorrow and get supplies. You know we can order anything we need on Amazon. I can have it delivered to my P.O. box and pick it up there. No one will know anything if we order clothes for you through Amazon.

"David, how can I have a baby and not tell my family or Joel?"

"Okay, let's sit down and figure everything out. Maybe when I call the detective I can ask if you can send letters or something to the family. Maybe we can get a secure line at the police station so you can call people. I will find out everything tomorrow, so if it helps, let's sit down and make a list of questions I need to ask the detective."

"Can we do that after dinner? I'm starving."

"And there are the mood swings."

"Oh, you are so in trouble. I hope you're prepared for the cravings and all the other things this baby is going to require."

"I am looking forward to waiting on you hand and foot. I promise I will get you everything you need, and this baby will be just fine. Now let's get you some vegetables. You are going to need your strength and extra vitamins."

CHAPTER 24

DAVID

"Dinner is served. I made you some healthy baked chicken with vegetables and a side of baked potato."

"Thank you, David. If we are pregnant, you're going to be a great dad."

"Well, I have to say, I'm hoping you're pregnant. I always wanted kids, and I'm totally in love with you, so I think it's perfect. I know the timing isn't perfect, but I don't care. I want to have a family with you. Besides, Joel already picked your baby names, so that is one thing to check off the list."

"David, how am I going to do this?"

"First, we're going to see if you're pregnant, and if not, then you're worrying for nothing. If you are, then we will handle it together. We will schedule doctor's appointments and get you whatever you need. We can turn the extra room into a nursery. Everything will be fine. You have nothing to worry about. I promise everything will be okay.

"Come on, let's finish dinner, and after dinner I will do the dishes. I'm thinking we make it an early night. I think you could use some rest. And I don't want you stressing yourself out. How about a movie after dinner to relax, then we'll turn in early. We can watch a rom com. I know you love those."

"That sounds perfect. Maybe after dinner I will feel better about this situation."

"I'm sure after you eat, you will feel better, and that will take your mind off of everything. Now eat up before it gets cold."

CHAPTER 25

DAVID

"Okay, I am headed to town. I have the list. Is there anything you can think of that we missed?"

"No, I think I have everything on the list."

"Okay, I will be back later. You get some rest and try not to worry. I will bring everything we need, and everything will work out just as it should. Keep Maddie close because she loves the extra attention. Try to rest and not think about anything, just take it easy while I'm gone. When I get back, we can take the test and figure everything out. I promise I will be as quick as possible."

I headed to town.

After a 30-minute drive, I finally arrived in town. My first stop was the police station to check in with Detective Jordan.

"Sheriff Jones, how are you doing?" I said.

"David, good to see you. I am doing well today. How about yourself?"

"Sheriff, I couldn't ask for a better day. The sun is shining, and I am just in town to pick up treats for Maddie. I thought I would check in with New York and see how things are there."

"Yeah, it's been a couple weeks since you called and checked on that case. Let me get Detective Jordan on the phone for you. Detective Jordan, this is Sheriff Jones. I have someone here to talk with you.

Here you go, David. I will give you some privacy. Let me know if you need anything."

"Detective Jordan, is there any update on the case?" David asked.

"David, I am afraid there is no update yet. We are still looking for John. He has to be off the grid. We haven't been able to track him by phone or anything. He hasn't been to work lately, either. I'm wondering if he is hiding out or planning an attack. I don't think he has given up."

"Detective, we are running out of time here. Julie is going stir crazy. Is there any way she can talk to Joel or her family? Write letters, call, anything?"

"David, I am sorry, but she can't reach out to anyone. It's the only way to keep John from finding her. I think he is still watching Joel somehow. I can't guarantee he isn't watching or listening to phone calls. I wish there was a way, but for now, I think Julie being out of contact is the best thing. I can get messages to her family if we absolutely need to, but I would say emergency only."

"Okay, Detective, I understand. We were just hoping this would have an end in sight. I'll check back in a couple weeks. Hopefully I hear something sooner, but if not, I'll check in."

"Take care, David. I promise all this trouble will be worth it."

"Thanks, Detective. I appreciate everything. Thank you, Sheriff, I am all set. Have a good day."

Okay, that was a bust. Next stop was the doctor's office.

"Hey, Doc Jameson, how are you doing?"

"David, I am wonderful. What brings you in today? Everything okay?"

"Yes, Doc, I am good. I have a couple questions. I have to ask you to keep this conversation private."

"Absolutely, David. Doctor-patient confidentiality, as always."

"Doc, I have a friend coming to stay for a couple weeks, and she may need medical attention. Any chance you could do some house calls for her? She can't go out in public."

"David, that is an odd request. I don't usually do house calls unless it's an emergency or my patient can't come to me."

"Doc, I understand, but I promise that if she could come to you, she would. But that is not a possibility, and I promise I will make it worth the time. But I must insist that this remains private and no one knows you are coming to my place or tending to my friend. I can't have anyone know she is coming."

"I see, David. Is everything okay?"

"Yes, Doc. everything is fine. I just promised her no one would know she was with me. I can explain more when you are at my place. But it must be private."

"Of course, David. I trust you. I will come out tomorrow and meet with your friend."

"One more thing, Doc. What do you suggest for a pregnant woman as far as vitamins and things she would need in the first trimester?"

"David, is there something you need to tell me?"

"Doc, I promise that at my house I will explain more, but right now I can't elaborate on anything."

"Okay, David. I would suggest some prenatal vitamins and, of course, regular doctor's visits. Regular checkups will show any issues with the baby. David, is the patient I'm seeing tomorrow pregnant?"

"Honestly, Doc, I am not sure. It's possible, but I don't want to jump to any conclusions. I am just asking to cover all my bases."

"Okay, well, I will plan on coming tomorrow after lunch, and I will bring tools for pregnancy just in case. And I promise I will keep this appointment to myself. I won't put it in my calendar or anything."

"Thanks, Doc, I appreciate you doing this and the discretion. I promise it is necessary."

"No problem, David. I'm sure you're being cautious for a good reason. I'll see you tomorrow."

"Thanks, Doc. I'll see you tomorrow."

Okay, now I needed to grab everything for the kitchen renovation. I needed paint, backsplash samples, and a small sink, if they had one. I might have to order that online.

"Hi, Henry, how are you today?"

"David, I'm wonderful. How about you?"

"I'm doing well. Just thinking about redoing my kitchen. I need some samples to see what I want to do. And I'm thinking about a small sink to add to my island. Do you happen to have any?"

"Sorry, we do not have small ones, just regular size. But I can grab a book. You can pick one out, and I can order it."

"That would be great, Henry. If you could grab that and the backsplash tile samples, that would be great. I'm going to take a look at paint and see what color I want to do the kitchen in."

"Okay, here you go, David. Hope this helps."

"This is perfect, Henry. I grabbed a few paint samples, too. I thought I would be able to decide, but I'm just not sure what I want. Any idea what the wait time is for the sink? Couple weeks or couple days?"

"Honestly, they are a little behind. I would say at least two weeks out. Some of the tiles are a couple weeks out also, so keep that in mind. If you decide what you want, give me a call. I can get the order placed over the phone. I'll speed it up so you don't have to drive all the way back into town just to order."

"That would be great. Thanks, Henry, I will do that. I'll see you next week, Henry."

"Have a good weekend, David."

Next stop, pharmacy. Okay, now to find pregnancy tests and vitamins. I was glad they had self-checkout now so I didn't have to try to explain to Louise what I needed a pregnancy test for.

Okay, there were a couple tests. First Response, Clearblue. How do you know which one to get? This looked complicated. *You know what, I'll just get the two packs for each one and see which one Julie prefers,* I thought. *I can't tell the difference between these tests.*

Now for vitamins. I would need over-the-counter until she got a prescription. I wondered if she wanted gummy ones. I knew she loved gummies. *Yeah, let's get this one. It looks good, and the back label says it has a lot of vitamins and nutrients. This should work till she gets a prescription.*

All good, so time to check out and on to the next stop.

Okay, last stop. Now to get groceries. I looked at the list. Vegetables, chicken, broth, paper towels, sour cream, orange juice, milk, and bread. This wouldn't take too long. I would take a look at the meat and see what looks good, too. The sooner I got the groceries done, the sooner I could get home.

Hmm, I had an idea. I thought Julie would like a pizza for lunch. We hadn't had pizza in a long time. There was no delivery at the cabin, so why not grab a pizza? That would be a good surprise. I would have them put some veggies on it, too, so it would still be healthy, sort of. I'd stop in and order at Geno's. I'd probably have to wait a few minutes, but it would be worth it.

I checked my list to make sure I had everything. *Yup, I think I got everything. I'll grab a pizza and head home.*

Chapter 26

DAVID

"Hey Beautiful, I am home, and I brought a surprise."

"Ooh yeah, what did you bring?"

"Pizza. I thought we could have it for lunch today. It's been a while since we had pizza."

"OMG, it smells delicious. I had forgotten how much I missed pizza. Joel and I used to order it late at night and talk. I miss pizza. I'll grab plates. Oh, should we put the refrigerator stuff away first?"

"I will handle that. You go ahead and grab pizza before it gets any colder."

"Oh, good, because I am so excited. Is it weird that I am this excited about pizza?"

David laughed. "No, it's not weird at all. It has been a long time since we had pizza. Now, you get this excited over veggies, and I will start to worry. I also thought maybe some ice cream would be a good idea, so I picked that up. It wasn't on the list, but I was thinking that if you are pregnant, ice cream is a good thing to have on hand."

"Yeah, that might be a good idea. I mean, honestly, ice cream is a staple even if you're not pregnant. Okay, well, I'm going to eat pizza till I burst, then I will take the test. You did pick up the test, right?"

"Yes, that was on the list. I have the test. Actually, I got a couple. I didn't know what to get, so I grabbed options. Let me finish unloading the car. You go ahead and eat."

"Oh, good, because I'm starving. The pizza smells so good. OMG, this pizza is amazing. It's not New York pizza, but it will do. I didn't realize how much I missed pizza."

"Wow, apparently this country life has been depriving you of pizza."

"David, you have no idea. I used to order pizza almost once a week, so going weeks without pizza is hard. It's the little things you miss, like pizza delivery."

"Okay, I have everything unpacked. I left the test in the bathroom whenever you're ready. I'm going to grab pizza, if there is any left."

"Don't worry, I saved you a slice or two. Okay, well, as much as I want to sit on this couch like a lump and relax, I need to take that test. I have never been so nervous about something, not even court. This anxiety is crazy. I'm nervous and scared all at once. I've never put so much faith in peeing on a stick. I hope I can keep my pizza down. I'm so nervous."

"Relax for a couple minutes, then take the test. Let your lunch settle if you need to, there is no hurry."

"I know, but honestly, I just want to know. I'm not sure why I can't tell anyone anything. I can't even call Joel. But the fear of not knowing is killing me. I'm just going to go take the test. I can't wait anymore."

CHAPTER 27

DAVID

Julie came out of the bathroom and walked into the living room.

"We have to wait three minutes to get an answer," she said.

David was down on one knee, holding a box with a sparkling two-carat emerald-cut diamond ring.

"Julie, don't say anything yet. I want you to know that no matter what happens, it doesn't matter. I love you with all my heart, and pregnant or not, you are my life, my hopes and dreams. I have loved you since high school. Finding you again has been the greatest gift I could ever get. I can't imagine my life without you. Will you marry me?"

Julie was crying. "YES!"

David picked up Julie, spun her around, and kissed her.

"David, where did you find a ring?"

"Actually, it was my mother's ring. Dad bought for her on their twentieth anniversary. She always wanted me to hand it down to someone I truly loved. That was her only wish."

"OMG, it's so beautiful. It's perfect. I love you so much. I can't believe this is happening. Are you sure this is what you want?"

"Yes, I have never been more sure of anything. Baby or no baby, I want to marry you. I would today if we could."

"OMG, I forgot about the test. Three minutes are probably up."

"Remember, it doesn't matter what the result is. I'm marrying you no matter what. If you are not pregnant now, then it will happen in the future. I love you now and forever."

"I love you, too. Now to see what our future holds."

Julie went to the bathroom to check her tests.

She came out holding two tests. She was smiling and crying.

"I'm pregnant."

David picked her up and kissed her.

"I couldn't be happier," he said. "Are you okay?"

"I'm shocked. I thought it was possible, but two tests kinda makes it real. I got engaged and pregnant in less than 10 minutes. Are you sure you want to do this?"

"I have never been more sure of anything in my life. I can't wait to start a family with you. So now we have work to do. I was going to redo the kitchen, but in light of this new information, I think I will start on the spare room and make it into a nursery. So you need to pick colors."

"David, what about doctor's appointments and stuff? I can't leave the house."

"Don't worry about that, I took care of everything. First, I picked up some over-the-counter prenatal vitamins, just in case. I also stopped by the doctor in town and set it up so he will make house calls, and he has also promised to keep everything private. No one will know when he is here. You have an appointment tomorrow afternoon. He will come by and take care of everything. You don't have to worry about anything. We are going to have a healthy baby, and you are safe here with me."

"David, I'm scared. If John finds out or finds me, I don't know what he will do."

"You don't have to worry. I talked to the sheriff and Detective Jordan while I was in town. He is still working on the case. They have no new information. But he is still working on the case and tracking John. He will show up eventually, and they will catch him, I am sure of it. You are safe here. I put cameras and a warning system in just in case. John has no idea where you are. And if by some chance he finds us, then Maddie and I will protect you. You have nothing to worry about. I promise you are safe with me and Maddie. No one except detective Jordan knows where you are. Joel doesn't even know. There is no one to tell John anything. He will do something stupid and get caught, and then we can go back to everyone and tell them we are engaged and pregnant. We can have a huge baby shower and plan our wedding."

"Why wait? Let's start planning. Where do you want to get married? Big or small wedding? OMG, I have a wedding to plan and a baby to prepare for. How are we going to get clothes and a crib?"

"Amazon delivers, Sweetheart. You can have everything sent to the P.O. box, and I will pick it up. Use my account, not yours, just in case. There are stores in town, and maybe we can do a drive to some town way far away to shop. Maybe we do a weekend getaway shopping spree to get some large items, like a crib and a stroller. We can go anywhere except New York. Maybe we could hit Boston. It's only a couple hours from here, and I highly doubt John would be looking for you in Boston. How about next time I check in with the detective, I ask if that would be okay? We could load up the truck with lots of baby items. Maybe some wedding things, too. Anything you want."

"David, that would be amazing. Just to get out of the house for a day would be amazing. I'm going a little crazy cooped up in here. I love this home you have made, and I love being here with you, but honestly, I do miss working and Joel and people. I miss my apartment, too, even though John made it a scary place. I miss my stuff."

"I understand. When I left my house to move here, it was a big adjustment, and I got to bring things with me. You came with a bag, and that's it. So I understand this is hard, but it's not forever. Unless you want it to be. We could live here together if you want and raise the baby here, or we can move back to New York after John is caught. It's up to you. I will go anywhere you want. As long as I am with you, then I am happy."

"David, I never thought about not going back. But I never thought about being engaged and pregnant, either. Life is changing so fast. How do I figure everything out?"

"Well we take everything day by day. Tomorrow you have an appointment to confirm your pregnancy, and then we can set up appointments. The rest we can decide later. We can get the baby's room ready, and hopefully John is caught soon, and we can go back to New York and have the baby closer to friends and family. But if you want, we can have the baby here, so it really is up to you. You are my life, and I will do everything in my power to make you happy every day. If that means moving to New York, then as soon as it's safe, I will pack us up. If that means a move to Japan, Hawaii, or Alaska, then I'll pack us up. Whatever your heart desires is where we go."

"David, you're making this too easy for me. I don't want to give up my job. I love working, and I love New York. I can get pizza in the middle of the night."

"Well, no worries. I will stay home with the baby while you go back to work, and if that doesn't work, then we can get a nanny or daycare or something. But for now, we are stuck here, so you need to pick paint colors, and we need to get a move on. I'm going to need some time to get that room ready. Besides, this will give us something else to keep us busy."

"Where do we start, David? The wedding, or the baby and clothes? I'm going to need new clothes. I need Joel. I need to tell him. He always calms me down."

"Well, unfortunately Joel is out of reach right now, so calming you down is now Maddie's job. Just pet her, and she'll make everything better. I promise."

"David, I'm spinning out. Everything is happening so fast."

"Stop and think. We have plenty of time before the baby comes, and we have our entire lives to get married. I am in no hurry as long as you are here with me. We can go as slow or fast as you want. I will marry you tomorrow or in ten years—it's up to you. So don't worry about that. We have months to prepare for the baby. We will be ready, I promise. And you will be a great mom. Everything is going to be fine. Here, look at this."

"What is this?"

"Cute baby stuff on Amazon. I logged into my account, so pick out some cute items that will relax you. The P.O. Box is already loaded in there, so you can just pick out some cute things and ship them there, and I will go to town and pick them up."

"OMG, this little outfit is so cute. And it has matching booties."

"We're going to need blankets and diapers. You know, I should start making a list."

"Making a list of baby items you think we need is a great idea. I will start working on the room. I need to clean out all the old boxes and the closet. We need to figure out if we want to keep the spare bed up."

"Oh, yes, we want the bed. I may sleep in there after the baby comes."

"Okay, that was an easy decision. See, everything is going to be just fine."

CHAPTER 28

DAVID

David said, "Good morning to my fiancée."

"Oh, that sounds weird. I feel like yesterday was a dream."

"Oh, it was my dream come true, my love."

"So, are you ready for this afternoon?"

"Yeah, but what if we're wrong? What if I'm not pregnant?"

"Well, then you only have to worry about planning a wedding, and we keep trying to have a baby."

"David, I'm serious. What if we jumped the gun on this baby thing?"

"Stop worrying. If we did, then it's fine. It will happen when it's time. Either way, I am marrying you. You said yes, no take backs."

"OMG, you're such a dork."

"Yes, but I am a happy dork. What would you like for breakfast? Doc will be here around lunchtime, so you should eat."

"I'm really nauseous. Maybe just some toast. Maybe it's just nerves."

"Could be nerves. Here is some toast and jam and your vitamins. Don't forget those. I need you to be healthy."

"Are you going to be this pushy and protective the entire pregnancy?"

"Yes, and I think you're going to be nauseous and moody the entire pregnancy, too."

"Oh, I hope not, and I'm not moody. You're just too cheery and annoying."

"I love you. Now eat some toast."

"Ugh, you're so annoying."

"So I have some ideas for the baby's room. I was thinking of moving everything to the barn for now, except the bed and dresser. I'll clean out the closet, too, and we should have enough room for a changing table and crib. Maybe even a second dresser if needed. Just out of curiosity, do you still have your clothes in that dresser? Any chance you want to move into my room now? We are engaged. I think we can share our dresser and closet now."

"I never even thought about that. I guess I can move my stuff into our room."

"Great, I already cleaned out a few drawers for you, and I am boxing up some closet stuff to make room for you, too."

"David I only have a few days of clothing. A drawer is fine."

"Um, Sweetie, I hate to remind you, but you're pregnant, and you're going to need more clothes, so you're going to need more than a drawer. Besides, most of the stuff in our closet is old junk I just haven't had a chance to go through. I'm sure it's mostly my Dad's stuff. I just wasn't in a hurry to go through anything when I moved here. I did the dresser, then I started working on the house. So it needs to be done. Besides, I want you to feel like this is your home, too. You finish breakfast, and I will start the closet."

David worked on cleaning out the closet while boxing up old clothes and items he found. Julie finished breakfast.

David headed towards the living room. "Hey, Honey, I found these old lamps in the closet. Do you want them for the baby's room?" He saw Julie sleeping on the couch with Maddie snuggled at her feet.

"Good job, Maddie. You keep an eye on her. She's our world now."

David headed back to the bedroom.

"David, where are you?"

"I'm back here, in the bedroom."

"How long was I asleep for?"

"Maybe an hour or so, not long."

"I didn't think I was tired. I sat on the couch with Maddie. Next thing I knew, I woke up."

"Hey, I found these lamps in the closet. Do you want them for the baby's room?"

"Oh, those are pretty. They might be antiques."

"I'm sure they are old. I think they were my parents' old lamps from years ago."

They looked hand-painted and had a metal base and glass lamp shade.

"The flowers painted on the shade are beautiful. I think they will look beautiful in the baby's room, and since they are from your parents, I think it will be sweet."

"I thought it would be a nice touch, too."

"I'm going to jump in the shower. The doctor will be here soon. I'm all dusty and gross from cleaning. You should relax and grab a snack. I'm sure Maddie would like her treats, too."

"I can't eat. I'm too anxious to see what the doctor says."

"Honey, you know the doctor might not say much. I mean, he doesn't have a lab to confirm pregnancy or anything, so it might just be a quick appointment."

"You're right, I just think I'm excited or anxious or something. I need a glass of wine to relax."

"Um, no wine for you."

"I know. I just wish, it would help relax me."

"I understand. Maybe doing some yoga or something would be helpful?"

"Yoga, seriously? Is that all the suggestions you have?"

"I'm sorry, we are a little out of my expertise. I don't know what to suggest. Hopefully the doctor has some ideas."

"I'm sorry, I'm just on edge. This isn't exactly what I expected or planned for. This whole John mess is more than I can handle, and adding a baby to the mix is not what I planned."

"I get that, Julie. I didn't expect it either, but we're not sure of anything yet, so let's just wait and see what the doctor says. There is no use in getting worked up over something that might not be. Especially since we can't control anything at this point."

CHAPTER 29

DAVID

"Doctor Jameson, it is good to see you," said David. Doctor Jameson arrived wearing a tan suit, pants, and a white shirt. He was carrying his doctor's bag.

"Hello, David. I hope I'm not too early. I thought I would come during lunch so no one suspected why I was out of the office."

"No, Doc, that is fine. Anytime works. Right now, the sooner we know what is going on, the better. Let me introduce you to Julie. Julie, this is doctor Jameson. He is our town doctor."

"Hello, Julie," said Dr. Jameson. "It is nice to meet you."

"Hello, Doctor Jameson, it is nice to meet you. Thank you so much for driving out here to meet with me. I really appreciate it," said Julie.

"It is not a problem at all, Julie. David has informed me a little of your situation and need for privacy. I have set everything up so that you will have a patient number instead of a name, and you will be referred to as Jane Doe. If you are pregnant, then the baby will be Baby Doe. David and I are the only ones who will know anything about your treatment. I will also not leave your file in our normal files, just in case.

"So, let me tell you a little about what we will be doing today. I will take a blood sample to run back to the lab and confirm pregnancy. But it sounds like that is a formality at this point, since David tells me you took a couple home pregnancy tests."

"Yes, Doctor, that is correct. I took a couple, and both came out positive."

"Okay, well, I will confirm with bloodwork. That will also tell us how far along you are. I am here to basically draw blood today and answer any questions you may have. I also brought you some info about pregnancy, like what to expect and how your appointments will work.

"Normally, I would do all this after we confirm your pregnancy, but since you took a home pregnancy test, and we don't have a lab available, we are doing this a little out of order. But that's okay. We need to handle your case special, so as far as our appointments go, I will come out once a month until you get further along. Then we will go to every other week, then once a week when you get about six weeks from delivery. If anything changes, we can change everything up. Whatever works for you. I also have contacts at large hospitals in case we need testing or ultrasounds, so we can get those done under Jane Doe. Everything will be kept private. I also brought you some prenatal vitamins to start. I will bring you a monthly supply each time I come rather than giving you a script to get filled. So what questions can I answer for you?"

"Doctor, I am such a ball of anxiety right now. How can I do this?"

"Julie, I meet with women all the time who find out they are pregnant and the anxiety kicks in. That is perfectly normal. There are many exercises you can do to keep your anxiety down. I do want to let you know that you do need to keep your heart rate good. That causes issues with the baby, so keep an eye on it. If you feel like you're not going back to normal anxiety levels, have David call me, and we can monitor your blood pressure. I think you finding this out and dealing with your current situation is causing your anxiety, but give it a couple days. I think as everything settles in, you will feel better."

"Doctor, being trapped in this house is not helping."

"I understand, but you're not on bed rest or anything, so you do need to take it easy on lifting and strenuous activity, but you can continue as normal. Get into a routine of exercise around the house and eating healthy. The healthier you make your body, the easier the pregnancy will be. In the paperwork, you should find some healthy food suggestions and some things to not eat at all, like caffeine and fish. Caffeine can be had in small amounts. Everything in moderation. Remember, I am always here for questions. You or David can call me anytime. I can always take a nice country drive and check on you if needed.

"I will plan on calling later today with test results. But going forward, most of our visits will be in person, unless you need me for something. I know David said he was trying to limit phone use and any out-of-the ordinary trips to town. I can put you on my schedule during lunch so it doesn't look like I have a patient at that time. Do you have any other questions?"

"I don't know, this is all happening so fast."

"I totally understand, Julie, and that is the normal response I get from patients. So what I will say is that after I leave, your mind will start running. Write all your questions down, and when David comes to town, he can stop in and ask them, or I can answer them at our next appointment here. Honestly, with the internet now, you can find most of your answers there. There are a lot of groups for parents online and some great resources for first time moms. I suggest you check out some of the groups online to see what you find. If you need some suggestions, please let me know. I think I have a handout of websites to visit for new and expecting parents."

"I will definitely check out those websites and things. I have plenty of time to research online. You're probably right about the questions, too. I'm just shocked. I guess this wasn't planned, and this isn't the best time, either."

"Well, Julie let me honestly tell you that I don't know of a patient who had an unplanned pregnancy who thought it was the perfect time. I also don't have any patients who thought everything went perfectly just as they planned or thought it would. With babies, I have found that nothing goes according to plan, so don't worry about that. Every baby is different, and every one of them comes on their own schedule. You are better off worrying about where the baby will sleep right now, or clothes and names. There is nothing you can do other than take care of yourself. Lots of rest and healthy food, take your vitamins. If you have any issues or are concerned about anything, call me. I will help as much as I can."

"Thank you so much, Doctor. I really appreciate everything."

"Okay, well, if there is nothing else, let's get this blood drawn and back to the lab for analysis."

Julie held her arm out, preparing for the blood to be drawn by Doctor Jameson.

"Okay, there we go. That should be everything. So I will get this to the lab and call you with the results. In the meantime, if you have any questions, do not hesitate to call or pop in to my office, whichever is easier for you. As I told David when I called, I won't refer to you by name. It will be a number, since we are keeping everything private. I will also make sure no one knows I am coming here. These house calls will also be private.

So I will see you next month, unless you need me sooner. Please don't worry about anything. That will cause you more stress than anything. Just try to relax and imagine how wonderful your baby is going to be. David, it is always good to see you. I will call you later."

"Thanks again, Doc. I really appreciate your coming out."

"Of course, anytime, David. I hope I was able to help set Julie's mind at ease a little."

"Yeah, I'm sure after everything sinks in, she will be fine. It's just an adjustment. We will be just fine. Thanks again, Doc."

Doctor Jameson headed out of the house and to his car to head back to town.

David headed back to Julie.

"So, any chance you feel better after meeting with the doctor?"

"Yeah, actually, I do. I think he's right. No one is one hundred percent prepared to have a baby. I need to worry about things I can control and not worry about what I can't control. Besides, I think I always wanted kids. I just didn't expect it to be right now. And I am engaged to the man of my dreams, so who could ask for more? This baby will be loved and spoiled beyond belief."

"Well my soon-to-be wife, I guess we have a few decisions to make. Starting with some paint colors and baby furniture."

"David, don't you think we should at least wait until Doctor Jameson calls and says for sure I'm pregnant?"

"Sure, we can wait if you want, but I'm excited. I'm going to marry the love of my life and have a baby. What more could I ask for?"

"Well, I'm a little concerned about how Joel will take this news. I wish there was some way to tell him what is going on. I could really use his advice, and he is the only person who can really keep me calm and sane. He was my rock the entire time I was leaving John and moving, changing my entire life."

"I understand that you need Joel, but right now, it's not safe to reach out to him. But I promise that as soon as it is safe, I will make sure you talk to him. Until then, we can plan our lives together and start planning a room for our baby."

"You're right, I know. I just miss my best friend. How am I going to know when he has his baby? He must be excited. The baby should be here in a couple months. Sarah was already a couple months pregnant when we left town. She must be at least four or five months along by now. So the baby will be here in a couple months, and I am going to miss it. The police need to catch John so I can go home before Sarah and Joel have the baby. I don't want to have our baby trapped here in this house, either. I want to be able to take Lamaze classes and go shopping for the baby. I want a baby shower and a bridal shower."

"Sweetie, I know, and I want all those things for you, but we have to think about your safety. Right now it might not be possible, but who knows? Next month, when I call the detective, maybe things will have changed, and we can go home. Until then, this is our home, and we will start getting ready for the baby. Hopefully we will be able to end the

John chapter of our lives soon and move on to our happily ever after. Until then, we can have fun planning our happily ever after."

"You're right, there is so much to do. We have less than nine months to plan this baby's life and our wedding. David, would you be okay with getting married after the baby comes? I really want my family and friends to be at my wedding, unless this craziness ends soon. I don't see how I can plan for a wedding and a baby, especially when I can't even talk to anyone."

"Hey, don't you worry about me. Whatever you want for a wedding is what you'll get. I want this to be your day, all about you and everything your heart desires. If you want to wait, we can wait. If you want to get married quickly at City Hall, then I am there. I want you to be happy."

"Thank you, David, for being so understanding. I honestly don't know what I would do without you."

"Well, you wouldn't be pregnant, that's for sure."

"Well, I guess that is true, but I also wouldn't be as safe as I am. Who knows? If I wasn't staying with you, John could have found me."

"Let's not think about that, let's plan our lives instead. So, Trixie or Thompson? Do you want a boy or a girl?"

"We are not naming our kids Trixie or Thompson. Just cause Joel said it was his pick doesn't mean I have to use those names. I wonder what he decided to name his kids. I am missing out on so much. I'm supposed to be the godmother. I should be there for him."

"Look, I know Joel understands. He wanted you to be safe. Don't worry about him, he is fine, and I am sure Sarah is fine, too. I will see if I can get the detective to deliver a message to him. Maybe that would be an easy way to communicate. Maybe he can get an update on Joel and Sarah. For now, let's worry about our baby and what color you want the baby's room. I brought some samples to look at. I was going to paint the kitchen, but I think now we may want to paint the baby room instead. What do you think?"

"David, do you want to know if it's a boy or girl, or do you want to be surprised?"

"Huh, I hadn't thought about it. I kinda like the idea of being surprised, but I think I want to know so we know better how to prepare. Knowing if it's a boy or girl might help us decide on colors for the room, too."

"I wonder if we will be able to find out the sex. I don't know how I will go to an ultrasound appointment, or any appointments that I might need. We're limited to doing everything here at the house. How will we find out the sex or even get a little ultrasound picture to hang on the fridge?"

"Don't worry about that. We're not there yet, and Doc said he knew doctors at larger hospitals if we needed anything. I'm sure we can go to a different hospital, just not one in New York. We will figure everything out, don't worry."

CHAPTER 30

JULIE

The phone rang. David headed over to pick up his phone.

"Hello."

"Hi, Doctor Jameson. How did everything work out?"

"Well, David, it is a definite now, and it looks like you're about five weeks along. Does that help with your project?"

"Yes, Doctor Jameson. Thank you so much for the information. I will stop by your office next week to discuss our project. Thank you, Doctor. Have a wonderful day!"

David said to Julie, "That was Doctor Jameson. He said you are definitely pregnant and about five weeks along."

"OMG, David it's really true. I don't know what to do. I'm so excited. I want to call Joel. I know I can't, but I can send him margaritas."

Julie grabbed her phone and texted Joel a bunch of margarita emojis.

"Hopefully that makes him think something wonderful is happening. I don't know how else to tell him I'm pregnant and engaged."

David grabbed Julie, put his arms around her, and kissed her. "I love you so much. I can't wait to marry you."

"I love you, David. I can't believe we are having a baby. My life has changed so much since I found you again. I can't wait to start our lives together with this baby. So now we need to pick paint colors and start looking for baby furniture. Do you want a changing table in the baby's room?"

"I hadn't thought about that. Let me get you some paper and a pen so we can start a list of items we need and what we want and don't want."

"Oh, why don't you grab the tablet and we can look for a baby furniture list? We might need to order some things soon if they are on backorder."

"Okay, we need a wedding list and a baby list. I will also start a grocery list."

"Why do we need a grocery list? You just went to town and got groceries."

"Well, Sweetheart, you're going to have to eat much healthier. And you can't have certain foods. Here is the paperwork Doc dropped off with a list of foods you should avoid. You need to make sure you are taking care of that baby."

"Really, you're going to start with me about being healthy and eating right? Baby liked the pizza, so I think what baby wants, baby gets."

"Oh, well. We can discuss that after you take your vitamins. Here is some water and a vitamin."

"You know I will take the vitamins every day. I promise I want this baby to be healthy. I am going to do everything I need to do to make sure this baby is happy and healthy. If that means cutting back on certain foods, then that is what I'm doing. Except for pizza."

David laughed. "Okay, I think we can work something out on the pizza. Now let's start these lists."

"Let's not start the lists. Instead, let's enjoy this moment."

"Oh, really? What did you have in mind?"

Julie kissed David passionately.

"Ooh, I think I like this idea." David picked Julie up and carried her to the bedroom.

CHAPTER 31

JULIE

"Sweetie, come take a look at the baby's room. I think I have it close to done, at least with painting, then I can put some of the furniture you ordered in. What do you think?"

"Ooooh, I love the green. It's not too pale. It's the perfect pale green but not pastel. I think it will be perfect for the baby."

"Good, the last color green I tried was too bright, so this has to work, and we're running out of time to get things ready. You're already four months along, and I still need to put the crib together, and apparently I'm not getting to the kitchen remodel anytime soon."

"I'm sorry, David, but that last green was too bright. I want everything to be perfect. But it took a month to agree on green."

"Well, I'm glad I got some of the kitchen done while you were deciding on paint for the bedroom. I'm glad we put in that extra sink on the island with the baby bottles and stuff. I think we might need it just for the baby."

"You're right, it took some time and lots of samples to find the right green. I suppose it would help if we knew if we were having a boy or girl. Then we wouldn't need a gender-neutral room."

"I did get some stuff ready. The changing table is put together, and you have lots of clothes already. I think you have a year's worth of diapers."

"I do not. I ordered a couple cases of sizes one to three. I'm sure we will go through them much faster than you think. Babies poop a lot."

"I know, I'm just joking. But I honestly didn't realize babies needed all this stuff. I go to town each week, and the pick-up truck is full. The postmaster must be wondering what I'm building out here. I keep telling them I'm doing renovations. Don't forget you have a doctor's appointment later today. I know I want to find out if we are having a boy or girl, but I don't know how we can go to get an ultrasound."

David came up behind Julie, putting his arms around her. "Hey, we will get to do an ultrasound. I am sure of it. We just need to be careful and make sure it's safe. When I go to town this week, I will call the detective to get an update and let him know we need to go to an appointment. Hopefully we can keep it quiet."

"I hope so. I really need to get out of this house. I'm going stir crazy here alone. I know I'm not totally alone, but you know what I mean. I miss Joel. What if he had the baby?

I will see if there is any news from the detective. Honestly, honey, I'm sure Joel had the baby by now. I mean, they were a few months along when we left. We have been gone over six months, so if they haven't had the baby, I'm sure they are close to the due date. Look, the doctor is coming today. We can ask about the ultrasound and maybe whatever else we need to do at the hospital. Maybe we can make a nice day of it and eat out somewhere."

"I know you're right. I just feel like I'm getting huge as a house, and my hormones are crazy. I just want to cry and call Joel. I was supposed to be there for the birth."

"Hey, it's alright. Joel understands, and he knows that as soon as you can, you will be home to help with the baby. How about we watch that show you love? That will make you smile."

"It's not on yet. It starts on Wednesday. I watched all the other seasons. I've been waiting for the new season to start. I watched all the previews."

"Honey, I don't know how you watch that show, but if it makes you smile, I am all in. I promise that as soon as it's safe, I will take you out on a date. Candlelight dinner for two. In the meantime, we'll have dinner alone together every night."

"Yeah, that is exactly what got me so pregnant to begin with. Look at me, I'm huge. I feel like a house. I know the doctor said it's normal, but I feel like I'm bigger than I should be."

"Well, we can ask him when he comes to visit later today. How about I make you some lunch? You feel like anything?"

"No, I'm not really hungry. I had a lot for breakfast."

"Okay, that is a lie. You're always hungry lately. You're hoping Doc comes with a pizza, aren't you?"

"Maybe. He's been bringing one when he came to the last two visits, so I'm kinda hoping, I guess."

"I'll get one when I go to town this week if he doesn't."

"How about you bring one even if he does bring one?"

"Seriously, you want two pizzas this week?"

"I can't help it, your baby loves pizza. It's half your fault. Be happy I don't send you to town every day to get pizza. Those frozen ones don't always cut it, you know."

"I will gladly go every day if it will make you smile."

There was a knock on the door.

"Oh, that must be Doc. He is early."

"I'll get the door, and you relax for a minute."

"Good morning, David," said Doctor Jameson. "I hope it's okay that I'm early."

"Of course, Doc. You're welcome anytime."

"Oh, good. I brought your usual order: pizza and vitamins."

"Thank you. Julie will be so happy. She really looks forward to this pizza. Apparently the baby really craves pizza."

"Well, good, I'm glad I can make the baby happy. I do have some news, too. I received a letter to my office from a Detective Jordan. He had the sheriff bring it over in some medical files I was asked to review for an opinion. Well, that is the rouse we worked up to get information back and forth as needed. So here is the letter. I have no idea what it is about. I was just asked to deliver it."

"OMG, David, what does it say?" asked Julie.

"Well, I'm not sure it's addressed to you," he responded.

"Gimme, gimme! Oh, a letter! I haven't gotten mail in months. David it's from Joel."

Julie started crying.

"Joel had the baby. They had a little girl. Her name is Isabella. He sent a picture, too. Oh, I missed it, I missed everything."

Julie started crying again. "This is my goddaughter, and I missed it. David, I am missing everything. Joel is a father, and I promised I would be there to help, and I'm trapped here."

David walked over to Julie. "Honey, don't cry. It's okay. Joel knows that you love him and that you will be there as soon as you can. Doc is here to check you out. Let's do that and have pizza. I know you want pizza."

"Okay, Julie, I made an appointment for you in Boston," the doctor said. "I have a personal friend who is a doctor there. He is going to take care of everything so there is no trace of you actually in the hospital records. Since it's a busy hospital, they won't notice anything. On Friday, you're going to go get an ultrasound. They will print some nice pictures for you and let you know the sex of the baby if you're interested in knowing. I will have them do some more extensive bloodwork while you're there, too, just to check things out as a precaution. This is the doctor's information. When you arrive there, do not check in. Just go to the desk and ask for this doctor."

Doctor Jameson handed Julie the paper with the doctor's information on it.

"Do not tell anyone your name. Just tell them you are family from out of town and popped in. When they call the doctor to tell him, he will know it's you. He will not know your name other than Jane Doe. He will answer all your questions and mail me the report, since he is not putting it in the system. It is going to take a few days for the report to come to my office. But if there are any problems, he will call and let me know."

"Doc, are you saying I'm going to get to see my baby?"

"Yes, Julie, you will get to see the baby and get a picture to keep. I know this has been hard for you, but I was hoping this news would cheer you up. You get to leave the house and see your baby."

"OMG, I'm so excited. Can we leave now?"

"The appointment is Friday, so I suggest leaving early Friday morning. You have a few days to plan. But in the meantime, there is pizza to keep you happy. I also brought you this month's supply of vitamins. So let's go ahead and get started. Let me check your heartrate and the baby's and get your measurements. Then you can have pizza."

"Doc, I will do whatever you ask. You just told me I get to leave for a whole day and have pizza. I'm good with whatever you need."

Doc Jameson laughed. "Huh, it only takes pizza and a road trip to make her this happy.

David, you're going to have a hard time getting her to come back home."

"You have no idea, Doc. She has been asking to leave this place since she got here."

"Are you kidding, David, the fresh air and sun on my face? It's going to be great. Wait, what about Maddie? We can't leave her all day."

"Well, I can stop by and let her out if you need me to," said Doctor Jameson.

"Doc, I couldn't ask you to drive all the way out here. You already do so much for us. She will be fine for a few hours. It's only a couple hours' drive there, and we are not doing anything other than going to the doctor's. She is fine for the day. If we can't make it back, I can call you, Doc, to come check on her."

"What? Wait, what about dinner or lunch? Can we eat out? Something, anything, please?" Julie asked.

"Sweetie, we can figure all this out. Don't worry. Worse case, we hit a drive-through. Don't worry. We can discuss everything. And I will ask Detective Jordan when I go to town tomorrow how much he thinks we can do. I promise that if there is a way to go out to lunch or dinner, then we will."

Julie said, "Doc, one thing: am I supposed to be as big as a house, or am I overeating?"

"Julie, you are not overeating, and everyone is different. Each baby grows at its own pace. That being said, you are a little bigger than I expected, which is why I want you to have the ultrasound. I want to make sure we have our due date correct. I'm a little worried you might be further along than the original bloodwork showed. But there is nothing to worry about. Everything looks good, your heart rate and the babies are great. I'm just being extra cautious. Okay, well, I am all set here. I have everything I need. So I am going to let you two enjoy that pizza and talk. If you have any questions, drop by my office tomorrow or give me a call."

"Thank you, Doc. Let me walk you out."

"Thanks, Doc, for the pizza and for getting Julie out of the house. You have no idea how great this will be for her."

"Not a problem, David. Just be extra careful out there. Make sure you watch your back. I'll see you next week. Please stop by my office next Wednesday when you're in town to make sure everything is okay.

If you happen to come to town sooner, stop in to let me know how everything went."

"Will do, Doc. Thanks again."

"Julie, it was good seeing you. Have fun on Friday."

"Thanks, Doc. I promise I will."

CHAPTER 32

JULIE

"Okay, Julie, I'm headed to town. I have the grocery list and the list of questions for Detective Jordan. Anything I am forgetting?"

"Maddie is low on treats. Can you pick some up for her, please? And maybe a pizza."

"You just had pizza yesterday, and I think there are still a few slices in the fridge."

"Um, no, the baby got hungry last night. And, well, I had to feed the baby, so the pizza is gone. So please bring pizza."

"Okay, I will see what I can do. Anything else I need to pick up?"

"Just the mail, sweetie. Thank you." Julie kissed David goodbye.

"I'll be back as soon as I can. I know you want your pizza."

David headed to town.

"Well, Maddie, it's just you and I, so what do we do while we wait for pizza and treats?" Julie said. "I know, let's start putting some of the baby clothes in the baby's room. How about that? David got everything painted, so we should be able to start getting some stuff ready. I know I bought a hamper. I wonder where we put that. You know, Maddie, this room needs a wall border, or maybe those cute character stickers. Let's go look and see what we can find online. I'm thinking of animals or teddy bears. What do you think, Maddie?"

Maddie barked. "Puppies, huh? that's a good idea, too, Maddie. Let's look at those, too. Oh, look at this, Maddie. They have the cute border and matching stickers for the walls. Matching sheet set, too. Oh, look at these, the cutest little bath towels. Add that to the cart. I think we should ask Daddy what he would like for the wall border. He should be home in a bit. Let's go take a nap. I'm tired from all this shopping. You listen for Daddy. I'm going to lay here and take a nap."

Julie yawned, and laid on the couch.

CHAPTER 33

JULIE

"Hey honey, I'm back. Got your pizza." Maddie barked at David.

"Hey, Maddie, where is Julie?" David found Julie sleeping on the couch.

"Oh, shhh, let's let her sleep. She will wake up when she smells the pizza. I'll get the rest of the groceries."

David finished unloading the car.

"Oh, HI, I didn't hear you come in," said Julie.

"That's okay. How was your nap?"

"It was good. I didn't intend to take a nap, but I got so tired talking with Maddie. Not sure why. I was looking at the border and stickers for the baby room."

"So now we need borders and stickers. I thought you liked the green."

"I do. I love it, but it looks a little plain, just like it needs a little pop of color. I was thinking about maybe baby animals or something. We could get matching mobile and crib sheets. I guess I want a theme for the room, maybe."

"Oh, yeah, that sounds nice. We could do that. Animals would be nice for a boy or a girl."

"I found some teddy bear ones, too. We can look at that."

"I like baby animals. I think that would be great. And when the baby gets older, we can take him or her to the zoo to see the real animals."

"I never thought about that. I think that is a great idea. It will be a great way for the baby to grow to love animals, too. We can have stuffed animals, too."

"Whatever makes you happy. By the way, I picked up your pizza. Here you go. I'm sure you are hungry after your nap."

"Oh, you have no idea. I'm starving, especially for pizza."

"After lunch, I thought I would show you what came in the mail. I got a few boxes. I think there are a few things you have been waiting for. I also thought we could talk about Friday. I plan on leaving a little earlier if that's okay, just in case we hit traffic."

"Are you kidding? If you want, we can leave now."

"Well, it's Wednesday, so I think that would be a little too early. Anyway, I got everything off the list, including Maddie's treats. I did call Detective Jordan also."

"Really? What did he say? Did they catch John? Can we go home?"

"Hold on, I will tell you everything. Well, Detective Jordan suggested we go to Boston and back with no extra stops. They still haven't found John. They do have some leads, but he has been able to avoid them. He also suggested we keep your pregnancy a secret as much as possible. If John finds out, it might send him over the edge. So no telling Joel. Or anyone, for that matter. And that means no dinner on Friday either. Hospital and back, that's it."

"Ugh, I was hoping for some time out. This hiding is killing me. David, I can't keep doing this much longer. I'm going stir crazy."

"I know, honey, but we have to lay low until they catch John. You know it's not safe. If he finds you, who knows what he will do, and now that you're pregnant, we really need to be careful. Detective Jordan thinks it isn't safe even in a different town. He's afraid John has some idea of where we are, or he might have some tracker on us somehow. Anyway, he can find us, and that makes it dangerous. So being careful is the best option for now. We just have to be careful. John is still dangerous, and no one seems to be able to find him."

"Fine. The hospital for the ultrasound, then back to captivity."

"It's not that bad."

"Says the guy who gets to leave the house and go to town every week."

"Okay, I get it, this totally sucks. But Friday is going to be a great day. So let's focus on that. Besides, that new show you love starts up on Wednesday night, so we can watch that, too."

"That's right, the new season of *Survivor* starts. I'm so excited. I have been waiting for this for months. I read all the blogs on the new Survivors."

"Okay, well, now we have two things to do. Along with picking out new borders for the baby room and getting that all set up."

"I can't wait. This season is going to be great. I have no cases to work on, either, so I can watch everything without any distractions.

"Okay, so Friday, hospital, and Wednesday, date night, followed by no distractions TV show."

"Yes, and now more pizza."

"The baby is going to pop out as a pepperoni or asking for pizza. I'm not sure which one yet."

"I can't help it. The baby loves pizza. It could be worse. I mean, if we lived in New York still, I would be ordering pizza every night."

"Yeah, that is true. I guess once a week isn't that bad compared to what it could be if we had delivery out here. So let's take a look at the borders you picked out and get those ordered so I have stuff to pick up next week. I put some boxes in the baby room that came this week, so

I have lots of stuff to put together apparently. What did you order? Did the crib come?"

"No, I haven't found a crib yet that I like. I did find a cute mobile that will match the border. I found some bath towels, too."

"Well, can I suggest we start to narrow down the crib? Especially if Doc thinks you might be further along. If that happens to be true, then we have less time to get ready. I don't want to be putting a crib together after the baby is born."

"You're right, we should pick a crib. I just can't decide if I want to do a nice wood color or white."

"Sweetheart, I am fine with either color, but if you're doing a border, you might want to see which one will match the border. Green will match either color."

"I know, but I can't decide, and then whichever color I pick, the changing table will need to match. I just don't want to pick the wrong thing."

"Honey, the baby won't care. It really is up to you whatever you like better."

"I know. It's just that I feel like this is a big deal. Besides, it needs to be safe, too, and I keep doing research on cribs and crib safety, then I wind up down a rabbit hole for crib deaths. I don't want to pick the wrong one."

"So how about we ask the doctor on Friday when we go if they have any suggestions on what to look for. Maybe the doctors know something we don't."

"Okay, we can do that. If nothing else, it will make me feel better about my decision."

"Right. So now let's look at these borders and unpack some boxes. After that, we can look at some more of your borders if you want, or we can watch a movie and relax. Any chance you're going to want anything for dinner other than pizza?"

"Nope. I'm good with pizza. But I would like something for dessert. Do we have any cookies?"

"Yes, I bought a new box of cookies when I was in town. And I think if you look, there might be a couple other options for cookies in the bags. I got some microwave popcorn for us to snack on when we watch movies and stuff, too."

"Ooh, yummy. That sounds good, too. You did great for groceries this week?"

"Of course I brought the treats too."

"Oh, good, because I gave her the last one from the treat canister earlier today."

"You know, she really is going through the treats lately."

"Yeah, I know I've been over doing the treats, but it's hard to sit here all day. When she's such a good girl, she deserves treats."

"I know, but try to make them last until I can get to town to refill them. I don't want to run out. Then we will really be paying the price."

"So, what would you like to do tonight?"

"I don't know. A movie and popcorn is sounding fun. After you look at the borders. I really need to pick out the crib, too."

"Okay, how about we look at borders and cribs, then we watch a movie on Netflix and have popcorn."

"Yes, deal. That sounds so fun. I hope there is something new on Netflix. I think we have watched just about everything."

"I'm sure there is something to watch. Besides, we can always watch some old movies again. There are some timeless classics that we haven't seen, or maybe something we haven't seen in years."

"Oooh, that sounds fun. We can do an 80's night and watch old movies from the 80's. Tomorrow we could do the 90's."

"Sure, we can do that. Watching old movies might be fun."

"Oh, we could watch The *Breakfast Club*. I haven't see that in years. Or *Pretty Woman*."

"I think *Pretty Woman* was a 90's, film so we could watch that tomorrow."

"Oh, yes, that sounds fun."

"But you know, we could watch some more classic films, like *Gone With the Wind*, *Casablanca*, or *Breakfast at Tiffany's*."

"Aren't those black-and-white movies?"

"Some are, but they are classics. We could watch classic films."

"Yeah, I guess we could try that, too. I'm not big on black-and-white films, but sure, why not? We are running out of things to watch, so how about we pick one night a week and watch a classic movie. It can be like date night with classic movies. But I'm still getting popcorn. And as soon as this baby comes I'm getting wine, too."

"So, theme nights for our movies. Any chance that will keep you occupied in finding some movies for us to watch?"

"Actually, that might help. I can make a list of movies we want to watch and what theme night they go on. I can search great movies and see what I find. I'm sure there are some crazy movies we haven't seen in forever."

"We could do a comedy night, too."

"Yeah, or we could do a thriller night."

"But not too scary. I don't want to scare the baby."

"Deal. No really freaky movies."

"Theme movie nights sounds fun. I just wish I could have wine with my movies. I miss wine so much. Wine and a nice bath would be amazing."

"Well, you can still take a bath."

"I do, but it's not as hot as I usually like it. I wasn't sure if the heat bothered the baby, so I keep it a little warm, not hot. I like a hot bath with my wine."

"I see. Well, you will be able to have hot baths and wine soon enough. But for now, we can have tea and popcorn to go with our classic movies. And on bath days, you just will need to have tea to relax you instead of wine."

"Oh, and on Wednesday, we can have pizza party night. Should we find pizza themed movies to go with pizza party night?"

"Um, that might be pushing it a little. Maybe we can do one night of pizza themed movies."

"Yeah, I know, it's just not the same. Nothing is lately. Especially my size. I feel like an elephant. The hallways all got narrow, and I keep bumping into stuff. I can't see my feet. The swelling...jeez, I swear my feet get swollen and none of my shoes fit. I had to order slippers to walk around in."

"I'm sure the hallways are getting narrower. It couldn't be that you are pregnant. But if you want, I can put wider hallways on my to-do list after I get to the kitchen remodel. I know it's hard, but it's going to be worth it. This little baby will be so loved. Wait till Joel finds out about the baby. You and him can raise your kids together, and who knows? Maybe they will grow up to be best friends."

"Oh, what if we have a boy, and he marries Isabella, and Joel and I are in-laws? Then we'd get to be grandparents together. Oh, wouldn't that be amazing, David? We could all be related and spoil our grand-children together."

"I think you're getting a little ahead of yourself, sweetie. Maybe we start with classic movie night and finding out the sex of our child on Friday, then we can plan his life with Isabella."

"You know, I hate to say this, but you and Joel are a lot alike."

"What is that supposed to mean?"

"Well, you're planning your son's future with Isabella, and Joel was planning your future and naming your kids not too long ago."

"I don't like it when you put it that way, David."

"I'm sorry, but I call it like I see it."

"Yeah, well, close your eyes."

CHAPTER 34

DAVID

"It's Friday, David! Wake up, lets go!"

"Julie, it's early. We don't need to leave for a while."

"I know, but I thought we should get an early start. You get in the shower, and I'll start breakfast. Then you can take Maddie on a quick walk while I jump in the shower, then we can head out early in case of traffic."

"Okay, I get it, you're a little excited to go on our road trip."

"Yeah, maybe just a little. I get to see the baby today, so yeah, I'm excited. So, be honest: do you want a boy or a girl?"

"I want a healthy child, preferably one who doesn't like pizza."

"Funny. You know, just for that, we're getting pizza for lunch."

"Oh, no, we were not. I don't know of any place that has a drive through for pizza."

"We can order it, and you can run in and pick it up."

"No way. We are eating something different. There are tons of great places where I can order and pick up. We can have pizza here at home, but we're going out, so I think it calls for something different: steak, burgers, or anything you want except pizza."

"Fine, but it better be good. You know I love my pizza."

"It's too early to have this conversation. We still need to shower and get ready. I will start breakfast, you shower. Then I will take Maddie out for a walk. You might want to pack a few snacks for the trip, too, just in case. The less we stop, the better, according to Detective Jordan."

"I get it. I'm going to shower, but then we're heading out early. Yes, I'm anxious to get out of this house. I love it here, but I'm going a little stir crazy. It will be so nice to see something other than the inside of the house. And people. I get to talk to people at the hospital. Not to mention we get to see the baby. So let's get moving."

"I'm going, I'm going. You get in the shower, and I'm making breakfast."

"Come on, Maddie, let's get moving before Hurricane Julie comes through again."

David headed to the kitchen to make breakfast.

• • •

"Breakfast is served. I made a couple of eggs and some toast to keep it simple since someone is in such a hurry to get on the road. So here you go, beautiful. I am jumping in the shower, then we can head out. Right after I walk Maddie."

"Yum, I'm starving. I packed a snack bag, too, so we're all set after you get out of the shower."

"Yes, I get it. I'm going to shower quickly. I still need to walk Maddie."

"Okay, well, I will be waiting in the truck just as soon as I finish breakfast, so hurry up."

"Seriously, you're getting in the truck already?"

"Hey, I'm ready. I just want to make sure you know I'm ready and waiting."

"Okay, I will hurry. I'm getting in the shower. I still need to walk Maddie."

"Well, you better get a move on, because I'm waiting."

David quickly showered and changed to get ready to go.

"Now, Maddie, let's get you outside for a quick walk before we head out. I got you a couple treats, so I know you will be a good girl while we're gone. And when we get back, we will be able to tell you all about the baby. Wouldn't you like to know if we're having a boy or girl, Maddie? Today is going to be a great day for us. I just wish you could come, too."

David and Maddie walked for a little while and finally returned to the house.

"Okay, Maddie, let's get you inside and get treats. I have to get going. Julie is already waiting in the truck, I see. So I better hurry."

David bent down to pet Maddie before heading in.

"Maddie, I really hope I'm going to be good at this dad thing. I'm nervous and scared, and I don't want to tell Julie. She's already nervous enough. What do you think, Maddie? Are we going to be a good family together? Maybe I'm just crazy. I don't know. Ugh, we better hurry. Let's head inside. Thanks for listening, Maddie. You are always there when I need you. Okay, here is your treat. Now, you be good while we're gone. I promise we will be back tonight. Keep an eye on the house."

"Finally! What took you so long?" Julie asked.

"Well, I had to shower and take Maddie out for a walk, and I had a talk with her about treats, and she said she would like more treats."

"Oh, well, I will make sure we put that on the to-do list. So did you decide what we are doing for lunch?"

"Actually, I thought we could see what is around the hospital and check out some reviews. See if anything sounds good. Besides, who knows? You might have some craving by this afternoon."

"Yeah, I'm craving pizza."

"Um, no, we agreed on something different for lunch. But let's get on the road, and we can figure it out later."

"Okay, so it's almost a three-hour drive to the hospital, and we are leaving with two extra hours. So we have lots of time to figure out what you want for lunch. So what do we talk about on the way?"

"Well, we can decide on the border for the baby's room, or we can discuss baby names."

"I thought Joel hooked us up with baby names."

"Uh, no. We are not naming our baby Thompson or Trixie."

"Okay, well, then what do you suggest for baby names?"

"I don't know, David. Do you want traditional names, like Jacob, Thomas, Sarah, or Emily? Or do we break the mold and pick something different, like Colton or Ava? Or do we go really crazy and be unique and name them Zara or Bixby?

"Well, honestly I haven't thought much about names. I thought it might be easier to pick after we know if we are having a boy or girl."

"You're probably right, but what if they can't tell the sex of the baby? Doc said it's possible they can't tell. I read about it online, too. Sometimes the baby hides from the ultrasound technician. Honestly, I can't wait to see the baby. I will love a boy or girl. But I kinda want a girl. Wouldn't it be fun to have our baby grow up with Isabella as her best friend?"

"Sure, that will be fun, but I thought you wanted a boy to marry Isabella."

"Oh my God, David, that would be so awesome. I admit I had a dream about that last night after our talking about it. I dreamt that Joel and I were in-laws, and our kids had twins named Thompson and Trixie. I wish I could call Joel and tell him all this. Just to tell him I'm pregnant and then listen to his speech about protection."

"Well, in our defense, we thought you were on birth control. So it really was accidental, but it is the best accident ever, and I wouldn't change a thing."

"I'm really excited about seeing the baby and picking a name."

"You know, we still have a wedding to plan, too."

"Yes, I was thinking about that, too, but we we're kinda stuck until after this mess with John gets resolved, so we can plan, but we really can't pick a date or venue until I can come out of hiding. We can decide on a destination wedding or church. Small or big wedding. We can probably even nail down the guest list."

"Well, Julie, I am good with whatever you want. I already did the wedding thing once, so this time you pick everything. I will just show up and say 'I do.'"

"Well, nice try, but you're not getting off that easy. You're helping with this wedding."

"You're right. I will help with everything I can, but I give you final say."

"Oooh, I like that idea. Can we adopt that for everything? I get final say on everything."

"Woooah now, I said you get final say on the wedding, but every-thing else we decide together. Marriage is a two-way street. So we do everything together. The baby's room is our decision, along with the baby name. But the wedding is all you, sweetie."

"Okay, I can work with that."

"So, baby names. What are your thoughts?"

"Well, I would like something normal. Traditional is fine, but I like our child also being one-of-a-kind, so I'm open to anything. As long as we both like it and agree. I don't want something that our child will be made fun of for at school. I want our children to have a normal child-hood, at least as normal as possible."

"Well, I think we're on the same page with that. So no Bixby."

"No. Isn't that a phone app?"

"Oh yeah, maybe. That might be where I heard it. Okay, let's figure that out later, after we know the sex."

"So, border for the baby. Animals or teddy bears?"

"I thought we decided on animals."

"We did. I just want to make sure we are on the same page."

"Yes, I like the animal idea. I'm hoping our kids love animals."

"I think our kids will love animals, especially if we decorate their room with sweet little animals."

"Okay, so the border is decided, which helps decide the crib bedding, too, and the mobile. So we are getting a lot accomplished on this trip."

"Okay, so how about the wedding? Big or small?"

"I'm thinking small. What do you think?"

"I think small would be great, and honestly, since we can't go look at venues, it might make it easier to find a place. Honestly, if you want, we could elope: just me, you, and the baby."

"No, I need Joel at my wedding. He would never forgive me if I had a wedding and a baby without telling him. This is already hard enough to do without talking to him every day."

"Okay, you have a point. We need Joel. You know, most men would be jealous of such a close relationship with another guy. But I am totally okay with your relationship with Joel."

"I know, and I appreciate the fact that you and Joel both love me and care about me, and that you don't get jealous of Joel. Don't think I don't know how lucky I am to have you."

"I'm just happy that Joel is a happily married man with a new baby. I'm pretty sure that keeps him more than occupied."

"True. I am sure Joel is going crazy being a new father. I just wish I could be there to see him in action. I really want to meet Isabella, too. I feel like I am missing everything. This crazy mess is costing me my entire life."

"You can't think like that, honey. Think about it this way: if you hadn't gone through this mess, then you wouldn't be pregnant. You would have had your phone, and you wouldn't have missed your birth control. And we wouldn't be having a baby together. So think about it that way. This mess has brought us together and made us into a family. I have to be thankful for that."

"You're right, without my crazy life, we probably wouldn't be pregnant. So, speaking of pregnancy, how about Cameron if the baby is a boy?"

"Cameron, huh? How about Kirk?"

"Really, David? Kirk Cameron?"

"Well, if I remember right, you had a huge crush on him."

"Oh my God, how did you remember that?"

"I remember lots of things, especially about you. I just can't believe you want to name our son after your crush from the 80's."

"Okay, you're right. Bad idea. But I do like the name."

"Fine, we can put it on the maybe list. How about Jessica for a girl or rabbit? LOL."

"Haha, you're so funny."

"Well, I just thought if we were going with our old crushes. You know she was mine. But on the serious side, how about Kayla for a girl?"

"Hmm, Kayla. That is pretty and a little different. I don't know any Kayla's. Did you date any Kayla's?"

"No, I didn't. I read it in a book, and I liked it. I also like Samantha, which is a little old school, but I like it. It's simple, and there aren't many girls named Samantha anymore.

Hey, I'm going to stop in this country store for gas. Do you need anything?"

"Yes, please. Can I have a cold water?"

"You sure can. I will try to be quick."

David returned from the store.

"Here is your water. I also found a bunch of magazines in that little market. They had everything in there. It must be one of the only markets in town, it looked like they had groceries and everything. I found a bunch of magazines. I grabbed you some wedding ones and some baby ones. Thought it might keep your mind busy on this drive."

"Oh, yes, I need some ideas on this wedding. I honestly don't know where to start. Do you pick the date first or the venue?"

"Well, I think you should start with the venue and see what openings they have. That might help pick the date. But I thought we were keeping this small."

"We are, but do we get married in the park, on the beach, or in a church? Maybe we do a small ballroom in a hotel. How about the Plaza in June?"

"The Plaza is a little over the top."

"I know, I was just kidding. I want to keep it small and simple. But seriously, some of these gowns in this magazine are amazing."

"Well, you know, you could keep the wedding itself simple and classic and do the dress up as amazing as you want."

"Yeah, that is an idea. Of course, I would need killer shoes to go with it."

"Oh, of course. The shoes make the dress, or so I am told."

"Yes, but right now, I would need a tent and flip flops. I can't fit into a wedding dress or even great shoes."

"Don't, worry in a couple months you will have the baby, and your feet will fit into your shoes again. But just look at the future."

"So, anything else good in those magazines?"

"Yeah, the dresses are great, but there are some great checklists, too, that will be helpful, and some great party ideas."

"So, how big do we want to do the reception? Do we want to keep it small like the wedding, or do we want a huge, invite-everyone-we-know blowout?"

"Well, I'll be honest with you, I don't have many people to invite besides family. Most of my friends are still enlisted and won't be able to get time off. So I would prefer to keep things small."

"Good idea. I like it. Small wedding, small reception. Now, colors."

"Oh no, I am not picking any colors. Those are completely up to you."

"Okay, colors are up to me. Do you want to wear a tux?"

"Well, that is up to you. I am fine with a tux, but if you want to keep it casual on the beach or at the park, then I am up for that, too."

"Okay, so if we do it at the beach or a park, we keep it casual. If we do it at a church or reception hall, we can do it up big with tuxes."

"Sounds like a plan. You know, we could always do a simple justice of the peace and just a few people."

"I will pretend I didn't hear that. I want an actual wedding with my friends."

"Okay, you win. We can do a wedding, and you can have whatever you want. Like I said before, give me the date, and I will show up. Now, how about dinner tonight? Any ideas on what you want, other than pizza?"

"Well, I was thinking about a nice steak dinner at some swanky restaurant. Some nice candlelight and a bottle of non-alcoholic wine. What do you think?"

"It sounds amazing, but you know we can't have dinner at the restaurant. We can order takeout."

"I know. I'm just wishful thinking."

"I promise when this mess is over, we will go to a nice dinner and have a beautiful night out."

"You say that, but by the time this is over, our kid might be a toddler, and we might not be able to get a sitter."

"You're being a little overly dramatic."

"I know, I just really want this nightmare over with and this baby to be healthy. I'm a little worried about the doctor's visit. Aren't you worried?"

"Yeah, I'm worried, but I really want to see this baby. I want to know if we are having a boy or a girl. Mostly I want the baby to be healthy. I can't wait to get a picture of this little one. We can hang it on the fridge and see it every day until the baby is born. How about Joshua for a name?"

"I like that name."

"I was thinking about the middle name if it's a boy. How about Robert, after my father?"

"Hmm, I like that. Okay, so we have a middle name for a boy. How about a first name and a girl's name."

"Well, I came up with the middle name, so I guess it's your turn."

"Hey, we're almost to the hospital, but we are very early. So do you want something to eat and to wait in the truck, or do you want to just go and wait at the hospital?"

"Um, eat, please. How about pizza for lunch?"

"Really, you want pizza? We were just talking about steaks."

"Well, that was for dinner. This is about lunch. Baby wants pizza."

"Okay, how about I get you a pizza, and after the appointment we get something for takeout."

"Perfect."

"I'll see if I can find someplace to get a pizza. Then we get to the hospital and see our baby."

"Yes, this is going to be the best day ever."

"How about that little place? I see a pizza sign. One pizza for you and the baby. We can eat in the truck. Do you want anything else besides the pizza?"

"Nope, I'm good with pizza and water. See if they have any cookies. That would be great for dessert."

CHAPTER 35

JULIE

"Hi, we are here to see Doctor Chase. We are his extended family that dropped in to town to have lunch with him."

"I will page Dr. Chase and let him know you are here. Please have a seat over there."

Dr. Chase came over and shook Julie's hand.

"Hi, cousin, it's good to see you. Come on back into my office. Hi, I am Dr. Chase. I am good friends with your Doctor Jameson. He explained a bit of your situation. So, tell me, what shall I call you?"

"Um, you can call us Chuck and Cindi, I guess."

"Great. Cindi, Dr. Jameson has given me a little bit of medical history. We are going to do some tests and an ultrasound and keep everything confidential. I have my nurse doing everything herself, so there will be no paperwork. Dr. Jameson and I have a call scheduled after work today to go over everything anonymously, of course. And I will mail him copies of everything, but they are going in the regular mail, so it might take a couple days. I will send them registered so he has to sign for them just to make it a little more secure. So, tell me, are you having any issues?"

"Um, no, just craving pizza a lot. I am a little concerned about my weight. I just feel huge. I'm not sure I'm supposed to be this big this early. My feet are so swollen. Is that normal?"

"Yes, swelling in the feet is totally normal, but we can check and make sure your bloodwork is good and there are no issues. And we will check everything else to make sure this baby is perfectly healthy. Then we will do an ultrasound and take a picture of the baby, and we will have a much better idea of everything going on with the baby. This is my nurse practitioner, Janet. She will draw the blood, and then we will do the ultrasound. After that, we will go over the results and then get you guys out of here. Janet, you go ahead and get the blood work going, and I will be back in a minute to check vitals."

Janet drew blood and asked Julie if she was okay.

"Yes, I'm good. Thank you."

"No problem. If you have any questions, please feel free to ask."

"Honestly, I just want to make sure the baby is healthy. I feel like a beached whale."

"How far along are you?"

"About five months. But I feel like I look eight or nine months pregnant."

"Don't worry, everyone handles pregnancy differently. Each mother is different, and each baby is different. Babies grow at their own rate. You really don't have anything to worry about. I am certain that Doctor Chase will go over everything with you and make sure everything is perfect. And we will get you a beautiful picture of your baby before you head home. So let me go grab the ultrasound and let Dr. Chase know you are ready to see that baby."

Dr. Chase came into the room.

"Okay, let's take a look at that baby. Janet dropped off your bloodwork at the lab with very specific instructions."

Dr. Chase started the ultrasound.

"Okay, let's see what we have here. We're going to take a few measurements of the baby and make sure everything is good. Do you want to hear the baby's heartbeat?"

Dr. Chase held doppler on Julie's stomach, and Julie and David heard the baby's heartbeat.

"Huh, okay, I see what Dr. Jameson was concerned about."

"What? Concerned about what?"

"Oh, no, don't worry. Dr. Jameson had a few small concerns, and he wanted me to check things out, which is why we are doing this ultrasound. So it looks like the baby is fine. Everything looks good here, and I do have some news. It looks like you're having twins. I see two babies, which is why you are a little bigger than you think you should be. Dr. Jameson had suspected you might be carrying twins, but he wasn't sure, which is why he sent you to me."

"Oh my God. Are you sure, Dr. Chase?"

"Yes, I am certain, and I am printing pictures of both babies. And if you look here on the screen, here is baby one. This is the face right here, and baby two is snuggling right in the shoulder of baby one. Do you want to know the sex of the babies?"

"Yes. Yes, I want to know. Are they boys or girls?"

"Well, baby one is a boy, and baby two is a girl. So it looks like you're having one of each. And from their size, it looks like you are just over five months along. So you are right on schedule with what Dr. Jameson thought."

"David, we're having a boy and a girl. Twins. David, I only planned on one baby."

"Don't worry, everything is going to be fine. We will order another crib, and we will be just fine. This is going to be great. Two babies. I can't wait. Sweetheart, you see, you were worried about nothing. Everything is fine, and we're having twins. Twice as much to love."

"That explains the weight and the pizza cravings. I'm eating for three, not two. This is crazy. Now we're having two babies. How am I going to do this?"

"Don't worry, we will get through this. Dr. Chase and Dr. Jameson are going to make sure everything is okay. That is why we came today, to make sure everything goes perfectly."

"I know, I'm just worried. I have been so worried about having a baby, and now I'm having two babies. I just don't know what I'm going to do. I didn't plan any of this, and now I'm going to have twins."

"Okay, don't worry, we can figure everything out. I promise everything will be okay. Now we know, and look, we have these beautiful pictures of our sweet little babies. So let's go and get some dinner to take home, and we can figure out names and what comes next."

"I can't believe this is happening. I don't know where to start. We were thinking about our wedding. Now I have to plan for two babies. I'm so confused, and I don't know what to do first."

"Don't worry about it right now. We will figure everything out, I promise. We have the entire car ride home to talk about things and figure things out. And we have the rest of our lives to get everything right."

"Okay, well I know this has been a lot of new information," said Dr. Chase. "I promise I will update Dr. Jameson today, so he will have all the latest info. I will also send him copies of everything without your names attached to keep everything confidential. But for now, you're all set. You can head out, and I will make sure to call Dr. Jameson. It was really nice meeting you both. I hope this pregnancy goes smoothly for you. Please, if you need anything else, don't hesitate to call. We can set up another discrete meeting if needed anytime. If you just have questions, you can call my office and ask for me or Janet, and we will answer all your questions.

"Thank you, Doctor. We really appreciate everything, especially our first baby pictures. Sweetie, let's head out, and we can talk all the way home."

"Yeah, you're right, we have a lot to talk about. Thank you, Doctor Chase, for everything."

"You're welcome. It was good seeing you again, Cuz."

Julie and Dr. Chase laughed.

CHAPTER 36

DAVID

"You're awful quiet, Julie. Do you want to talk or just head right home?"

"Um, can we pick up dinner and head home, please? I just want to go home. This is just a lot to process, and I really miss Maddie. She always helps me think."

"You know, I never thought you and Maddie would be so tight."

"Well, since she is all I have to confide in, she tends to keep my secrets, and she is always great with advice, too. She is my best friend. And you know she always takes my side."

"Well, what would you and your bestie like for dinner? We can grab something here, or we can grab something on the way home."

"Can we just get something on the way? I'm not too hungry yet."

"Sure, sweetheart, we can do whatever you like. If you see something that looks good, just say something, and that will be dinner tonight. If you want, there is still pizza left from lunch, too."

"Honestly, I'm just overwhelmed. I don't know what to think or how to feel about this. I can't believe we're having twins. I never thought that was why I was getting so big. I just thought I was eating too much. David, our lives are going to change so much now. A baby is one thing, but twins? They are going to be a lot of work. Do you still want to do this with me? I would understand if you changed your mind."

"Are you kidding? I am excited to do this with you. I am all in, I promise. Nothing is going to change us. Our family is growing, but we will still be the same. A lot less sleep, but everything else will be the same, I promise. Yes, it will be hard, and yes, there will be a lot of crying and dirty diapers. I'm sure I will be doing most of the crying, but we can get through it."

"As long as you're sure. I know this isn't exactly what we planned. I just want to make sure you're okay with everything."

"Julie, I love you, and I love this family we are building. I know twins wasn't what we were expecting, but I'm happy. As long as I have you, I'm happy. Maddie will love having the babies to play with. I will love you and the babies. So now let's talk about wedding and baby names."

"David, how can you think about a wedding? My mind is racing trying to keep up with the idea of twins."

"Well, I am a happy guy, and I want to make sure that I get to marry the woman of my dreams, so I am more than happy to think about a wedding and twins."

"You think this mess with John will be over soon?"

"I think either he will never turn up and just run away, or he will mess up, and they will catch him. Either way, it should be over soon. If he gave up, it might already be over with now, and we just don't know it."

"Detective Jordan would have told us if he was gone, and he thought this mess was over. I just have this feeling that he's still out there, and he will find me."

"Julie, even if he does, he isn't going to hurt you. I won't let that happen. I promise I will always take care of you and our family. You are my world."

"David, I know you will protect us. I'm just worried. I want this over with. I want my life back. I want to get married in front of my family and friends. I want to call Joel and tell him I'm pregnant. I want to go back to work. I just want normal again."

"I know you do, honey. I want that, too. Hopefully we don't have to hide much longer. Detective Jordan said he was working on it. But honestly, I am enjoying having you all to myself. I think it has given us a real chance to get closer than we would have ever gotten just dating."

"I know, I enjoy being with you, too, and you're right. This has made us a lot closer, but I just want this mess over with. I want a normal life where I can be married and pregnant in public and go to doctor's appointments and use my real name. Is that too much to ask?"

"No, it's not, and I'm sorry things have to be this way. I wish there was something I could do to change it."

"What if we just go back?"

"What do you mean?"

"What if I go back and start living my life? If John comes for me, the police will catch him, and then it's over."

"Honey, we can't take the chance of you getting hurt, especially since you're pregnant. What if something happens to the babies?"

"You're right, I know you're right. I just want this over."

"I know you do, but we have to do what Detective Jordan says. Right now, we need to figure out dinner. Then we can get home and figure out what to do next."

"Dinner sounds good. I'm actually getting a little hungry."

"Good, let's get you and those babies fed. You still want steaks?"

"Yeah, that sounds good. Maybe get one with a bone in it for Maddie if you can find somewhere to stop on the way."

"I'm sure there is something on the way home. Don't worry, I'll stop and get dinner and gas."

"Sounds perfect. So, baby names. We need a girl and a boy name. What do you think?"

"Well, we had a middle name for our son. Are you still good with that?"

"Yeah, Robert is a great middle name, but the baby needs a first name, and we need a girl's name. Any ideas?"

"How about Sophia? And Cameron?"

"I like Sophia, but not too sure on Cameron after the Kirk discussion earlier."

"How about Lucas and Sophia, or Aubrey? I like Aubrey or Zoey."

"What about Levi for a boy?"

"Levi Robert Thomas."

"I actually like that name now. What about a girl name?"

"I still like Aubrey. How about Aubrey Samantha Thomas?"

"I like those names, but I'm sure you will change your mind a couple times before we settle on them."

"Yeah, you're probably right. I did change my mind about the paint a few times."

"Look, let's just think about the names, and we can make a list just like we have with everything else. We can narrow it down, or when the babies come, we can see which one looks like their name. Until then, we have a room to get ready and lots of things to learn about taking care of these kids. It isn't going to be easy."

"You're right. I've gotten really good at lists, so we can do that, and that will help keep my mind from going crazy."

"Great. Here is a town that looks like it has nice restaurants. Let's see if they have any steaks we can get to go, and I can get gas."

"Great, can you grab me another water too, please?"

"Sure. Is there anything else you would like me to get while I grab our dinner?"

"No, just the water and dinner should be good. Honestly, I'm anxious to get home, if you can believe that. I want to check on Maddie and get some things ordered for the babies."

"I understand that. We're almost home. Don't worry, sweetheart. And you have a lot to look forward to because next week starts your favorite show."

"Oh, that right, the new season of *Survivor* starts on Wednesday. I am not missing that, no matter what. Joel and I used to watch every week together, and we never missed an episode. If we weren't together, we talked on the phone while we watched together."

"Seriously, you and Joel are that strict about *Survivor*?"

"Yes, David, it's a big deal to us."

"Okay, I am sure we will get dinner done early and make sure dishes are done and everything is put away so we can have a nice relaxing night on the couch with popcorn."

"Yes, which means I need to get everything on my list ordered tonight or tomorrow."

"What exactly is there to get ordered?"

"Well, I need another crib and more blankets and bath towels, and I want a baby names book. There is so much to do, and now that we are having twins, there is twice as much to buy. Since I'm not working, everything is going to cost twice as much."

"Honey, don't worry about the money."

"How can I not worry? I had to take a leave of absence from work, so I don't have an income, and I had to use Cobra to make sure I had insurance, which is crazy expensive."

"Well, once the babies are born, I can cover them under my insurance, since I am technically retired military. Once we are married, I can cover you also."

"Yeah, but until then, insurance is way overpriced, and I have no choice but to pay it. At least my checking is on auto pay, so it pays my accounts each month."

"Look, honey, I know this isn't ideal, but let's just get dinner, and we can talk about everything over a nice dinner tonight, okay? I'm going to run in and see how long it will take to get dinner. You sit here and relax, okay?"

"Sure, try not to take too long. If we wait too long, we can go somewhere else."

"Okay, I will let you know."

David returned from the restaurant.

"Okay, sweetheart, I have dinner. There wasn't a wait at all, so I have our dinner, and we can head out and check on Maddie. I got your water, too. Grabbed an extra couple bottles, one for each baby, just in case."

"Very funny. Let's head home. I miss Maddie. And I'm sure she has to go out."

"Yeah, I'm sure she does. She has gotten used to you being home with her all day."

"She is probably going to love having babies to play with all day, too."

"Yeah, I'm sure she will be really protective of them."

"David, I really want to call the detective when we get home. I want him to draw out John and end this mess when we get home. I don't want to have these babies with John still out there."

"Julie, that is dangerous. I don't want you in danger."

"I know, David, but I need to do something to end this mess so we can move on.

"Look, we can discuss this later, but for now, we need to concentrate on the babies. I don't think that's a good idea. We can discuss it, and when I go to town next week I can talk to Detective Jordan and see what his thoughts are about it."

"Okay, as long as you ask him about it. I don't want to have these babies while I'm still in captivity."

"I understand, Julie, but we need to still be safe about how we do things."

"You're right, and I promise to be safe in whatever we decide to do."

"Good. We're almost home, so we can figure this mess out then. As soon as we get home, I will take Maddie out, and you can relax and put your feet up."

"Yeah, that sounds good. Maybe I can have some tea and calm myself down a little. I'm so worked up over the twins and John. I swear I just go from calm to crazy in two seconds. My emotions are all over the place, too. I just want to cry. I can't keep myself calm. I just start thinking about things, and I want to cry. David, how am I going to get through this mess? How am I going to safely have these babies? How can I plan a wedding and two babies coming when I can't even control my emotions? How can I do all of this?"

"Julie, don't worry. Everything will be fine. You just need to relax and remember that you're not alone. We can do this. And as soon as John is caught, you will be back with Joel and your family. Then you will have so much support, you won't know what to do. Honestly, they will be driving you nuts with all their advice and support."

"You're right, I know you're right. I can think about it, and I get it, but my emotions are so hard to control."

"Maybe we watch a comedy when we get home. Maybe that will help you. Something funny to keep you laughing and get your spirits up."

"Yeah, we can watch a comedy tonight. That might help make me feel better."

"Yeah, I'll pop us some popcorn, and we can sit by the fire and watch a funny movie. Any suggestions on what you want to watch?"

"I don't know. Whatever looks funny, I guess."

"Okay, well, after I get Maddie taken care of and dinner, then it will be comedy night."

"We could watch a standup routine."

"Yeah, that could be fun."

"Okay, well, let's get home, and then we can figure it out. We should be there in couple minutes. I bet Maddie will be so excited to see us."

"She really has gotten used to being with you. I think she would pick you over me."

"You bet your ass she would pick me. I give her way more treats than you do. She loves me more."

CHAPTER 37

DAVID

"I slept so hard last night. How did you sleep?"

"I slept good. How about breakfast? I just took Maddie out for her morning walk."

"Breakfast sounds great. These babies are hungry."

"How about some pancakes for breakfast?"

"Oh, that sounds yummy, and while you do that, I am going to get some stuff ordered off my lists. I want to get a baby name book ordered and another crib."

"Well, you do that. I will get breakfast, and you know, you should order some magazines about having twins and being new parents and planning weddings, too. Anything you find that will help us."

"Yeah, I will see what I can find. There has to be some lists I can print or something."

"I'm sure there are lots of lists. You start looking, and I will start cooking."

"What time is your show on Wednesday?"

"8 p.m., why?"

"I just want to make sure I have everything done and ready and popcorn popped and ready for you. It will be our date night."

"Ooh, that sounds fun."

"Yes, I am planning an early dinner, and dishes will be done and in the dishwasher before 8. So how does this show work, anyway?"

"Oh my God, you're going to love it. I can't believe you have never watched it. They drop people off on an island to fend for themselves. They form teams and have to compete for food and luxury items."

"This sounds like the craziest show I am ever going to watch, but if you like it, then I am all in. Breakfast will be ready in a couple minutes. How is your list going?"

"Good, I have a few things in the cart. I am getting an identical crib to the one we already have, and I found a baby name book and a couple other things. I need another mobile and more baby blankets and towels. I just didn't realize how many things babies need. I guess we will need baby food, too, eventually. Wonder if we need formula. I'm not sure if I will be able to feed both babies. I might need to ask the doctor about that. I don't know if I will produce enough milk for two babies. I have so many questions. Guess I should order more diapers and more wipes. I only planned for one baby, now we're having two.

"David, how much bigger am I going to get? I'm already wearing sweatpants because I can't fit into my clothes. What am I going to wear? I feel like a beached whale already. I still have a few months to go. I already have a list of questions for Dr. Jameson when he comes, starting with how big I am going to get. I can't see my feet, but I can feel they are huge."

"Look, you know you're carrying twins, so you're a little bigger than you planned. Besides, it will be over soon. You only have a couple months left. You said it yourself. Here, eat some breakfast. Then we can finish some more of that list. And you can relax."

"I'm going nuts. I have so many lists. Baby room, clothing lists, wedding lists, food, kitchen remodel, TV shows, and to-do, and none of these lists have anything to do with work. I'm so over this confinement. I just want to go back to Joel and my work. I'm going crazy being trapped here. I love you, David, but I'm going nuts being trapped here."

"Julie, I know this is hard, but you have no choice. It's not safe for you out there. John is still out there looking for you. It's not just you anymore. Now it's our babies, too. If he finds you, he could hurt our babies, too."

"I know, David. I would never put the babies at risk, but it's driving me crazy."

"Just relax. Doctor Jameson will be here later to go over everything with us today. You can ask him all the questions you want. I'm sure he will have lots of information for you, which will probably lead to more lists for us, too. Then on Wednesday, we have your *Survivor* premier, so we have a big week to look forward to."

"Do you think Dr. Jameson is bringing pizza?"

"I would think there is a good chance Dr. Jameson is bringing pizza. I also think there is a good chance there will be no leftovers. Hey, maybe on Wednesday, I should plan a pizza party instead of a nice dinner."

"Oh, that would be awesome. Yes, can we have different kinds of pizza, too, like meat lovers and thick crust with tons of leftovers? And breadsticks?"

"You know, I think you're getting a little overly excited about this."

"Wednesday is going to be a great day. Pizza party and *Survivor*. It's going to be great. I think I have my list of questions ready for Dr. Jameson. So many questions. I really didn't think having a doctor's appointment last week would lead to so many more questions this week. I thought it would answer questions, not lead me to more questions. This twins thing really threw me for a loop."

"Yeah, it threw me for a loop, too. I didn't expect to be having twins. I'm happy, though. I'm happy both our babies and you are healthy, especially with everything you have been going through. Dr. Jameson will be here pretty soon, so I'm going to jump in the shower and get cleaned up. You relax and finish working on all your million questions to make sure you didn't miss anything."

"I don't know how I missed anything. I have questions about everything: food, milk, my size and weight, and the hospital. I'm more confused now than I ever was."

"Dr. Jacobson will get us through everything. Don't worry so much. It will be fine."

"I know. I'm just alone again, that's all."

"Don't worry. I'm going to shower, and then we can talk, okay?"

"Yeah, I'm fine. Go shower."

CHAPTER 38

JULIE

"Dr. Jacobson! Hi, how are you today?"

"I am great. How is my favorite patient? Doing okay?"

"Just okay."

"Yeah. Does this pizza I brought help?"

"Definitely."

"Julie is a little concerned," said David. "She has a list of questions since our last visit to the doctor in Boston."

"Of course. I talked to Dr. Chase after your visit. He filled me in on everything, and I understand congratulations are in order your having twins, a boy and a girl."

"Yes, we're very excited about twins, but it's a lot to take in," said David.

"Of course it is, David. It changes a lot of things. What are your concerns, Julie?"

"First, how much bigger am I going to get? I already can't see my feet."

Doctor Jameson laughed a little. "Julie, each expectant mom is different, and each baby is also different, so depending on the size of each baby, you will have to adjust for the growth of each baby. But I assure you that you're growing within normal amounts for twins. You're not too big. I know it feels like a lot, but you're not by any means overly large. I think you feel that way because it's your first pregnancy. You're almost six months now, so think about it this way: if you were only carrying one child, you would only be half this size. So you wouldn't feel so big. It's only because you're carrying two children that you feel bigger. You're really not that big. I've seen a mom carrying twins who was much larger. I promise you're not that big, it just feels like it."

"Okay, Doctor. I'm very concerned about breastfeeding two babies. Is that possible?"

"Absolutely. Most mothers can breastfeed both babies, just maybe not at the same time. Some mothers chose to nurse one at a time, and some chose to pump and store bottles to feed later. But it is possible to use breastmilk to feed both babies. How you choose to feed the babies is up to you. Now, I have had some mothers who were not able to breastfeed. They did not produce milk with enough nutrients to sustain the baby and had to use formula. You will know within days of giving birth if you do not have the nutrients to sustain the babies, and then you can decide to use formula. You can have a can on hand just in case, if you want. I will tell you that it has nothing to do with anything you eat or anything you did wrong. That is usually a genetic gene or an anomaly, so do not think you need to do anything to change that outcome."

"What about the hospital? How am I going to have these twins if I can't go to the hospital?"

"First of all, we can deliver in town if we need to in an emergency. I have a team available 24 hours a day. My concern is if you go into labor early and have premature babies, which tends to happen with twins. We do not have the emergency equipment, and we would have to send you to the next town, which is doable. However, we would not be able to keep your identity a secret, but the babies' safety would take priority, and I would call Detective Jordan to come and safeguard you, so I do have a plan if that were to happen. I have been working with Dr. Chase in case we do need to prepare for an early delivery. He has offered to help with that if needed. We are hoping that this ends before that becomes necessary."

"Well, David and I are hoping this ends soon, too. I keep making lists and questions. I'm trying to be prepared for the worst, just in case."

"Honestly, that is the best you can do. Julie, you are doing everything right. Lists are the best idea right now. It keeps you focused and keeps your mind busy. It also allows you to make sure you don't forget anything."

"I'm just so concerned about my weight."

"No need to be concerned about that, you are just right for carrying twins. Honestly, you're a little low, so if you overeat on the pizza, you're okay."

"Seriously, I'm low on my weight for twins? Are you saying I can eat more pizza today?"

"Absolutely, you're eating for three. Your blood pressure is good, and your heartrate for you and the baby is good. From everything Dr. Chase told me, you're good. Everything I see here today and everything from the ultrasound looks good. You and the babies are in good health. I don't see anything out of the ordinary."

"Doc, can I ask if heartburn is normal?"

"Yes, heartburn is very normal. Are you using over-the-counter antacids?"

"Yes, David got me some from the market, and they seem to be working. They take a little bit to kick in, but they work okay."

"I can get you some prescription ones. Have David pick them up on Wednesday when he comes to town. I will have some samples to try, and you can see which works better. Pizza might be making it flare up a little, too."

"Doc, speaking of food, I've been reading all these magazines and books about feeding these babies and caring for them. Is there anything I need to know that would help?"

"Well, honestly, you should speak to a nutritionist. That would help. Breastmilk is always best, but what you put in your body goes to the babies. And then when you start to feed the babies, alternate food. You will need to slowly introduce foods to them. Organic may be the best option. There are great books. I will get a list together and send that with David on Wednesday, along with the name of a nutritionist I recommend."

"That would be great. I'm kind of struggling with being a first-time mom while not being able to ask any friends or family any questions."

"I totally understand, and like I said before, I am always here to answer any questions. When in doubt, feel free to Google, too. Google can answer anything. It just doesn't bring pizza. Oh, I almost forgot, I brought you this CD. It's a copy of the ultrasound. I had Dr. Chase send it overnight to my office. I made a copy for you. He couldn't keep it in his office, so he sent it to me. I thought you might like a copy."

"Thank you, Dr. Jameson, this is an amazing gift. I really appreciate it."

"I will see you next Monday. You guys have a great week."

"Thank you, Dr. Jameson. This is wonderful."

"You're welcome. David, I will see you Wednesday to pick up a few items for Julie."

"Yes, of course, I will stop by. Thank you," said David. "Well, sweetheart, do you feel better?"

"Yes, I do. Doc said I can eat more pizza. I'm underweight for someone having twins."

"That is all you got out of the visit?"

"No, that is not all, but I feel a lot better about not being able to see my feet. I feel better about feeding the babies, too. He said I would be able to feed them both. He said my lists were helpful, too. He said I'm doing everything right. He even said he had a plan for having the babies in case they come early. He is planning ahead, just like we are."

"I honestly hadn't thought about having the babies early. That hadn't crossed my mind. All these books and magazines, and I hadn't thought about premature babies. Dr. Jameson has. He has a plan already just in case. He knew we were having twins just from how huge I was. That is why he sent us to Dr. Chase. He had the idea, he just had to confirm it."

"Julie, are you okay?

"No, David, I am not okay. I am losing my mind again. I am alone. I hadn't thought about any of this stuff. Did Dr. Jameson know about all of this? And I had no idea and these babies are inside me. I had no idea this could even happen."

"Julie, Dr. Jameson is a doctor. It's his job to think ahead and to plan ahead. He has seen all of this. He deals with babies and premature babies and twins. This is your first pregnancy. You need to stop putting this all on yourself. You can't think of everything. You can't think of everything that could possibly happen either. You may not have premature labor. You may not have to go to the hospital out of town. We might be able to end everything and tell everyone soon. We didn't plan on anything."

"I know I'm just letting this get to me. I just get something in my head, and it runs rampant. I'm trapped. John has me trapped here. I keep thinking the worst case, and the worst case is that the babies are premature and need help, and we are trapped, and I can't get to the hospital, and we can't get help."

"That is not going to happen. Dr. Jameson already said he has emergency services available. He has a plan already in place. As soon as he found out you were expecting twins, he put a plan in place. Dr. Jameson is already looking out for us. I know we will be okay. I will go and talk to Detective Jordan, and I will explain the situation and that we need to come out of hiding soon."

"You promise you will tell Detective Jordan we need to come out?"

"Yes, I will tell him it's for the babies."

"Okay, hopefully we can make it a little longer."

"I hope so. David, I don't want to have these babies early. I keep reading about stress and it causing issues with babies. This entire issue with John is nothing but stress. What if it pushes me to have the babies early?"

"Honey, don't think about it. You need to relax. Stress is not good for you at all, you know that. You're only six months along, so do not stress yourself out thinking about John or anything. You need to relax. It is way too early to even think about having the babies. We have three more months to go. Why don't you go lay on the couch, and I will get you some more pizza to relax with. And then you can tell me about *Survivor* and what I can expect on Wednesday."

"Good idea. I could use another slice."

"We need to discuss baby names, too."

"I thought we did that."

"Yeah, we did, but I keep thinking we can do better."

"What, you don't like Cameron?"

"I really like Sophia still."

"Yes, Sophia is a beautiful name."

"How about Sophia Rose? And Robert James."

"What do you think of those names?"

"What happened to Levi?"

"I like Levi, but I don't know. I'm still thinking."

"I like both of them. Robert, after my father. And James, after your father, I assume."

"Yes, what do you think?"

"That way it's one from each of our families, and I just love the name Sophia, since Joel isn't here to put his two cents in or make me pick his names. I can veto them. And if he asks later, I can totally throw you under the bus."

"Okay, so we have baby names. But we can always change them if you change your mind. Nothing is set in stone until it's on the birth certificate."

"I can check that off my list now."

"You seem more relaxed."

"I am. It helps to talk things out, and now we can try to figure out which baby is kicking me all the time."

"I wonder which baby is going to be the soccer player."

"Maybe it's a football player."

"If he's a football player, then he is definitely a placekicker."

"Maybe it's Sophia and she's a cheerleader practicing her cheerleading," David said, laughing.

"You know what, maybe it's both of them, and they are fighting and punching at each other. Like siblings do."

"Can I ask you something? We never talked about having kids or even getting married when we were talking, and now we're engaged and pregnant and expecting twins. I know this conversation is a little late. How many kids do you want?"

"Honestly, I hadn't thought about it. I always wanted a family. I know I wanted to get married and have kids. I never thought about how many. I just figured I would know when we were done."

"Really, you never thought about how many you wanted? I only wanted like one or two. I think only because I still want my career. So, do you still plan on working? Do you plan on going back to the military when this mess is over, or do you plan on doing something else?"

"Honestly, I hadn't thought much about it. I planned on doing something, but my focus has been on you. Before you, my focus was Susan. Now I guess my focus will be on Sophia and Robert. Or will we call him Bobby?"

"Huh, I hadn't thought about that. Should we call him Bobby? Usually kids develop nicknames. Bobby seems natural for Robert. Sophy and Bobby. I like it."

"Now, back to you and your career."

"Yes, I plan to go back to work in some way, shape, or form. I do not know what it will be yet. I'm sure it will be after you go back to work. I wanted to find out where we were going to be now that I know we will be married with kids and probably living in New York."

"When you came to live with me, we weren't dating, so I wasn't sure what would become of us. Now were engaged and expecting. So things changed. So I know you want to go back to work, and you work in New York."

"I am such a terrible fiancée."

"Why do you say that?"

"I didn't even think of you and your career. I just assumed you would move to New York and live wherever. I want to raise our kids in New York. I didn't even think of what you want or where you want to live. We never even talked about it. I just assumed that when this mess was over, we would move to my apartment, restart my life in New York, and live there with my husband and our kids. I never even thought about your life here. I'm horrible. You're giving up everything to be with me. You have done everything to be with me."

"No, stop. I love you. I want you in my life. I will do anything to be with you."

"That's the problem, David. You love me and will do anything for me. You are doing everything to be with me. You have done everything. You gave up your life to protect me. Now you're going to give up your life and drop everything to move to New York and marry me and raise our kids. I never even asked what you wanted. I just assumed that was what we were doing. Okay, so let's stop and have this conversation. What do you want?"

"I want you, period. I want Sophia and Robert. I don't care where we live or what career I have. I did my military career already, so where we live is irrelevant, and what I do, I can do in any town. I want you and my family. Besides, the Marines kept me moving around, so I am used to picking up and going anywhere. What do you want, and where do you want to live?"

"I want you and Robert and Sophia. I want to live somewhere close to pizza. I want a career as an attorney and with Joel."

"Okay, so back to New York, as long as Joel is still there. They do have the best pizza, and they deliver, so I wouldn't have to go get it. I do have one more question. Do you want more kids?"

"Hmm. Honestly, a couple years ago I would have said no, I only wanted one or two, but I'm not sure anymore. I like our life right now. I guess I have to say I'm not sure. I might like having lots of kids. Can I get back to you on that one?"

"Of course. Besides, who knows? we might get a surprise again. Maybe that's how we get all our kids."

"Don't say that. If there is more than two in this belly, I don't think I could handle it."

"No, for sure. Two is plenty for now."

"I do have another question. House or apartment? Since we are having twins, should we be considering getting a house?"

"I hadn't thought about that, either. I just got my apartment. My lease...oh, wow, my lease will be up very soon, wont it? I hadn't thought about that, either. It's been almost a year since I signed my lease. Wow, this year has been a whirlwind."

"What do you think?"

"Honestly, I think if we did an apartment for the first year or two, we would be okay, but we would need to look into a house within a year or two. The kids really do need a backyard."

"Yeah, you're right about that."

"And I'm sure Maddie would appreciate someplace with a yard. I can't imagine her going to an apartment after having all this yard here."

"How did Joel find a house in New York with a yard?"

"Yards are hard to come by. Apartments and condos are the big thing there. Well, we could do Staten Island or Brooklyn, or maybe outside New York."

"Well, maybe we could keep your apartment for another year, and while we live there we could look for a house. That would give us time to find a place while we have a place to live."

"So what I'm hearing is, you want a house."

"Yes, but I also want us to have a place to live."

"We could find a fixer upper, too, and I could fix it up, since I'm not exactly working right now."

"That would work, too."

"What exactly do you want to do?"

"I'm not exactly sure yet. This would allow me some more time to figure it out."

"You know, you could always stay home and raise the kids."

"I could do that, too. Would you like me to do that?"

"I'm not saying that I'm offering that option. If you would like to do that, it is available for you to do."

"That is very diplomatic of you."

"David, I don't want you to feel like you need to stay with the kids."

"Julie, I know I don't need to stay with the kids. We can get daycare or a nanny. Right now, you're staying with the kids. Later, maybe I will. I'm not sure yet, but for now, we need to figure out if they are going to live here in this cabin in the woods, or in New York in a house or in an apartment."

"Okay, look we've been talking for hours. Do you want dinner tonight, or are you full from snacking on pizza all day?"

"Honestly, I'm still full from pizza."

"All this talking is making me really tired. I just want to go to bed. I have a lot to think about tonight. Now I need to really rethink a lot. When you go to town Wednesday, can you ask the detective to ask my landlord about my lease and how I deal with that when I'm not there?"

"Of course. Joel actually signed everything before. I'm sure if we asked, Joel would handle it again."

"I'm sure he would, but do we want him to, or do we want a house? And if we do that, do we want to go look at houses? Can we do that virtually? This is just a mess. I need this to be over, David. I'm exhausted thinking about it. Good night."

Julie kissed David.

"Good Night"

CHAPTER 39

JULIE

"Good Morning."

"Breakfast is ready. I made you some eggs with bagels and cream cheese."

"Eggs? No fluffy pancakes or waffles?"

"Sorry, I thought the bagels would take the place of the fluffy cakes. Besides, I thought you might like the change of pace, and I also thought you might still be full from all the pizza yesterday."

"It's not for me. Sophy and Bobby really like the pizza. I do it for them."

"Oh, I know, honey."

"Eggs are good for the babies, too, so I made them special for the babies. I have to go out and cut some wood for the fireplace. It's starting to get colder at night, and we are getting low on wood. We have to stock up for winter just in case we are here for the winter."

"What a winter. Seriously, you think we are spending winter here? David, I thought we talked about this yesterday."

"Julie, we did, and I am just playing it safe. Besides, maybe we will be in New York, and I can rent this place out. If so, then the tenants will need fire wood. So then I still need to cut firewood. So I am going to go out and make sure there is enough wood for the winter. I know Dad had some in the barn, but I try not to touch it, if possible. I try to go out and cut our own, so I'm going to go out and cut some trees since it's a nice day out. So if you need me, I'll be out in the woods."

"Okay, but you promised you were talking to the detective about getting us out of here."

"I promise I still am. I'm just doing this to be on the safe side, okay? Then Maddie and I will be here working on our lists today and cleaning."

"You know, Julie, if you need something to do, you could look at houses in New York to get some ideas. Just look. Not seriously, just the idea of yards and rooms or areas. Start making lists of areas and number of rooms. That kind of thing. You know, a must-have list and what I would like if I could have."

"Yeah that's a good idea. I can do that. I'm getting really good at lists."

"Okay, Maddie, breakfast dishes are washing so now, what I need is to put my feet up for a bit. They are killing me. How about we work on that house list David wants us to look into? What do you want on the list, Maddie?"

Maddie barked.

"Fenced back yard? You think so, Maddie? Yeah, that's a good idea. The kids would like that, too, I think. Let's look at some neighborhoods and make a list.

"Oh, let's see, we need at least three bedrooms, I think. With two kids right off the bat, yeah, at least...wait maybe four bedrooms. If Jody comes, I want her to have somewhere to stay, and if we ever have any visitors, like parents, they need somewhere to stay. And if we ever have any more kids, they will need a room, unless we plan on putting kids in another room together.

"Maybe we need a four-bedroom house. Or maybe a three-bedroom with a study or an office. We can turn into a spare room. A garage would be nice, too. How am I going to find this in New York? This is going to be way too expensive. I might have to look in Staten Island or Brooklyn. Maybe Joel will have some ideas. His house is small, but he

221

makes it work. He drives a ways to work, but it's not that bad. It takes about a half hour on a good day.

"You know what, Maddie? Let's do this how David suggested:

Must have three bedrooms. Prefer four bedrooms. Must have fenced back yard. Prefer garage. This could work, Maddie. Must have dishwasher. Must have two bathrooms. Prefer three bathrooms. Learned that one from living with David, and now with kids on the way, ugh! Definitely going to need more bathrooms.

"Prefer two sinks in kitchen. Must have laundry room. Prefer basement. Deck to watch kids play in yard. Grill on back patio. Prefer fireplace. Must have master bath. Must have safe school district.

"That's a pretty good list, I think, Maddie. David should be happy with that. I am. Now I need a nap. Then we can work on some more lists. But for now, I just need to sleep. I am totally exhausted. These babies are playing soccer or football or something in there, and it is totally exhausting. I never knew being pregnant was so much work. I hope they let me get a little nap in before dinner. Maddie, you keep watch. Let me know when David comes in."

• • •

"Hey, Maddie, is Julie sleeping? Let her sleep. Let's get dinner started. How about some pork chops for dinner tonight? How does that sound? I have to get a shower before I start dinner, but let me get those chops out of the freezer, then I will jump in the shower so I can start dinner after I shower. Here we go, chops in the sink with some water. So, those can thaw, and now I can hit the shower. You stay with Julie. I will jump in the shower. Good girl, Maddie."

"David is that you? David?"

"Yeah, I'm in the shower."

"Okay, I just heard water running."

"I'll be out in a few."

"Hey, Julie, you're up."

"Yeah, I heard water running."

"Sorry, I was trying to be quiet."

"No, I told Maddie to wake me when you came in."

"Well, I told Maddie to let you sleep. I was just about to start dinner. We're having pork chops for dinner. How did your lists go?"

"Actually, I got a lot done on the list you asked me for."

"Really? The house list?"

"Yes, I worked on the house list just in case you want to talk about it."

"I would love to discuss that after dinner."

"Great, I will print it out. I also printed out the grocery list and my pizza list."

"Wait, there's a pizza list?"

"Yes, you said we were having different kinds of pizza tomorrow, so I kinda got excited and figured I would make a list for pizza."

"How many pizzas are there?"

"Well, I thought maybe we could do halves. You know, half the pizza meat lovers and half pepperoni and half supreme. You get the picture."

"I feel like we're going to have pizza for days."

"I feel like we won't have enough pizza, David. I'm eating for three. So I need at least three pizzas, one for each of us. Oh, wait, did you want pizza, too? Because then I need four. And if you want leftovers, you might want more than four."

"I get it Julie, you love pizza."

"I also love ice cream lately. I can't say I will love it tomorrow. I can't say what I will want on any given day. These babies tell me what I will want, but pizza seems to be the norm. I can't get enough of it. I'm sorry. It just is that way. The babies love pizza. I can't explain it, and I can't get enough of it."

"You're right, Julie. I will get pizza. Tomorrow I will order lots of pizza. I will see if we can get them special ordered with half pepperoni, half meat, half another way, however you like them. Maybe I can see if we can get some uncooked pizza that I can cook here or keep frozen to cook here. I will see what I can work out tomorrow. I'm sorry. I will see what I can do to make these wonderful babies happy. I know they love pizza. I wonder if when they are born they will love pizza this much. I'm going to start dinner. Then I thought we could talk about your lists."

"Great. I printed everything out."

"Okay, let me get dinner started. I'll get it put in the oven, and we can talk. What would you like with the pork chops? How about some roasted potatoes and green beans?"

"Yeah, that sounds good."

"Just good? If I offered you pizza, you would be drooling."

"Well, tomorrow, I guess I will be drooling. Tonight, it just sounds good."

"I guess I will take it."

"You want some help cooking?"

"Sure. If you want, you can cut up the green beans."

"I can do that."

"Just throw some olive oil and spices over them on the pan with the chops, and then when I finish the potatoes, we will be all set."

"How about that?"

"Yeah, that's good. Now we can put them in the oven, and we should be good to go talk while everything cooks. So, where is this house list?"

"Oh, I have that right here on the end table. Take a look and tell me what you think. Is there anything I missed?"

"Fireplace. Four bedrooms. Do we need that many?"

"Well, I think we need three, but I want four in case Jody comes to visit."

"Okay, that makes sense, and in case parents come to visit. Three bathrooms."

"Yes, I definitely want more than one. It has really been hard with only one bathroom."

"I agree that we need more than one bathroom, and when these kids are teenagers, I'm not sure two will be enough, so I get three bathrooms. Fireplace, I like that. Romance and warmth on cold nights. Fenced back yard is definitely a must have for Maddie and the kids. Safe school zone, yes, for sure. Master bath, yes, for sure. Maybe a nice big shower? Should we add that to the list?"

"Huh, guess I missed that on my list. So we can add that to the list."

"This is a great starter list for a nice starter home."

"I think when we get back to New York we will have a good list to start looking at houses. Any ideas of where you want to look at?"

"Honestly, I'm not sure. I was thinking about that."

"It's expensive to live in New York and to buy a house there and raise kids. I don't know how we could afford it. I was thinking Staten Island or Brooklyn, maybe."

"So you're open to moving out to the areas around New York to raise the kids?"

"Yes, I want to be as close to New York as possible to work, but it has to be affordable, too. David, is there any way this is possible?"

"Yes, it's possible. I will find a way. I just need the list of things you want in the house. I can make it happen. It won't happen right away, but it will happen. I just need to find a way."

"How, David?"

"Julie, I'm not sure yet. It's going to be hard. We're not rich. It would be helpful if we were. But we are not. So it will take some work. But I'm very handy, so maybe I can find a fixer-upper, and I can buy it cheap and work on it."

"So it's possible."

"Yes, Julie, it's possible."

"I saw the list, and I figured that in New York, there wasn't any way I would ever be able to have that for our kids."

"No, it's possible. It's not possible to get it brand-new tomorrow, but it's possible to get it eventually. It might take time. We may need to sell this place."

"David, I don't want you to sell this place. This was your dad's home."

"Julie, we are building our kids' futures. My dad would want us to do whatever we need to do in order to give our kids whatever they need. If that means selling this place to provide a home for them, then he would want that. Besides, we may need the money for a down payment to buy a house in New York. Houses there are really expensive, and we might need money to buy materials to fix up the house, especially if you still rent your place. Unless you want to commute from here."

"That's a long commute. Maybe we need to let my apartment go."

"If we do that, where do we live?"

"Well, you own this place. I only rent my apartment."

"Yeah, but you work in New York. You can't work from here if you work in New York."

"But I can work from here if I live here."

"But you love your job."

"I love you and my family more."

"Now, we can figure this out. We aren't losing the house or anything. We're trying to move to New York. We just save some money before we move. The kids will be fine in the apartment while we save up. We got a couple years to figure it out. The kids won't even notice until they are toddlers. We have time to figure this out. I think we're jumping the gun on this."

"You're right, we're going too fast on this. The kids aren't even here yet, and we're worried about where we're going to raise them."

"Let me check on dinner. What else did you do today?"

"I cleaned mostly. Maddie and I talked a lot. Went over our lists."

"Dinner is done. Hope you're hungry. You stay there. I will bring dinner to you."

"Oh, we're eating on the couch?"

"Sure, we can eat there. It's just us. We might as well while we can. Once the kids come, we might not be able to do this much anymore."

"What do you mean?"

"Well, once the kids come, they'll start crawling, and soon enough they'll be grabbing everything, and you can't leave anything out, so dinner is at the table, or the kids will grab it. So we might not be able to eat on the couch or even together. We might have to eat in shifts because one baby might be crying or need to be fed or changed. So I think we should cherish our dinners together and our date nights and watching TV together. Our lives are going to get a lot more hectic after the babies come, so let's make the most of these next few months."

"I never thought about that. I guess you're right. This is our last few months of it just being us. In a couple months, it's going to be us and the kids. We won't have any time alone anymore. We will never be alone again. We may never have the chance to even make a brother or sister for Sophy and Bobby."

"Don't you worry about that. Uncle Joel will babysit, so we can at least have a date night."

"Only if we can see Uncle Joel."

"Julie, I promise this mess will end at some point. It has to. You know that it can't go on forever. I'll call the detective tomorrow and see what's going on. I will also tell him we need a way out. So something will change soon. Now we finish dinner, then we can go to bed early so you can rest because tomorrow is a big day. It's *Survivor* day. I know you're excited about that."

"You have no idea. We should have ordered a cake and made it a party."

"Okay, I'm just going to tell you, we are not doing this pizza party every Wednesday. This is just for the premier. Don't plan on this every week."

"Fine. But I still get my pizza every week, right?:

"Yes, you still get a pizza every week. Not a bunch, but one pizza for you and the babies to share."

"I can handle that."

"But next season, we are having a premier party. I know Joel will help me plan. Maybe we do a taco theme."

"I would think you would do island themed, since it's on an island."

"Oh, yes, we can do that and margaritas. Since I won't be pregnant."

"Woah, wait, who says you won't be pregnant?"

"Not funny, David."

"You never know, Julie. "You could be pregnant again. We could have more kids."

"No, not next season. You need to wait. I need time to recover."

"We can discuss it."

"Let me do the dishes, then we can relax."

"I'll help."

"Okay, can you feed Maddie real quick?"

"Maddie, did David forget to give you dinner?"

"I didn't forget. I was just trying to get the dishes done."

"Sure you were. I will feed you. Maddie, you are my bestie. Here you go, Maddie."

"The dishes are done, so how about we sit on the couch and relax a little? Maybe I can try to get my arms around you."

"Very funny, David."

"Julie, I really just want to sit and hold you. I really wonder how many times we will be able to do this. Especially after the babies come."

"Well, then come on the couch and hold me. Maddie can come sit, too, when she's done with her dinner. You think the couch will be able to hold all of us if I keep getting any bigger?"

"Well, if the couch makes weird noises, then maybe we need to think of getting a new one. This one is kinda old."

"Well, we can just be careful and relax, sit here, and cuddle. It's kinda nice to just sit and relax. Here, put your hand here on my stomach and feel this."

"What is that?"

"I think it's a foot. Wait a minute. Just leave your hand there."

"Holy crap. What was that?"

"That was either your son or your daughter playing soccer."

"Someone kicked hard. Do they do that a lot?"

"Yes, all day, and sometimes all night. Makes it a little hard to sleep. It's been getting stronger every day. Babies are very active. Some days they don't kick much, but lately they have been really kicking. Today it was really a lot."

"Sweetie, that is amazing. I can't believe that. It must be so weird to you."

"It feels weird, but I love how it feels, too. I feel the babies turn over sometimes, and then a kick here and there. I wanted you to feel it, too. It's weird, but it's nice."

"I'm glad you let me feel that. I didn't realize the babies kicked that hard. I knew they kicked, and I had held your stomach before, but never like that."

"They have gotten a lot more active these last couple weeks. I just started noticing it. I'm hoping as they grow it gets more often so you get to feel it, too. Hopefully just not at night."

"Are you about ready for bed?"

"Yeah, I am actually exhausted. It's been a long day, and tomorrow is going to be a busy day."

Chapter 40

JULIE

"Good morning."

"Would you like breakfast?"

"Yes, but nothing big, something small and light. I want to save room for all my pizza I'm planning on having later."

"Really, you planning on eating that much pizza?"

"Yeah, I am, I can't help it. You know that."

"Okay, so how about some toast for breakfast? Or some eggs and toast?"

"No, just toast. And jam and a donut."

"That sounds good. Yeah, a donut. Do we have any donuts in the freezer?"

"Can you check the freezer for donuts to see if there is a glazed donut in there? That sounds so yummy."

"Okay, let me check the freezer. I think there are a couple donuts in the freezer left. Not sure if there are any glazed left, but there might be a couple other ones left. You sure you don't want pancakes or waffles or something?"

"No, I'm saving room for pizza today."

"Okay, I'm going to check the freezer, then hit the shower and get ready to head to town. I have a lot of stuff to get done in town today and apparently a lot of pizza to pick up and lists to get checked off."

"Yeah, you're right, you need to get a move on. But please check the freezer first. I really want a donut."

"Yes, dear, I will do that right now. Okay, I didn't find a glazed donut, but I did find chocolate-covered and a cinnamon-spiced. Which do you want?"

"I will take the cinnamon one. Leave the chocolate one for tomorrow."

"Of course, my dear. I will pick up a glazed one for you for later while I am in town if you add it to the list. Now I am jumping in the shower real quick, okay?"

"Yes, you do that. I am eating this donut."

"Can you feed Maddie, too, please?"

"Yes, of course. I will give Maddie her breakfast."

David headed to the shower.

"Okay, Julie, I'm ready to head to town. Do you have all my lists ready?"

"Yes, of course I do. Here is the grocery list, pizza lists, and detective list."

"Anything else I need?"

"I can't think of anything else."

"Okay, well, I am going to head out since I have a lot to pick up. You and Maddie have fun while I'm gone. Take care of my babies while I'm gone, Maddie."

David kissed Julie goodbye.

"I love you. I'll see you soon."

"Drive safe."

"Okay, Maddie," said Julie. "It's just us. What shall we do while David is off shopping again? I say Netflix. What you think?"

Chapter 41

DAVID

David arrived in town to Doctor Jameson's office.

"Doctor, I thought I would stop by and see how you are doing."

"David, hi, I am wonderful. I have some samples for you to try and some paperwork for you to pick up. Come on into my office, and let's take a look and see what I have. Here is everything you need. I left instructions inside for you."

"Thank you, Doctor. I will call if I have any questions."

"Great, I will plan on seeing you next week, then. Have a great day."

"Thanks, Doc," said David. "Okay, I'll cross that off the list. Now on to the grocery store. Let's see what is on the list: Maddie's treats, milk, bread, donuts, bagels, frozen pizza, ice cream, yogurt, eggs, butter. You know what, I see a cake there. Let me grab that. I think Julie will love that. It will be a nice surprise for her party tonight. Okay, what else do I need? I think I have everything on the list, so I should be good.

"So I can get the pizzas. The pizza place is going to think I'm crazy when I order so many pizzas for myself. And when I ask if they won't cook them all and then if there is a way to freeze them, man, I am going to look crazy. The things we do for love. I still need to call the detective. I can call while I'm waiting for the pizza. Then I can head home and wait for *Survivor* with Julie. I can't believe she is so *Survivor* crazy. Anyway, I think I'm done here, so I'll check out and then head to order the pizza and call the detective. Let me get these groceries in the car and get the ice cream in the cooler, and then I can head to the pizza parlor to place the craziest order ever."

David arrived at the pizza parlor.

"Hi, um, I have a couple weird questions. I have a kid's party tonight, so I am wondering about pizza. Can I order some cooked and some raw? And can any be frozen?"

"Sir? Are you kidding?"

"No, I wish I was kidding."

"Um, okay, yes, I can sell you raw pizza I guess, and yes, pizza can be stored in a refrigerator for three to five days and frozen up to three months. However, we don't suggest more than a month."

"Okay, then can you make me several pizzas, with different items on half of the pizzas?

"Sure, I guess I can."

"Great, I need four pizzas: one half with pepperoni and half meat lovers, and another half veggie and half supreme, and another half everything and half Hawaiian, and the other you can pick the two other halves. Cook one pizza, then leave the others uncooked, please."

"So, you want four pizzas, only one cooked?"

"Yes, please, and can you please also give me some breadsticks?"

"Sure. Give me 30 minutes, and I will have it all ready."

"Perfect, thanks so much. I'll be back in a half hour."

David talked to Sherrif Jones next.

"Hi, Sheriff Jones. How have you been?"

"I am great, David, how are you?"

"Good, just doing my weekly supply run."

"Everything still okay?"

"Yes, it is. I need to make a call if you don't mind."

"No, not at all. Please use my office. I need to go for coffee. I'll be back in a couple minutes."

"Thanks."

In the office, David called the detective. "Detective Jordan, please. Detective Jordan, this is David Thomas."

"David, how are things?"

"Not the best. Julie is going a little crazy. Have you caught John?"

"No, we haven't had any luck yet."

"Well, Detective there have been some changes here. Julie needs to get back to her life. She is going crazy being here alone. Its really starting to get to her. The last doctor's appointment really changed a lot of things."

"Is she okay?"

"Yes, she's okay, but we are expecting twins, and that complicates the pregnancy. It makes it more likely she may go into early labor."

"David, that's wonderful. Twins are great."

"Yes, it's great, but it puts her at a higher risk for complications, which means we need to be able to go to a hospital, and she wants to talk to her family and friends. She misses them. She needs a support system other than me."

"Okay, I understand. We need to do something to find John. I will see what I can do to push him to show himself."

"In the meantime, I was hoping you could help me with another project."

"Sure, what can I help with?"

"Well, Julie and I will need to find a house. She wants to live in the New York area, Staten Island or Brooklyn, somewhere close so she can still work in New York and make the commute, but we can't afford to live there still with a family of four or more in case more kids come along. We need a house since we can't look. I was hoping you could reach out to Joel for us to start looking. Julie's lease will be up soon, so we're not sure if we want to renew or buy a new house."

"Actually, David, I may be just the person to help Joel with this. I have a few ideas. I will reach out to Joel with this info. I have a contact that might be able to find a foreclosure or tax repo house, which you could get really cheap and fix up."

"That would be amazing, Detective I would greatly appreciate any help in doing this. Since we can't go ourselves, this would be great."

"Yeah, I can reach out to Joel, and we can work on it. I'm sure he knows Julie's taste, so we can narrow down some options. Should I tell him about the twins?"

"I don't know, should you?"

"Honestly, I would say no, probably not. If we do, then John may find out, and I'm hoping this ends soon. So let's keep this information between us for now, but if it goes on for much longer, then we can let him in on it."

"That's probably best, but I will reach out to Joel about the house search. I will do it in person to make sure no info will pass on to John or anyone else. Maybe it will lure John out, too."

"Let's hope that's exactly what it does."

"Thanks, Detective. I hope this works I'll give you a call next week."

"Good luck."

"Thanks." David hung up.

"Thank you, Sheriff. It was good to see you. I will see you next week."

"Yes, good to see you, too, David. I will see you next week. Have a good day."

"Hi, are my pizza's ready?"

"Yes, sir, they are ready. Perfect. That will be 68.27."

"Here you go. Keep the change."

"Thank you, sir. Enjoy your party."

"Okay, pizza, check. Cake, check. Talked to detective, check. Talked to Doc, check. I think I have everything done on my list. I think I can head home to Julie."

CHAPTER 42

JULIE

"Hey, honey, I'm home. Are you ready for a pizza party?"

"Yes, I am so ready for pizza and *Survivor* tonight. Did you get everything on my list?"

"Of course. Do you think I would dare come home if I didn't?"

"Oh my gosh, how much pizza did you get?"

"Oh, well, my love, I found out I can purchase a cooked pizza and uncooked pizza and freeze them for us to cook later."

"Are you kidding me?"

"No, I am not. So we can put one in the fridge for tomorrow or later tonight and a couple in the freezer for your cravings for later in the week."

"David, you are the best fiancé ever. Tonight is going to be the best party. I just wished it was for more people."

"I know. I wish Joel and Sarah and our friends could be here, too, and their new baby. It would be amazing to have a big *Survivor* blowout, but you know we can't do that. But next year, we can have a big party. And just because it's the two of us doesn't mean we can't have cake."

"What? You got a cake for tonight?"

"I got us a cake to celebrate our first *Survivor* party together."

"This is perfect. We are going to have a great party. I just wish I didn't have to do everything alone. I'm tired of being locked away. I want to enjoy life and my family and friends. I want to go outside. Take long walks. These babies are making it hard to do anything. I just want to go out and shop a little for some clothes and have a baby shower. Plan a wedding. Simple things that normal women can do."

"I know, and soon you will be able to do those things. I promise. I talked with the detective, and he is checking into some options. He is trying to speed things up and get us out of this captivity. So for now, the best we can do is just enjoy our pizza party.

Just relax and think about your show tonight. that will relax you."

"That will not relax me, that will get me more anxious and excited. I can't wait for you to see the show. I still can't believe you never saw the show before. It's been on for so long. How have you never seen it?"

"Honestly, I probably saw the commercials and never paid attention. I was also in that Marines thing. It kept me kinda busy. You know, once we have the babies, you might get too busy for *Survivor,* too. It might get replaced with that baby shark thing."

"No way, don't you even suggest that."

"I'm just saying."

"You're not funny David. I would love to call Joel and ask if he is watching *Survivor* tonight. This is what I have been looking forward to all summer. I have been waiting for the new season to start since the last season ended. Joel and I discuss it every week and who we think will win. You know, there are even betting odds on this and fantasy Survivor groups, too. I miss the internet. I'm so limited. Before, I used to use Facebook and online shop and surf the web. Now I can't post anything or do anything. I have to use your account to do anything.

"My Paramount is the first time I have ever used any of my accounts since leaving New York. We always used your Netflix account, and I haven't checked my email or anything. It's been hard to give up my life and just walk away. I never thought going technology free would be so hard."

"I know, honey. But Detective Jordan said to leave everything behind. The less technology, the better. I know email and cell phones can be tracked. So we are going old school as much as possible."

"I know, David, but being without my phone and laptop is really hard. I never realized how much I rely on those things. I miss my laptop and surfing the internet for stupid cat videos and Joel sending me stupid things. Joel used to send me the dumbest videos. I bet my email is full."

"Julie, it won't do any good to sit here and think about it. You're just going to miss it more. Why not think about the great things that we have because of this experience? We painted the baby room and started the kitchen remodel."

"I know, David. I just miss so many things, and I want to call Joel and my mom and Jody. I didn't get to tell her what was happening. She is probably so worried. I hope Joel told her I was okay. It's almost time for her spring fling, too. She won't have anywhere to go."

"Seriously, you're worried about her having somewhere to go for her spring fling?"

"I'm worried about all my friends. I miss everyone. I'm missing all their lives and everything. By the time this ends, everyone will have changed, and I will have missed it all. It's like watching a TV show every day, and all of a sudden they just stop airing it and leave it on the cliffhanger and never start the next season. I need to know what is happening with my friends' lives."

"Julie, I know it's been a while, but it hasn't been that long."

"I know. I just feel like I'm missing everything."

"It will be over soon. Here, have some pizza. That always makes you feel better. I made some popcorn to go with our show, and we have cake for dessert."

"I have Maddie all taken care of for her dinner, so we can relax and enjoy the show on the couch."

"Is there anything you need before the show starts?"

"No, I think I have everything: pizza, water, cake, popcorn. I think I am all set. Nope, wait, I need to pee. I swear, I go to the bathroom so much, I may need a TV in there. I swear these babies are kicking my bladder just to make me go to the bathroom more."

"Okay, well, I have everything set here, so you go to the bathroom. I will let Maddie out again so we can watch the show. It starts in about ten minutes."

"I guess I better hurry. It takes forever to waddle down the hall."

CHAPTER 43

DAVID

"So, what did you think of *Survivor*?"

"It wasn't what I thought it was going to be. The challenges were different. There is a lot of drama for people who don't know each other. These people know they are going to an island. Why do they not dress for it?"

"Well, they don't always know when they are going to the island. I think they tell them they are going to a cast meeting or something."

"Okay, but if you sign up for the show, know how to swim and make a fire. These people don't know how to do those basic things."

"I agree with you that they should know how to do those things. But other than that, what did you think?"

"It was alright. I can handle watching it once a week."

"Good, because you're watching it once a week, even if you hate it."

"I figured that, so I figured I better like it one way or another."

"But I'm glad you like it so we have something else to talk about. I'm running out of things to talk about. It's hard not having work to discuss. All we have is babies and a wedding. You know, we could go back and watch all the *Survivors* from the beginning if you want."

"Maybe we save that for after this season is over and you need something to do. I can handle it once a week, but I'm not sure I can watch it from the beginning. Besides, I think I would mix up the seasons if we did that. How long has this show been on?"

"Years. Over 20 years, I think. I've been watching it since I can remember."

"We can watch the past seasons after this season is over. Hopefully after this season, I will be back to work and too busy to watch with you."

"Oh, well, if that happens, then I will wait for you. I wouldn't want to watch it without you."

"Okay, I see how you are."

"What? I just think this can be one of our shows we watch together now. At least until you and Joel can watch it together."

"Okay, fair enough. I wonder what Joel thought of it."

"I bet he watched with Isabella."

"I doubt it. I'm betting Isabella slept through it."

"I wish I could call him and find out."

"Soon, honey, soon. Pretty soon I will be yelling at you to get off the phone and let Joel go to bed."

"I never realized how hard it would be to not talk to my family and friends. Even not talking to people at work is hard. I miss the daily interaction. Sometimes I would just be happy going out and talking to a tree. Do you remember calling to hear the weather back in the 80's? I would do that at this point if I could."

"Well, if you want, we can order an Alexa to talk to you."

"Well, that would make me feel pathetic, but honestly, I might take you up on it."

"How about we go to bed, and you get some rest. Things will look better in the morning. I promise."

"Okay, maybe I will dream about talking to people or trees."

"Okat, let's go get some sleep. Come on, Maddie. Bedtime."

CHAPTER 44

JULIE

"Good morning. How did you sleep?"

"Good, I guess."

"What would you like for breakfast this morning?"

"How about waffles? Babies like their fluffy dough."

"Okay, but do waffles count as dough?"

"No, but they are fluffy and filling and a good substitute for rolls and pizza."

"Then waffles it is. Do you want hashbrowns or anything with them?"

"Ooh, yeah, that sounds yummy. You know you're spoiling me, right?"

"Oh, I don't want you to ever tell Joel I didn't take good care of you."

"Good point. You should stay on my good side."

"Not to mention those babies should always be happy and healthy."

"So, what shall we do today?"

"Well, is there anything on the lists we need to do?"

"I'm sure there is a lot on the lists. Honestly, I don't feel like dealing with the lists. I really want to talk to people. Or a tree, at this point."

"Are we still in that discussion?"

"Maybe we should get some plants for me to talk to?"

"Honey, I think you're just feeling lonely. This will pass. Just give it time."

"I am past lonely. I am feeling like I am in prison. I think going to the hospital made it worse. It gave me a taste of talking to real people. I was used to the silence and living alone, just you, me, and Maddie, then I went to the hospital and saw real people. Now I went back to reality, and it's back to silence. It's like giving me the internet for a day and then taking it away, or giving me a new car and taking it away the next day. This just sucks. David, I can't keep doing this. I can't keep living my life in a cabin without my friends and family. We can't raise our children without our friends and family."

"Hey, don't think that way. We will have our friends and family. I promise we will find a way to work this all out. I will go on Wednesday and call the detective and tell him we need to figure a way out of this mess one way or another. You need to get your life back, okay?"

"It's just, seeing the babies made this so real, and not being able to tell Joel or my family is hard. I can't talk to anyone and tell anyone. I only have you. I love you, but I need my family. I need help. I'm a huge whale, and I don't know if all these changes I feel are normal or not, and I can't ask anyone or tell anyone. Google can only help so much. I just feel so alone. Maddie can't answer me. I talk to her when you're gone. I feel like she is my best friend. I'm talking to myself. David, I have no one. I am going insane and driving myself crazy. I didn't realize how hard this was going to be. I thought I could handle being here with just you, but I didn't think it was going to be for months, and I wasn't pregnant. My life has changed so much, and I can't tell anyone. I need my family and friends."

David hugged Julie and tried to comfort her. "Julie, I get it. we need to get your life back and your family. I promise I will call the detective, and we will figure this out. I won't stop until we figure this out. But you will have to be patient."

"Yes, you're right David, I am so very happy, just lonely. I miss family and friends. That's all. I promise I am happy. I just wish I could tell everyone how happy I am. I wish I could ask my mom questions about being pregnant and what to do about the wedding. And invitations and the ceremony. I just want my friends and family I want to know their thoughts and what to do. Even Joel's bad jokes about my weight and not seeing my feet. I need my friends."

"I know you do, sweetheart. I wish I could give you that. I would do anything to give you the wedding of your dreams and let us tell the world about these babies."

"Why don't you take a relaxing bath? I need to go chop some wood for the winter. When I get done, we can figure out what you and those beautiful babies want for dinner tonight."

"That sounds like a good idea. Maybe a relaxing bath is what I need. I wish wine was an option. Maybe I'll make some tea to go with my bath."

"Yes, tea. I can do that, and I will start your bath for you."

CHAPTER 45

JULIE

"That tea hit the spot. Now I'm dressed for this fall weather. I need slippers. It's getting chilly out."

Maddie's ears perked up, and she went to the door.

"Is David coming? It's kinda soon. He hasn't been gone long."

Maddie started to bark.

"Maddie, who's there? You don't usually bark at David."

Maddie started barking again and growling.

"Maddie, you're scaring me. Maddie, if you don't stop barking, I'm calling David."

Julie grabbed the phone and called David.

"David, is that you outside? Maddie is barking, and I can't see why."

"Go to the barn and take Maddie with you. I'm on the way to the house."

"Maddie, we have to go to the barn. Come on."

Julie headed outside to the barn with Maddie. She started running to the barn with Maddie through the leaves and the cool fall air.

Julie looked behind her to make sure Maddie was coming, then when she turned around, she ran into John.

"Finally, I have found you. It took a long time, but I knew if I waited long enough, you would eventually show up. I see our last time together was even more special than I realized. Why didn't you tell me you were having my child? Now we can get married and be a family."

"It's not your baby, John. These are my babies."

"Julie, you are mine. You will always be mine. We can raise our baby together and be a family. You can be my wife and take care of our child."

"No, John, I don't want anything to do with you. How did you find me?"

"Your love for *Survivor* led me right to you. I knew you would use your account eventually, and I would be able to track you. It took a while, but I found you. You were definitely worth the wait. Now I can't wait to start our life together."

"John, please, I don't love you anymore."

Maddie kept barking at John.

"Tell that stupid dog to stop barking."

"No, she's not stupid, and she won't stop barking at you because you're a stranger to her."

"Well, then we have a problem, cause she is going to tell people I'm here. So if you cant get her to shut up, then I will need to make her shut up."

"Don't you hurt, Maddie. John. You have done enough to ruin my life. Don't you dare touch my dog."

"Julie, I dont want to hurt your dog. I just want you to come back to New York with me and live our lives together with our child. We can live happily ever after. You can bring your dog, too, if you want. I just want you forever."

"I will never go with you, John. I don't love you. I never will love you again. You ruined my life, and I hate you. I want you to leave me alone forever."

Julie pushed and fought to get away from John. She struggled, screaming for help. Maddie ran and jumped at John and bit his arm. John pushed Maddie off of him. Julie took off running towards the barn, calling for Maddie to come.

A loud pop went off.

Julie turned around, screaming, "Maddie!"

Julie saw John on the ground. She stopped to see if John was getting up. John stayed still.

David emerged from behind a tree, holding a gun.

David told Julie to stay back. "Don't go near John."

Julie called for Maddie again. Maddie went to Julie and sat by her. David went to John to see if he was okay. David kicked his leg and got no response. He bent down and checked for a pulse.

Nothing.

David went over to Julie. He held her.

Julie was crying, and David said, "It's over."

"Are you okay?"

"Yes, I'm okay. I'm scared. I thought he was going to hurt the babies. He thought they were his babies, David."

"He is crazy, Julie. I'm sure he thought he could win you back."

David grabbed his cell phone and called the detective to tell him what happened.

"Detective Jordan is calling the sheriff to come out and take care of everything here. We need to go inside get you calmed down. The sheriff is on the way, and we will have to give him our statements. Maddie, you're such a good girl." David bent down and pet Maddie's head. "You did exactly like we practiced. Good girl. Let's go inside and wait for the sheriff."

"I don't want to contaminate anything. Just in case."

"Julie, can I get you anything? Please tell me what you need. Are you okay?"

"David, I'm shocked. I don't know what to do. My ex is dead outside on the ground.

I don't know how to feel. Free, and excited that I am free? Or sad that my ex is dead? I don't know what to do or how to feel. I'm overwhelmed."

"Here, have some tea. This will relax you. Just sit here on the couch and relax. Don't think about John. Think about the babies and how we can start our lives. Think about how everything is finally over. We just have to get through all this with the sheriff. Just tell him everything, and then it will all be over. Are you sure I can't get you anything? A blanket? You're shivering."

"Oh, I just can't believe it's over. I guess I am a little chilly."

"Let me get you a blanket, sweetheart. You relax and sit here with Maddie, your great protector."

"She was great, wasn't she?"

"She sure was the best dog ever. She is really going to be great with the babies. I know I will never need to worry about you or them when she is around."

CHAPTER 46

JULIE

There was a knock on the door.

"It's Sheriff Jones," said David. "Sheriff Jones, thanks for coming so quickly."

"Of course. David, will you show me where John is and tell me what happened? I will need to talk to you and Julie. Separately, of course."

"Of course. Julie is right here on the couch. You can talk to me here, or I can show the deputies where John is while you talk to her."

"That would be great, David. Thank you. Julie, please tell me everything that happened. Don't leave out any details."

Julie went over everything with the sheriff.

"Julie, I will give all this information to Detective Jordan. I don't think there will be any issues showing cause for David killing John, and I don't think there will be any charges. David has given us access to the camera footage. And we have taken the weapon in as evidence just in case, but I think we have everything. According to Detective Jordan, the case against John is strong, so I think everything will be fine. I believe David is talking to Detective Jordan now, so I'm sure he will update you, too."

"Thank you so much, Sheriff. I appreciate everything."

"You're welcome. Try to get some rest. Do you need me to get you a doctor or anything?"

"No, I think I'm okay. I'm just shocked, I guess. I'll call doctor Jameson if I need anything."

"David, thank you for assistance with everything. If we have any other questions, we will contact you. I think the coroner is all set, so we should be finished."

"Thank you, Sheriff. If you need anything, please call my cell. I'm taking Julie away for a few days."

"I think that it is a good idea, David. Get away from this mess for a while. Maybe get her checked out by a doctor to just to make sure everyone is okay."

"I will call if we need anything, take care."

David turned to Julie. "Okay, let's go."

"What? Where are we going?"

"Home, Julie. We're going to see Joel. I packed a bag while you were talking to the sheriff. So, let's get in the car and go. Me, you, and Maddie are headed back to New York. At least for a few days. You can call your family and friends and get an update on everyone. Or you can surprise everyone. Your choice."

"Oh my God, yes! Lets' go. I get to see the baby. I'm so excited."

"Okay, I packed the car. Our bags are in there, and there's some water for you and Maddie in there, so we just have to get in."

"What are we waiting for? Let's go. I will call my mom on the road. I can call Jody, too. I can't wait."

"What about Joel? Are you calling him?"

"No, I want to surprise him."

"Are you sure? It might be late by the time we get there. It will definitely be dark."

"He won't care, and I want to see my godchild."

"Where are we going to sleep?"

"Well, I was thinking we still have your apartment, so we can crash there. Since John is gone, there is no reason to be afraid anymore, so we should be safe there."

"Yeah, I do pay the rent still, so we might as well get some use out of it. I'm so excited. David, it's finally over. We get to live our lives and plan our wedding. We can have a baby shower."

"Yes, Julie, it's finally over. We can have everything you want, so now you need to decide where we want to have the babies, because I just put all that baby furniture together at the cabin, so if I have to break it down and bring it to New York, I need to know. So you think about it."

"Wow, all these decisions. And now I can call my mom and ask her help in making these decisions."

"Yeah, why don't you call your mom and Jody before it gets late?"

"Good idea. Then I can think about our wedding and baby shower and where we're going to live and have these babies. I haven't even told my mom I'm pregnant or engaged. She's going to be so happy. There is so much to do and plan now. I can't wait to see Joel's face when he sees me.

CHAPTER 47

JULIE

David arrived at Joel's house.

Joel came running down the driveway. "Julie, it's you! are you okay? Detective Jordan called."

David came around the side of the car to open the door for Julie.

Julie stepped out.

Joel saw Julie.

"Jules, you're huge!"

"Gee, thanks, Joel. Good to see you, too. I'm pregnant."

"I can see that, Jules. When are you due?"

"Few more months. I'm having twins. Now take me to Isabella. I want to meet my goddaughter."

Joel hugged Julie.

"Jules, I have missed you so much. Finally, you're home, and we can have real margaritas."

"Joel, I promise margaritas at the wedding, which will be after the babies come. Now tell me everything I missed. I have missed you so much."

"Wedding? Wait, you're engaged and pregnant? I think you need to tell me everything first. We are going to be up all night. Sarah, get out here! Jules finally got a man!"

"You're a jerk, Joel. God, I missed you. Did you see *Survivor* last night?"

"Of course I did," Joel said as they walked up to the house arm in arm.

David and Maddie followed Joel and Julie into the house.

"Come on, Maddie. I see a long night ahead of us."

THE END